"Sorry? Why I'd be sorry?"

Kent asked.

"I thought perhaps you've had second thoughts about having me right on your doorstep," Susan said. "What I mean is, sometimes impulse leads us into things we'd later as soon get out of."

Grasping her chin between his fingers, he made her look up at him.

"I think you know better," he whispered.

"I'm not too sure of anything these days, Kent."

His eyes were unwavering. "You can be sure of me."

His voice was warm, his words flowing over her like a gentle balm, holding the promise of healing she so badly needed. But there was heat to the balm, too, a delicious heat that began to spread through her, filling the spaces that had been cold and empty for so long....

Dear Reader,

Welcome to Silhouette Special Edition . . . welcome to romance. Each month Silhouette Special Edition publishes six novels with you in mind—stories of love and life, tales that you can identify with—as well as dream about.

This Valentine's Day month has plenty in store for you. THAT SPECIAL WOMAN!, Silhouette Special Edition's new series that salutes women, features a warm, wonderful story about Clare Gilroy and bad-boy hero Reed Tonasket. Don't miss their romance in *Hasty Wedding* by Debbie Macomber.

THAT SPECIAL WOMAN! is a selection each month that pays tribute to women—to us. The heroine is a friend, a wife, a mother—a striver, a nurturer, a pursuer of goals—she's the best in every woman. And it takes a very special man to win that special woman!

Also in store for you this month is the first book in the series FAMILY FOUND by Gina Ferris. This book, *Full of Grace,* brings together Michelle Trent and Tony D'Allessandro in a search for a family lost . . . and now found.

Rounding out this month are books from other favorite writers: Christine Rimmer, Maggi Charles, Pat Warren and Terry Essig (with her first Silhouette Special Edition).

I hope that you enjoy this book and all the stories to come. Happy St. Valentine's Day!

Sincerely,

Tara Gavin
Senior Editor

MAGGI CHARLES

THE OTHER SIDE OF THE MIRROR

SPECIAL EDITION®

Published by Silhouette Books New York

America's Publisher of Contemporary Romance

For Nonnie, who, for a lot of us, offers a very special kind of oasis where the Cape's real spirit lives on despite so many changes. May it ever be so!

SILHOUETTE BOOKS
300 East 42nd St., New York, N.Y. 10017

THE OTHER SIDE OF THE MIRROR

ISBN: 0-373-09795-6

First Silhouette Books printing February 1993

Printed in the U.S.A.

Books by Maggi Charles

Silhouette Special Edition

Love's Golden Shadow #23
Love's Tender Trial #45
The Mirror Image #158
That Special Sunday #258
Autumn Reckoning #269
Focus on Love #305
Yesterday's Tomorrow #336
Shadow on the Sun #362
The Star Seeker #381
Army Daughter #429
A Different Drummer #459
It Must Be Magic #479
Diamond Moods #497
A Man of Mystery #520
The Snow Image #546
The Love Expert #575
Strictly for Hire #599
Shadows on the Sand #647
As the Moon Rises #771
The Other Side of the Mirror #795

Silhouette Romance

Magic Crescendo #134
Keep It Private #840

Silhouette Intimate Moments

Love's Other Language #90

MAGGI CHARLES

wrote her first novel when she was eight and sold her first short story when she was fifteen. Fiction has been her true love ever since. She has written forty-plus romance and mystery novels and many short stories. The former newspaper reporter has also published dozens of articles, many having to do with her favorite avocations, which include travel, music, antiques and gourmet cooking. Maggi was born and raised in New York City. Now, she and her writer-husband live in a sprawling old house on Cape Cod. They have two sons and three grandchildren.

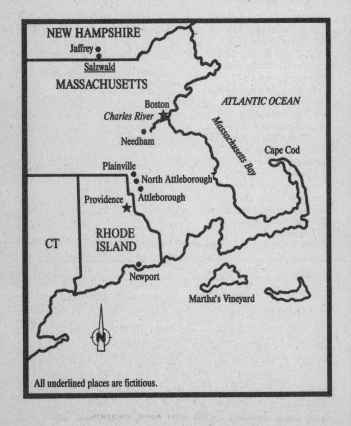

NEW HAMPSHIRE

Jaffrey ●

Salzwald

MASSACHUSETTS

Boston ●
Charles River

Needham ●

ATLANTIC OCEAN

Massachusetts Bay

Cape Cod

Plainville ●
North Attleborough ●
Attleborough

Providence ★

CT

RHODE ISLAND

Newport ●

Martha's Vineyard

N

All underlined places are fictitious.

Chapter One

She was standing on the opposite side of the room, the center of a small group of people. A hot needle of pain pierced Kent's chest, and he sucked in his breath. The shock of seeing her was overpowering, even worse than he'd expected.

God, how he hated her!

She was a ghost come to life, an insidious wraith with substance, back to haunt him. He strained his ears, expecting to hear the echo of her mocking laughter.

He recognized the people she was talking with: Phil and Heddy Donavan, Clark and Mandy Benedict, Bert and Lilian Whitfield. They'd all been in Salzwald on that ghastly, unforgettable weekend almost three years ago.

The pain needled again and Kent swallowed hard, his throat muscles constricting. The room, crowded with people partying, was overheated, but he broke out in a cold sweat.

What in *hell* was he thinking about?

He had known she'd be here. The party was in her honor. He'd thought he was ready for this, had expected to be in full control. Now the intensity of his reaction staggered him.

Dazed, appalled, he stared at her exquisite profile. She was standing near the fireplace with a glass of champagne held between slender fingers, a slight smile on her face as she listened to the others.

Her amber-colored dress was made of a soft fabric that molded the proud thrust of her breasts, clung to her slender waist, then flared to fullness over her hips and thighs.

Her hair was a shade or so darker than her dress, and fell in soft waves almost to her shoulders. Her eyes, Kent knew, were the turquoise of Caribbean shallows. And he could have traced her features from memory: the smooth forehead, the straight nose, the rather high cheekbones, the mouth that curved with such infinite promise.

Her features?

He fought back a bitter laugh.

At his elbow, Beth Farragut said, "Oh, there you are, Kent. I was beginning to wonder if you were going to make it."

"Sorry I'm late," Kent apologized. "I had an emergency case, and I had to be sure he was admitted to the Cardiac Care Unit."

Beth, dark-haired, petite and pretty, patted his hand. "Well, I'm glad you're here now."

Kent started to answer, but at that second Susan turned, and their eyes met.

This time the crashing shock wave threatened to knock the air out of his lungs.

He concentrated on some of the basics his profession had taught him—a certain ability to camouflage, discipline, self-control. He said to Beth, "Excuse me," and slowly but steadily crossed the room.

He looked down into those extraordinary turquoise eyes, and was surprised that his voice sounded so normal as he said, "Hello, Susan."

"Kent." She let him take her hand.

Her fingers were icy.

The Donavans, the Whitfields and the Benedicts greeted him simultaneously. It seemed to him that their smiles were too cheery, their cordiality a shade too forced.

"Kent, long time no see," Clark Benedict said heartily.

"Kent," Heddy Donavan complained, "do you spend *all* your time in that hospital?"

He managed to smile at Heddy. "Not quite all of it."

As he accepted a glass of champagne from a passing waitress, he asked Susan, "When did you break away from Washington?"

"Yesterday afternoon."

She looked as taut as he felt.

"How are your parents?"

My in-laws, Kent reminded himself.

"They're fine, thanks," Susan said. "They send their regards."

Some other people joined the circle. They all knew Kent, but many of them had never met Susan. Introductions were made, and then other long-ago friends came to claim Kent's attention and for a small spate of time he and Susan were separated.

He tried to focus on what was being said to him, but it was difficult. He hadn't realized how completely he'd lost touch with these people. And he was so aware of Susan, nearby, that it would have been hard to listen even if he'd seen them yesterday.

Susan saw him smile, a perfunctory smile that was equations away from reaching his dark eyes. He was not looking at her, which gave her a moment to study him, and she felt as if she were suffocating.

Beth Farragut loomed up at her side, and said softly, "You could use a little lipstick. Let's go freshen up."

The small bathroom to which Beth took her was off Harvey Farragut's study, well away from the main traffic pattern. Beth closed the door and sat down on the edge of the tub.

"You looked like you needed to be rescued," she said gently.

"I did." Susan splashed cold water on her face, then patted her skin dry with a monogrammed guest towel.

"I take it this is the first time you've seen him since..."

Susan nodded.

"It must be rough for both of you, and I should have thought of that." Beth added ruefully, "But it would have looked odd if I hadn't invited him."

Susan's response was swift. "Of course you should have invited him."

"I wanted this to be a pleasant, *comfortable* visit for you, Susan."

"Beth," Susan said, "you must be the best hostess in Boston, and I feel privileged to be your houseguest. Don't worry about Kent and me. Now that the initial jolt is over, we'll be fine."

But would they?

She had thought she was prepared to see Kent again, but how wrong she had been! When he'd come up beside her, she'd begun to churn inside.

Outwardly, he had changed very little. He was as handsome as ever, tall, classically broad-shouldered, trimwaisted; obviously he took care to stay in shape. His smooth hair, worn just a little bit long, still looked like midnight velvet. So did his eyes. They were as dark as his hair and they were gorgeous, edged by thick ebony lashes, accented by slightly arching, black brows.

Beth said, "Kent's become quite a loner, I don't think he's had a date since Elaine died. Of course we don't see much of him since he moved away from Louisburg Square."

Susan had been looking in the mirror as she touched up her lipstick. She swung around. "He moved away?"

"He sold his house not long after Elaine died," Beth reported. "You didn't know?"

"No," Susan confessed, "I didn't. I haven't had much contact with Kent since Elaine's death. My parents and I have pretty much lost touch with him. He sends them a poinsettia each Christmas, but that's been about it."

"Kent bought a small condo in one of those townhouses in the Back Bay they've converted into apartments," Beth volunteered.

There was a pounding on the door. Harvey Farragut called, "Beth, are you in there? People are beginning to leave."

"Be right out," Beth promised.

Though a few guests were leaving, there were still clusters of people in the big drawing room, and others spilled over into both the dining room and the adjoining library.

Susan was alone, briefly, as Beth went to say some farewells. Then the voice she'd heard so seldom in her life—but could never forget—asked, "Could you do with another glass of champagne?"

She gazed up into Kent's dark eyes and wished she knew what she was seeing. She didn't want to misconstrue. It would be so easy to be wrong.

She took the champagne he handed her and flinched only slightly when he cupped her arm with his hand.

"That couch in the corner is vacant for the taking," he said. "I want to talk to you."

As they sat down, he said gravely, "It's good to see you again."

Susan couldn't answer.

"I was delighted when Beth called to say you were coming for a visit. I didn't realize you and Beth knew each other."

Susan's voice was so low Kent had to strain to hear it. "We met at your house...after the memorial service. We talked quite a bit. We've kept in touch since."

He nodded, then said, "Something else. I didn't know you and Glenn had split up. Beth told me when she called to invite me to the party."

"Glenn and I were divorced over a year ago."

His smile was wry. "Should I say I'm sorry?"

Before she could frame an answer, he added, "I've heard it's usually wiser not to tell a person who's gotten a divorce that you're sorry, because often they're glad."

"Glad?" she questioned. "I don't know that 'glad' would be the right word. Relieved, maybe."

When he didn't comment, she went on, "Glenn and I came to the end of our road, Kent. Maybe it would be more accurate to say that for quite a while we'd been traveling along two different roads. When we realized we weren't reading the same signposts, we agreed to disagree."

"Is Glenn still in the service?"

"Yes. He's a major now. He's as much of a career military man as my father. I'm sure he'll make general one day, just as Daddy did.

"Speaking of Glenn," she added, "he remarried a couple of months ago."

"And you?"

"Marriage plans, you mean?" She smiled. "None," she stated firmly. "I like my current status."

Her smile faded slightly as she realized that, strangely enough, she was looking at the only man in the world she'd ever really wanted to marry. That, of course, had been impossible. Now, even though both of them technically were free, it was still impossible. Unless a miracle happened, how could they ever be at peace? She would be a constant reminder...

Kent said, "Beth told me you got your master's in art history. I think that's terrific. I understand you're into the French Impressionists?"

"Yes." Susan's throat went dry, but she managed the fib. "That's the main reason I'm in Boston. The Museum of Fine Arts not only has an excellent Impressionist collection, it has a curator who's an expert on Claude Monet. Presumptuous though it may seem, I want to write a book about Monet."

"Why should it seem presumptuous?"

"There have been scads of books written about Monet. I have to admit it seems as if every aspect of his life has been covered."

Susan latched onto this chance to talk about her Monet project. An impersonal subject would give them both a needed reprieve.

She said, "I'm hoping to unearth something that hasn't already been dealt with."

"Possibly you already have," Kent informed her.

"What do you mean?"

"Do you remember Joe Chase?"

The name didn't register immediately, and Susan saw a bleak expression sweep over Kent's face.

"You met him at the wedding," he said. He added quickly, "Joe says the two of you talked about art at the reception. About the Impressionists, matter of fact."

"Why, yes, of course." That conversation, Susan recalled, was her only pleasant memory of her sister's wedding day. "He was a big man, prematurely gray, and he had the bluest eyes I've ever seen. He's a relative of yours, isn't he?"

"Yes, on my mother's side. My mother and Joe's mother were third cousins. It was Joe's grandfather on his father's side who was an artist and had a connection with Monet."

Susan was amused. "I suppose this grandfather was an admirer of Monet's, and went to Paris and tried to paint like him?"

Kent smiled. "You're only part right. As it happens, Joe has a collection of letters Monet wrote his grandfather. They've never been published."

He wished he could photograph the expression on Susan's face.

He said, "After Beth phoned the other day and invited me to the party, I nearly called you. I didn't know till then that you were so deeply involved in art, or that the Impressionists were your favorites. But I decided that since you were coming to town so soon, I'd have the pleasure of telling you about Joe's treasure in person." His voice was soft. "I'm glad I waited."

Susan asked doubtfully, "Are you sure about this?"

"Yes. It seems that in the late 1880s a group of American art students went to France and studied with Monet...."

"Yes, at his place in Giverny. Some of those artists became very famous."

"So Joe tells me. His grandfather, however, didn't become a famous artist. His name was Henry Chase, and his family gave him a kind of sabbatical to go to France and study art for a year. They expected him to enter the family shipping business after that, and he did. Maybe he didn't have enough talent to make it in the art world. I don't really know. As it is, he died rich and successful, if not fulfilled as an artist.

"He and Monet, though, developed a special kind of rapport. For years, Monet and Henry Chase kept up a correspondence. I don't know exactly how many letters there are, but Joe inherited them all."

"And you think he'd consider letting me see them?"

Kent loved the eagerness she was trying so hard to conceal. And the reality of how disastrously easy it would be to love *her* swept over him.

Susan saw the light ebb from Kent's eyes until they looked like flat black stones. What, she wondered, had caused such an abrupt and disconcerting change? Then, with a sudden, crystal-cold awareness, she was afraid she knew. She imagined she could *feel* Elaine standing between them.

Kent stared at his hands as he said, "Joe can't wait to meet you again. He suggested the two of us come out to his place tomorrow afternoon. It's one of the few upcoming Sundays when I won't be on call. Can you make it?"

Susan hesitated. Kent was offering her a once-in-a-lifetime opportunity, if his cousin Joe actually owned letters Monet had written. Especially if those letters were virtually unknown.

On the other hand, she needed to be so careful, when it came to anything that involved this handsome and disturbing man who was patiently waiting for her answer.

Kent finally said, "If tomorrow wouldn't be a good time for you, Susan, I'll arrange another date."

She *couldn't* deny herself this opportunity.

She said, "I should check with Beth first to be sure she has nothing planned for tomorrow...."

"What's this about Beth?" Beth inquired.

She had come up to them so quietly, Susan hadn't heard her.

Kent asked, "Would it be okay if I borrow Susan for a while tomorrow afternoon? An old acquaintance of hers wants to see her again."

"Of course," Beth said. "Why don't you come back with Susan afterward, and stay for Sunday supper?"

"Thanks, but I'll have to check in at the hospital. This is supposed to be my weekend off, but I'm concerned about the patient I admitted to the CCU before I came over here." Kent stood. "Suppose I pick you up around three-thirty tomorrow, Susan?"

"That would be fine."

Kent turned to Beth. "Nice party, Beth," he said. "Thanks for inviting me."

A small silence followed in the wake of his departure. Then Beth reached for Susan's hand and gave it a slight tug.

"Come help me entertain some of the lingering guests," she implored.

There were always hangers-on at a party, and these guests stayed and stayed. Finally, admitting her exhaustion, Susan told Beth she needed to call it a night.

"I wish I could do the same thing," Beth muttered. "Some people never know when it's time to go home."

She went on, "Susan, sleep as late as you can tomorrow, then come along to my room. Sunday's my lazy morning. Martha brings up coffee and croissants."

"Sounds perfect."

Beth, shorter than Susan, had to reach up to give her a hug. "Sleep tight," she advised.

Sleep tight?

As she walked up the winding stairs to the second floor in the Beacon Hill mansion, Susan wondered if she'd be able to sleep at all.

The spacious corner guest room she'd been given was elaborately decorated in gold and white, and furnished with priceless French antiques. Alone, her door closed, Susan stood very still for a moment. Then she walked over to the window that looked out on Louisburg Square, and stared into the night.

The square remained both a charming and opulent small oasis in the heart of Boston. Across, on the other side, as imposing as this one, was the house that Kent had inherited, and to which he had taken Elaine as a bride eight years ago.

Susan pressed a palm against the windowpane. Three years ago, she and Glenn had flown from Georgia, where Glenn was then stationed, to attend a memorial service for Elaine in the ivy-and-brick church in Copley Square where the Davenports had been worshipping for generations. Later, they had gone back to the Louisburg Square house.

Kent was wearing a charcoal-colored suit that emphasized an almost ghastly pallor, and his eyes were so filled with pain Susan had found it unbearable to look at him.

That was the second time they'd ever met.

The first time had been five years earlier, at the wedding rehearsal the night before Kent's marriage to Elaine.

They'd sat on opposite sides of the table at the rehearsal dinner. Their eyes had focused on each other, and something so cataclysmic had happened that she'd never been able to find words for it.

It was as if there were a magnetic field between the two of them, the force of the currents incredibly strong.

Susan had felt as if her heart were being ripped out of her, and it was a gift she wished she could have offered this man who looked as stricken as she felt. But Kent Davenport already belonged to Elaine. Her sister. Her *identical* twin sister.

God, why hadn't she met him first?

The bitterness she'd felt then had never entirely faded. But despite it, Susan was painfully aware that there hadn't been a moment since Elaine's death when she wouldn't have given anything to bring her back. And to try, with everything she could give, to achieve the kind of closeness she and her sister had never shared.

If only their relationship had been different, she thought now. She and Elaine had never experienced the kind of intuitive affinity identical twins were alleged to have. They hadn't even been very good sisters.

She'd often thought that nature had played a mean trick on them, making them look so alike when they were so entirely different.

As children, she remembered, few people had been able to tell them apart, and their mother had fostered their similarity by dressing them alike until they were old enough to choose their own clothes.

Once they were in their teens, they'd begun to express their individual personalities by their choices of clothes and accessories. Susan couldn't remember their ever liking the same things, not even the same colors.

And the differences had run much deeper than that. She and Elaine had never even remotely shared the same mental and emotional wavelengths, Susan thought sadly. Their personalities, their desires, their ambitions, could not have been more different.

Eight years ago. Susan had been in Paris, taking some courses at the Beaux Arts. Their father had been stationed in Washington, and Elaine was living at home. She and Kent had met at a party, a whirlwind courtship followed, and a wedding date was set in no time at all.

Elaine had phoned Susan in Paris to ask her to be maid of honor, and Susan had flown to Washington just in time to make the rehearsal dinner.

How she'd wished she had missed that flight.

But, as it turned out, the day after she met Kent, Susan walked down the church aisle, fulfilling her role as Elaine's maid of honor. She still didn't know how her wobbly legs had held her up all the way to the altar.

She'd kept her eyes averted as Elaine and Kent spoke their vows, and she was determined to avoid him at the reception later. But that wasn't possible.

He came to her and said, "Just one dance," and there was no way she could have resisted him.

They circled the ballroom, Susan's pulse throbbing in tempo with the music. His hand was so warm, she felt like the back of her sheer lime-green dress was being scorched.

They didn't speak. They were both so intensely conscious of the way it was between them that it would have been stupid to try to cover up with words. Kent's hand gripped hers, his lips tightened and Susan thought she would as soon die, right then and there, melt into the floor, seep through the boards, because her life had gone dark.

She watched Kent and Elaine cut the wedding cake. She helped Elaine change into her stunning turquoise traveling suit. She watched the newlyweds climb into the limo that would take them to Dulles. At the very last instant, Kent looked back. Susan's eyes met his, and the ache of tears that couldn't be shed became excruciating.

Now she walked over to the gold-and-white bureau, foraged under a small stack of satin and lace lingerie, and took out an envelope.

It was an ordinary, business-size, cheap white envelope. There was a Boston postmark. Her name and address were typed in capital letters. There was no return address.

The letter inside, on plain white paper, was also typed in capital letters.

For at least the hundredth time, Susan read:

YOUR SISTER'S DEATH WAS NOT AN ACCIDENT. KENT DAVENPORT MUST BE MADE TO PAY THE PRICE. ONLY YOU CAN SEE THAT JUSTICE TRIUMPHS, SO THAT ELAINE MAY REST IN PEACE.

There were two long white envelopes under the top one. Each bore a Boston postmark, and each had a letter in it. But Susan left them where they were. She knew each word by heart.

The first letter had come a couple of weeks before the first anniversary of Elaine's death. It had mentioned only that soon it would be a year, and Elaine must not be forgotten. For, the writer had said, *Her spirit is not yet free.*

That had been sufficient to shake Susan, yet not enough to impel her into action.

Last year, shortly before the second anniversary of Elaine's death, there again had been a long white envelope in her mailbox. This time the writer had observed that two long years had passed since Elaine had been condemned to the misery of becoming a shackled spirit; and shackled she would remain unless Susan took steps to free her.

That letter had disturbed Susan so much, she'd nearly shown it to her parents, Susan remembered. Then she had decided it would not be fair to involve them. They still grieved enough for Elaine as it was.

This year's letter was the first to be accusatory, the first to name a name.

Kent's name.

For two nights after she'd received the letter, Susan had been unable to sleep. She'd stared through the darkness at her bedroom ceiling, trying to puzzle out the author's rationale.

It seemed to her that the writer must live in or around Boston, and must be a very troubled person. Someone who hadn't become reconciled to Elaine's death, and, as each anniversary date approached, found this way of venting otherwise suppressed feelings.

By the end of the second night of sleeplessness, Susan decided that she had to make a trip to Boston.

She owed it to Elaine.

Perhaps she also owed it to Kent.

Chapter Two

"Harvey's nursing a hangover," Beth said, when Susan wandered down the second-floor corridor to Beth's private suite late Sunday morning.

Beth's bedroom and an adjoining sitting room were decorated in green and ivory. Beth was wearing a pale green peignoir, trimmed in ivory lace. Martha—who, Beth said, had been with the Farraguts forever—brought fresh coffee and warm croissants.

Beth's eyes looked puffy. Susan wondered if she'd been crying.

"You never see Harvey in the morning after a party. You don't see much of him on Sundays anyway, for that matter. Sunday's his day, and," Beth said tolerantly, "he works so hard in that law office of his, he deserves it. He stays glued to news and sports on the TV in his study."

She sipped the fresh cup of coffee Martha had poured for her, and admitted, "I'm curious. Who's this old acquaintance Kent wants you to see?"

"Joe Chase, a cousin of his whom I met a long time ago."

Beth nodded. "I know Joe."

"Well, as it happens, he's also interested in the Impressionists." Susan was deliberately vague. She didn't want to talk about the Monet letters until she had some facts.

"I thought Kent looked more like his old self last night," Beth commented. "For a while, he was much too thin, and he seemed so uptight." She added, "He's making quite a name as a cardiologist, and that takes doing in a world medical center like Boston."

Beth snuggled up against her pale green pillows, and Susan tried to keep her mind from wandering as Beth talked about Boston and its multifaceted advantages. But she wasn't too successful.

She'd had a restless night's sleep, and in the small hours of the morning she had awakened to wonder how she could possibly see much of Kent without subjecting both her nerves and her heart to far too much havoc. Yet, paradoxically, she *had* to see him, or the real purpose of her trip to Boston would be defeated.

Also, at some point she was going to have to work up the courage to confront him with the anonymous letters—unless she could first find out who had written them and track down the writer's motivation by herself.

The way such letters could plant the ugly seeds of suspicion was terrible, she was discovering. It was very difficult to think that Kent could have had anything to do with Elaine's death. Yet there was no way she could simply erase the letter writer's accusation without first doing her damnedest to find out who the writer *was*.

She didn't like to think she knew anyone who would stoop to anonymity so that they could vent hate. And, that's what the latest letter was. A message of hate in which malice came through with every word.

Beth said, "Susan, you were a great hit with everyone at the party last night. Though ... I do have to admit that seeing you was a shock at first to some of Elaine's friends."

Susan winced inwardly as Beth's words brought her back to the present, but she managed to sound casual enough as she observed, "Well, we *were* identical twins, Beth."

She was thinking that a number of the people who'd been at Beth's party must have been in the White Mountains on that ghastly weekend three years ago when Elaine had died.

She remembered that Beth had told her—after the service for Elaine—about the close-knit group who went to the same place in New Hampshire each year at foliage time, some to rock climb, others just to relax and enjoy.

Undoubtedly she'd met some of those people at Elaine's memorial service, though they'd been too tactful to mention that last night. And, everything connected with the service was so hazy in her mind, as if she'd deliberately suppressed the memory. Only her conversation with Beth, and the vision of Kent's white, stricken face, were really clear.

Now Beth said, "I should tell you that everyone said Elaine's image faded, after they'd talked to you for a few minutes. You're very much your own person."

Beth's eyes narrowed slightly as she surveyed Susan. "You do look so exactly like her ... and yet you don't. She kept her hair blonder, for one thing."

"She always has," Susan remarked, unconsciously slipping into the present tense. "For a while when we were in school she was platinum."

Beth chuckled. "Well, at least that was one way for people to tell you apart. Incidentally, the Benedicts want us for cocktails next weekend, and so do the Whitfields, and so do the Donavans. Also, the Grahams and the Kellys..."

Susan laughed. "All at the same time?"

"That's what I said. I told them they'll have to settle some dates among themselves and then get back to us. They all want to entertain you, Susan, and that says something."

Maybe it says they're curious as hell, Susan thought. *Maybe one of them is the anonymous letter writer, and he... or she wants to see how I'm reacting to the letters...*

Beth rambled on about other things, mostly some of the charitable causes in which she was involved. She was chairman of a benefit bazaar to be held near Christmas, and had a thousand things to do, she complained. Then suddenly she observed, "Susan, you look sleepy."

Susan was so tired she felt as if she could curl up on Beth's rug and drift off. But she said, "I need to get out in this beautiful day and stir up my circulation. How about going for a walk?"

"Exercise?" Beth shuddered. "I'm too lazy to stir."

She gestured toward the TV and VCR in the corner, and Susan saw boxes of videotapes stacked on a nearby table. "Sunday's my movie day," Beth confessed. "My secret vice. News and sports for Harvey, movies for me. How about watching a couple with me?"

"Later, maybe, but my body's asking for a small workout first," Susan said honestly. And a few minutes later, as she strolled down Beacon Hill and along Charles Street toward the Boston Common, she thought it was a shame for anyone to hole themselves up on a day like this, even in a room as beautiful as Beth's.

On this last Sunday in September, the trees on the Common were beginning to show color. The sky was blue silk, the air, if bottled and properly labeled, could have been sold for a premium price. Susan inhaled deeply, felt vibrantly alive . . . and at once thought of Kent.

Driving a black Porsche, Kent wove skillfully through the Boston Sunday-afternoon traffic toward Newton, Susan at his side.

She had a hard time keeping her eyes off him. He was wearing a gray tweed jacket, navy slacks, and an open-throated sport shirt, and he looked terrific.

As if he was aware of her watching him, he glanced toward her and smiled. There was an unexpected sweetness to his smile that brought stinging tears to her eyes—something he didn't see, fortunately, for his attention veered to his driving again.

Susan tried not to focus on Kent as she finally let herself admit that she'd loved him for such a long time. She'd tried so hard to fight that love. She'd even managed for a time to convince herself that she'd won the battle, or she never would have married Glenn.

She'd gone into her marriage determined to make a success of it, and she'd failed. Maybe if they'd had a child, things would have been different. But she had become pregnant once, and then miscarried.

Kent said, "You're so quiet. Are you thinking great thoughts about Monet, and what you're going to say to Joe about him?"

Susan flushed, because her thoughts had been so far afield of the life and times of Claude Monet. Aloud, she said, "I think this should be my day to listen, not to talk, don't you?"

She loved the way Kent's lips curved when he was amused.

"Oh, I don't know," he said. "You're the expert. Joe isn't, as I'm sure he'll be the first to tell you."

She looked at him suspiciously. "Kent, are you sure your cousin really has genuine Monet letters?"

"In a few more minutes you'll find out," Kent promised.

She frowned at him. "You're a tease."

She felt Kent's eyes on her, and his voice was soft and sexy, and caressing as a muted violin solo.

"I could tease you forever," he began, and his tone as much as his words sent a shaft of exquisite pleasure spiraling through Susan. But then she saw him pull back, as literally as if he'd been wrenched away, and she heard his voice change.

He spoke with no inflection as he warned, "I should tell you that you'll find Joe changed. He was in a bad accident a few years ago. But the change is all physical. He's still the same great person he's always been."

Before Susan could comment, Kent added, "We're almost there."

Joseph Chase lived in a big, slate-blue frame house. The neighborhood was old, with thick-trunked maples shading the sidewalks. Chrysanthemums bloomed in vivid shades of yellow, rust, dark red, and an amber that almost matched Susan's hair.

Kent clanged the brass knocker, and a plump, middle-aged woman opened the door.

"Doctor." She smiled at Kent.

Kent smiled back. "Hi, Mrs. Bancroft." He introduced Susan. "This is Susan Evans. Susan, Mrs. Bancroft is Joe's housekeeper. Is Joe ready for us?"

"Ready and eager, Doctor. He's on the sun porch."

The sun porch, a glassed-in room at the back of the house, overlooked a small garden. Even now in late September, pink and red roses still bloomed against a latticed fence.

Susan saw the wheelchair first, and thought about the big, friendly man who had insisted that she dance with him at Kent and Elaine's wedding. She couldn't keep back a jolt of shock that she was afraid might be echoed on her face.

But then she concentrated on the man himself, and she smiled. Joe Chase was still a big man, with powerful shoulders, a ruddy complexion, a shock of silver hair, and the vivid blue eyes she remembered. And there was nothing of the invalid about him. Rather, he seemed to be bursting with energy. He looked as if he should be out on a golf course with a group of his peers, or maybe sailing on the Charles.

"Susan," he beamed, and his enthusiasm was contagious. "This is terrific! It would be wonderful just to see you again. But it's a real bonus to know that you're interested in my grandfather's friendship with Claude Monet."

Kent chuckled. "Watch it, Joe. Susan's going to challenge you about that."

"Kent," Susan protested.

"Don't pay any attention to Kent," Joe advised.

Kent grinned, sat down and stretched out his long legs as he said, "I can't wait to hear this. You and Susan are about to fill in a neglected area of my education, Joe."

"Don't believe that," Susan promptly advised Joe.

"I won't," Kent's cousin promised solemnly. "I have this feeling he's been sneaking a crash course in art so he can out-expert both of us."

The housekeeper appeared with tea, homemade scones and a cranberry liqueur that Joe informed Susan he'd made himself from an old family recipe. Susan watched Kent munch happily, and wished she could preserve this moment. He looked so carefree, so relaxed. Though there was certainly a good twenty-year difference in the two men's ages, Kent and Joe clearly had a special kind of camaraderie.

Susan was suddenly grateful to Joe for what he was doing for Kent—without even realizing it, she was sure. Kent needed that kind of friendship. So, she realized, did she. She began to unwind, and it was wonderful.

She said frankly, "I can't believe you've kept a collection of genuine Monet letters such a closely guarded secret."

"I haven't done it on purpose." Joe shifted the wheelchair's position so he was facing Susan. "My sister was interested in genealogy, but French Impressionists didn't mean a thing to her," he confided. "So she had no objection to my taking the letters when our father died. There were just the two of us left in our branch of the Chases. She was quite a bit older than I, and she's gone now, too. I'm the last of our line.

"Recently...well, it has occurred to me that I've reached a time of life when I should do something with material as valuable as this correspondence."

"You're going to live to be a hundred, Joe," Kent put in.

Joe chuckled. "Kent insisted on giving me a going-over a while back," he told Susan. "He said I have a heart like an ox, and I think he honestly believes that makes me good right through eternity."

His eyes rested on Kent, and Susan saw the genuine fondness in them.

"Now," Joe went on, "about the Monet letters. Maybe Kent has already told you that it's Henry Chase, my grandfather on my father's side of the family, we're talking about. So, Kent isn't related to him.

"Henry really was a talented artist. I have a couple of his paintings, which I'll show you. I don't mean to imply he could have become another Monet. Who could? But he and Monet *did* form an unusual friendship that lasted for over four decades. Monet was in his forties when he and my grandfather met, and eighty-six when he died."

Joe paused. "Stop me if I'm rambling too much."

"No, go on," Susan urged. "I'm fascinated."

Kent laughed. "Joe," he said, "you've really hooked her." His tone deepened as he added, "And I think I'm more than a little envious."

Susan couldn't help but look at him, and once she met his eyes there was no way she could hide the way she felt about him. Her long-denied love flowed like a river let loose to spill over a dam.

To Kent, she shone. She was radiant, and she sparked a desire in him so powerful he was staggered. He needed the reprieve of having her turn her attention to Joe again. And he tried not to fantasize about what he was sure he'd just seen in Susan's eyes, as clearly as if she'd spoken the words to him.

God, if only he could respond and tell her the way he felt about her. But he couldn't take that risk unless . . .

He heard Joe say, "I have eighty-nine letters Claude Monet wrote to my grandfather, Susan," and he heard Susan gasp.

"Joe, that's fantastic."

"I also have the letters my grandfather wrote him. Henry went back to Giverny after Monet died, and was able to get them from the artist's daughter-in-law. She'd kept house for Monet."

"I don't believe this."

"That isn't all," Joe added, with a twinkle. "There are the sketches."

Susan's skin prickled with excitement, and she knew that Kent must be watching her very closely, for she heard the amusement in his voice as he said, "She's going to need my professional services, Joe, if you come out with much more like that. So, all right. *What* sketches?''

"Now and then Monet would send my grandfather a rough sketch of work in progress.''

Susan's eyes widened. "Can you imagine the value of those sketches, Joe?''

"Their commercial value?''

"That, too. But frankly I was thinking of their artistic value.''

"They're in my will,'' Joe said. "They're to go to the Museum of Fine Arts here in Boston when I die. Meantime, I keep them here in the house. Don't blanch, Susan. A few years ago I took the precaution of having my attic fireproofed, and a special security system installed. Now the attic is as good as a vault. And—'' he glanced ruefully at the arms of his wheelchair ''—as difficult now for me to access as breaking into Fort Knox would be. Otherwise, I'd have a sample here to show you. As it is, I can give you the key, Kent, and perhaps you'd like to show Susan around.''

Kent said quietly, "I think that's something Susan might like to do herself, Joe, a bit further down the road. I have a hunch the two of you are going to be working together ... if Susan can stay in Boston long enough to get into all this material you have. I don't think she was expecting much more than a conference with a museum curator when she came here. Were you, Susan?''

Susan froze. There was no way she could tell him what her real motive was for coming to Boston. She deliberately turned away from Kent, and faced Joe. "This is up to you, you know,'' she told him.

"I'm not sure I understand you, my dear,'' he said gently. Joe had seen apprehension in Susan's eyes a couple of seconds ago, and he was puzzled. He'd had the distinct impression that her apprehension was connected with Kent, and that was disturbing.

Kent had enough on his plate, Joe thought grimly. He had hoped that Susan's coming to Boston might lighten up Kent's life, instead of making it more difficult. Now he wondered. Long ago, he'd been trained in people-watching for a very specific purpose. Though it wasn't a talent he'd used much lately, catching vibes most others might miss was still second nature to him.

Joe vividly remembered witnessing a potent emotional current flowing between Kent and Susan eight years ago. The only time he'd seen them together . . . until today.

The signs had been there then, he thought. The signs were there now. The way one looked at the other when they thought the other wasn't noticing. The nuances of voice tones when they spoke. Nothing had changed.

Eight years ago, he had watched them at the rehearsal dinner. By the time the organist began to play the wedding march the following day, he wished he had the nerve to stand up when the minister asked if there were any reason why the two at the altar shouldn't be married, and shout, "Yes."

It was a tragedy, Joe thought. Kent was marrying someone who looked exactly like Susan, but wasn't Susan. But he was committed, and it already was too late.

Joe thought about flying back to Boston after Kent's wedding, gripped by memories he'd thought he'd put behind him. Memories of Megan. He'd been surprised by the depth of his pain after the passage of so many years. Deep inside him, that same pain stirred when he thought of Megan now.

They had been such fools, the two of them. So young, so much in love, and so vulnerable. They'd had a stupid, ridiculous quarrel. In its aftermath, Megan had gathered up her pride and entered a convent where the nuns were cloistered. Joe had never seen her again.

He had never married. He never could have married anyone else. Then, a brother of Megan's had notified him when Megan died, shortly after her fortieth birthday. And for quite a long time he'd been inconsolable.

Long before then, he'd chosen his own life work, just as Megan had chosen hers. He had turned his back on the family shipping business and embarked on a career so filled with danger that the threat of death was a constant companion.

He sometimes wondered what his real motivation had been, in his career choice. Had he merely wanted adventure? Or had he harbored the hidden wish to blaze out of the world a hero, while Megan was still alive, so that she would appreciate what she'd given up?

He nearly *had* gone the hero route, he now thought wryly. But by then, of course, Megan was dead.

He said, his voice still gentle, "As you can see, some things have changed since the last time we met, Susan. For the most part, I'm wedded to this contraption." He lightly stroked one of the chair wheels. "I don't gallivant much these days, so my time and my household are at your disposal. If your schedule would permit your working on the Monet material, I would welcome you. More than that, I'd help you any way I could." Joe spread his hands wide. "I'm not a writer, or maybe I would have tried to do something with the letters myself."

"Susan is a very good writer, Joe," Kent said unexpectedly.

She glanced at him, surprised. "What makes you say that?"

"Do you mean how do I know you've written, and been published? Beth told me last night. In fact, she promised to lend me a couple of magazines your articles have appeared in.''

"About art," Susan said. "They'd bore you."

"You really think so?" he challenged.

There it was again, that magic between them. Joe saw it, and wondered if he hadn't been mistaken about his other impression. Maybe he'd only imagined that fleeting expression on Susan's face.

He knew better.

Susan bypassed further comment about her writing, and said, "As I told Kent, Joe, my dream has been to write a book about Monet." She shook her head. "This is so terrific."

"To coordinate everything I have into a book would take considerable time, Susan," Joe warned.

"Yes, I know."

Susan paused and stared thoughtfully at the roses blooming in Joe's tiny garden.

She knew she was on the verge of making a double-edged commitment. If she started this project with Joe, she could be in Boston for several months. But it might take that long to find out who'd written those harrowing letters.

She didn't see how she could give up on the anonymous letters, but she realized that coming to Boston and meeting people whom Elaine had known wouldn't be enough to discover the writer's identity. It would take effort, scrutiny, opportunity, caution and determination, among other things, to trace the author... if she ever could. But she had to give it a real shot, and that meant staying on the scene as long as necessary.

As for this unparalleled opportunity to tap into new material about Monet—how could she possibly not take advantage of it?

Joe said, "Susan, you don't have to make up your mind now. The letters have been in my attic for a long time. They can be there a while longer. I promise you, no one else will have access to them until you've made your decision."

Susan told herself there was no good reason to go back to Washington. Her parents had a full life with their old service friends, also now retired. They didn't need her. And there was nothing—no one—anywhere else to demand her attention.

She flashed Joe a genuine smile. "When can we start?"

"Well," he drawled, "I'd say right now, except I have a couple of old cronies coming over for Sunday supper and a poker session. Tomorrow? How would tomorrow be? Any time you say."

"Suppose we say tomorrow afternoon."

"Fine with me," Joe assured her. "There's an upstairs study that used to be my favorite place in the house, but now I can no longer use it. It would make good work space for you. It comes with a word processor and a printer, both of which should be in good shape and ready to use."

What a wonderful man he was. Susan's eyes were moist as she went to him and impulsively bent and kissed him on the cheek.

A few minutes later she repeated that thought aloud, as she got into Kent's Porsche.

"What a pity that he has to be in that wheelchair," she said. "Is there hope that one day he'll be able to get out of it?"

"He can walk to a limited extent, using crutches," Kent said. "But it's difficult and painful for him." He added, "Sorry to say, I think medical science has done about all it can do for him."

"You said he was in an accident. What happened, Kent?"

Kent said thoughtfully, "Perhaps I should let Joe tell you that. As I'm sure he will, before the two of you have been together very long."

"Mysterious, aren't you?" Susan teased.

"Perhaps," Kent conceded, and smiled. But, again, it was a smile that didn't reach his eyes.

Chapter Three

"I'll have to find a place to stay."

Susan was thinking aloud, so she was startled to hear Kent say, "There's a sublet available in my building."

Instinctively, she backed away. It would be difficult to handle that kind of proximity.

"I wouldn't hamper you where your work's concerned, Susan," Kent assured her. "I'm not around that much. I think I already mentioned this happens to be one of my rare Sundays off."

"Yes," she said. "And I appreciate your sharing it with me. Your free time must be very precious to you."

She looked guilty, and Kent didn't want that. He wished he could tell her that though his free time meant a lot to him, she meant so much more.

Instead, he stuck to the practical. "Fall isn't the greatest time of the year to get a rental around here," he pointed out. "The Boston area is loaded with educational institutions.

Students swarm into town in late summer and rent everything in sight.

"As it happens, though, a colleague of mine who owns a condo in my building went to Texas on a research grant a couple of months ago. He'll be away at least a year. He's a private kind of a guy, and he doesn't need money. He wasn't interested in renting his condo to anyone who might happen by. But he told me if I came across someone I could vouch for..."

"I don't know," Susan murmured doubtfully.

She was tempted, but her common sense told her this was a temptation that should be resisted. If she was to move into Kent's building, they would be bound to see each other, regardless of his schedule.

Well—that's what she wanted, wasn't it? Hadn't she come to grips with the necessity of seeing Kent, if she hoped to get to the root of the anonymous letters?

Kent's frustration increased as he watched a range of mixed emotions cross Susan's face. Something was bothering her very much, and he needed to know what it was. But there was no way in God's world he could ask her directly.

If he could persuade her to sublease George Bartlett's condo, at least he could keep an eye on her.

Susan said warily, "I wouldn't want to get involved in a lease, Kent. And I should imagine your friend will want one."

"Not necessarily," Kent retorted. "I think George would agree to a month-to-month rental provided the tenant is right."

Provided you speak up for me, Susan silently amended.

"I don't know," she hedged. "When I told Beth I was coming to Boston, she invited me to stay with Harvey and her. She insisted there was no time limit involved, but I don't want to impose on her hospitality." She paused for a moment, considering her options. "Before I commit myself to a rental, however, I should be sure things are going to work out with Joe Chase."

"Aren't you?" Kent asked.

Before she could answer, he frowned and said, "Susan, I'm not trying to influence you. I think George's condo would be just what you want, but that's up to you. Daisy Crandall manages our building. She lives in the basement apartment. If you like, I'll tell her you may stop by to see her tomorrow." He shrugged. "Why not take a look at George's place? If it doesn't suit, Daisy might know of something else that would. For that matter, the real estate broker I bought my condo from handles a few rentals, and he's reliable. I'd be glad to put you in touch with him."

"Kent," Susan began. "There's no need..."

He gave her a reassuring smile. "No problem."

Kent centered his attention on driving, and Susan stole a glance at his profile. It was inscrutable. She envied him his poise, and his ability to mask his emotions so quickly. A couple of minutes ago he hadn't been quite so casual.

He'd seemed both anxious and eager for her to rent his friend's condo, and she wondered why. She had a reason for needing to keep in touch with him, but what was his reason for wanting to have her around? He must know, just as she did, that the more they saw each other the more difficult it would be for them. It would be like swimming upstream against a strong current; they couldn't let go and give in to the flow of passion that was always there. At least, *she* couldn't, not until she found out who'd written the letters, and exactly what they meant.

The venom behind the latest letter suddenly hit her. It wasn't a plea for justice, she decided. Rather, it was the signal for a vendetta. The writer must despise Kent, and desperately want to hurt him.

Why?

Kent *couldn't* have had anything to do with Elaine's death. She had fallen from a mountain ledge, plunged hundreds of feet to the rocky shore of a glacial lake.

Her death had been an *accident*....

Susan shivered.

Kent suddenly pulled the car over to the curb, then sat back and looked at her. His eyes seemed very dark and deep, and unreadable.

He said, "Let's stop and get a drink someplace. We need to talk."

"I should go back to Beth and Harvey's," Susan said quickly. She didn't think she could face being alone with Kent at an intimate table for two.

His eyes didn't waver. "Are they expecting you at any special time?"

"No...well, not exactly. They have potluck supper on Sunday. I'm sure Beth would still like it if you could come back."

"I'll have to pass on that. As I told Beth last night, I need to check on a patient. I'll take you directly to Louisburg Square if that's what you want," Kent added. "But we still need to talk, Susan. Will you meet me for lunch tomorrow?"

She was surprised. "I thought you were so busy you didn't have time for things like lunches on weekdays."

"I'm busy," he said grimly, "but I'll make time. I know something's bugging you, and I can't shake the feeling it has to do with me."

"Kent—" she began.

He cut her off. "Don't try to deny it," he cautioned.

He swung back into traffic, and they were both silent until he turned into Louisburg Square and pulled up in front of the Farragut house. Then he said, "There's a little French place not far from the hospital. I'll jot down the address for you. Meet me around one, will you? You can go on to Joe's from there.''

He took a small leather-bound notepad out of his coat pocket, scratched a few words on a slip of paper and handed the slip to Susan.

''I know how difficult this must be for you,'' he began. But then he stopped, and shook his head. ''No point in going into that now,'' he muttered, as if he were speaking to himself.

Suddenly he smiled, a smile that was both sad and tender. Before Susan realized what he was about to do, he bent toward her and brushed her lips with a kiss that was a remarkable mix of lightness and intensity.

Susan was still under the spell of the kiss's astonishing impact as she climbed the steps to the Farraguts' front door. Carefully she touched her fingers to her mouth, smoothing her lips with a soft and telling gesture, as if by doing that she could seal in Kent's kiss, hold it to herself and preserve it.

Harvey Farragut opened the door. He was holding a glass half-full of amber liquid, and he looked flushed and angry. *Not exactly anyone's idea of a welcoming host*, Susan thought wryly.

When he saw who it was, Harvey managed to switch on a lopsided smile. ''Beth's in the library,'' he told Susan, and led the way.

Beth was sitting stiffly in a leather-upholstered armchair. She, too, was clutching a drink, and she was pale and tense.

Susan felt sure she'd interrupted the Farraguts in the middle of a hefty argument.

''What'll you have, Susan?'' Harvey asked, and indicated a well-stocked bar in the corner.

''A glass of sherry would be fine.''

As Harvey poured, Beth forced a smile and asked, "How did your meeting with Joe Chase go?"

"It was very enjoyable. We have a lot in common."

"We haven't seen him for quite a while," Beth said. "Not since his accident, which must be over three years ago. I understand he's in a wheelchair."

"Yes, he is."

"He and Kent always have been close," Beth went on. She took a sip of her drink. "Too bad Kent couldn't come back here with you."

Harvey laughed. "Don't tell me Kent had another engagement? Maybe he's finally decided to join the human race again."

"For all we know, maybe Kent's latched onto some new people who are more interesting than our crowd," Beth said tightly.

"For all we know, maybe Kent's not that keen about hanging round with us and our crowd." Harvey retorted. He gave Susan her sherry, and added, "Too many lousy memories."

"Harvey," Beth protested, and Harvey had the grace to look abashed.

"Sorry, Susan," he mumbled.

"That's all right," Susan murmured. But *nothing* was all right. The undercurrents were tense and murky. Maybe they only had to do with whatever disagreement Harvey and Beth had just been having. But, from Harvey's retort to Beth, Susan wondered if maybe her presence in Boston had stirred up things that had been carefully kept dormant for almost three years.

The Farraguts and their closest friends had been at Salzwald the weekend Elaine died, Susan reminded herself. Subsequently, Kent evidently had pretty much withdrawn from their social inner circle.

She needed to get to know the people in that inner circle, though it wasn't something she looked forward to. Naturally she reminded them of Elaine. Beth had already said so, though actually it hadn't needed to be said.

Well, she'd have to live with the realization that they'd be looking at her and probably thinking of Elaine. She still had to approach each of them. There was a good chance that one of Beth and Harvey's crowd had written the poison-pen letters.

Susan hoped the party guests would follow through with the invitations Beth had spoken about that morning. Once she moved away from here, she'd have to keep checking with Beth. Maybe if the Benedicts and the Whitfields and the Donavans didn't get in touch, she could arrange to do something herself before too long. A Sunday brunch, perhaps. Something simple and casual . . .

After a time, Harvey trundled off to his study to watch the Red Sox on television, and Beth suggested that she and Susan go out to the kitchen and find something to eat.

There was food left over from the party, plus casseroles that had been prepared so they could be heated quickly in the microwave; more to eat, Susan thought, than she'd ever seen assembled at one time in one place. She and Beth settled for chicken sandwiches.

Then it seemed that Beth hadn't finished her movie viewing for the day.

"Why don't you come watch with me?" Beth invited Susan. She giggled. "This one's X-rated."

"Thanks," Susan said, "but I'll have to beg off, Beth. I have a couple of letters I need to write tonight."

She thought about telling Beth that she might go apartment hunting in the morning, then decided that could wait. Beth was putting up a good front, but she still looked upset.

It was a relief to escape to the gold-and-white bedroom. But once in it, with the door securely closed, Susan didn't immediately start in on any correspondence. Instead, she took the envelopes out of the drawer and read the latest letter again, and this time the poison the words spewed seemed more odious than ever.

Though she had intended to write her parents and a couple of close friends in Washington, Susan couldn't concentrate on anything but the anonymous letters, once she'd stashed them away again.

She undressed, slid into bed and tried to read a book, but that didn't work, either. Finally she gave up and switched off the bedside lamp, but it was a long time before she fell asleep.

Daisy Crandall was a tall, slim redhead who looked more like a high-fashion model than a condo manager.

"Dr. Davenport said you might be stopping by," she told Susan. "Dr. Bartlett's place is on the fourth floor, which is also the top floor. Let's take the elevator."

The tiny elevator was tucked in a rear corner of the beautifully restored townhouse. The top floor condo looked out over Storrow Drive, and beyond to the Charles River and Cambridge across the way.

"Super view, isn't it?" Daisy Crandall commented. "Actually, Dr. Davenport has an even better one, though he's on the floor below this. He has a larger corner unit.

"As you can see," she went on, "this is just one studio room. But it's spacious."

The room was huge, with high ceilings and a wood-burning fireplace. Kent was right, Susan had to admit. This would be a perfect place for her. She could picture herself working on the Monet material on snowy winter nights, and it was a nice picture. But the realization that Kent would be just one floor below her was daunting.

Could she deal with that much physical closeness?

Also...did Kent really want her as a neighbor? Or, had his mentioning his friend's condo been an impulsive gesture? Because he knew the rental situation in Boston at this time of year really *was* difficult and he'd been kind enough to want to help her out?

Susan sighed. She was so terribly aware that every time Kent looked at her, he, too, must think of Elaine. That *had* to be so, regardless of the powerful feelings between the two of them.

She could imagine only too keenly how painful seeing her must be for him. How could it be otherwise? How could it ever be otherwise? For five years of his life he had been married to a woman who looked exactly like her.

Lost in unhappy thoughts, Susan was startled when Daisy Crandall said, "Dr. Davenport speaks highly of you, and he and Dr. Bartlett are good friends. So there's no doubt in my mind about your being the right person for the sublet. If you feel the condo suits you, I'd say we've made a perfect match."

It would be stupid not to rent the condo, Susan told herself. Stupid to let her imagination play tricks on her. The reality of this situation was bad enough without adding any new dimensions to it.

She made her decision, took a deep breath and asked, "When can I move in, Mrs. Crandall?"

Daisy laughed. "Immediately, if you like. That wouldn't be true with most people, but you come with a very special reference. Let's go down to my apartment. We can take care of the paperwork, and I'll give you a key."

* * *

Susan stood in the entrance of the French restaurant where Kent had asked her to meet him, looked around and didn't see him.

A gray-haired woman, her ample figure encased in black silk, approached and inquired politely, "Madame?"

"I'm to meet someone here," Susan said. "Dr. Davenport?" She wasn't sure whether Kent's name would be recognized.

It was. "Ah," the woman said with a smile. "You must be Madame Evans. The doctor telephoned to say that he has been delayed but will join you shortly. If you will follow me, please..."

The small back dining room had casement windows that overlooked a brick courtyard where there were round wrought-iron tables and matching chairs.

"The doctor prefers the outside," the hostess said, "but I told him, *il fait un peu trop froid* today. May I bring you an aperitif?"

"Yes. Cinzano, please."

She was sipping the aromatic vermouth when Kent arrived.

"Susan, I'm sorry," he said, as he slipped into the chair opposite hers. "I couldn't break away any sooner."

Susan looked at him and felt as if eight years suddenly had been telescoped into this single moment. It was as if she were seeing him again for the first time, and the impact was even stronger than it had been that first time.

People might scoff and say there was no such thing as love at first sight. But, though she had tried as hard as anyone could to disavow it, that was the way it had been with her.

She had been forced to deny her love, and no rite of exorcism could have been more difficult. But now, as she looked at Kent, she knew she could never go through that denial process twice.

On the other hand, how could she let herself love Kent as she so desperately wanted to love him if there was even the sliver of a chance that he had been involved in her sister's death?

Kent had been looking at her with a tenderness that threatened to undermine all her resolve. But now his expression changed, and he asked, "What's the problem, Susan? Please don't say there isn't one. Your face just now was a study in conflicting..."

He broke off as the hostess approached and put a stemmed glass at his place. "Your soda, Doctor," she said.

Kent managed to smile at her. *"Merci, Madame."*

"Do you and *madame* wish a little time, or must you order?"

"We'd like a little time, please."

Kent told Susan, "I warned the staff I was taking a long lunch hour."

He saw that she was rummaging through her handbag and he asked, "Lost something?"

"No. Here it is." She held up a key.

The significance of the gesture escaped Kent. He was still thinking about the changing expressions he'd seen on her face a couple of minutes ago, but he was beginning to realize that he needed to gain Susan's trust before he could hope to get her to confide in him.

Susan twirled the key between her fingers. "I rented your friend's condo, Kent."

Kent's heart took a quantum leap and beat a tattoo against his chest.

Susan looked at him anxiously. "Are you sorry I followed through?"

"Sorry?" he echoed. "Why should you think I'd be sorry?"

"I thought perhaps you've had second thoughts about having me right on your doorstep. What I mean is, sometimes impulse leads us to get into things we'd later as soon get out of."

Susan was staring at the tablecloth. Kent reached across the table and grasped her chin between his fingers, and made her look at him.

"I think you know better," he said.

"I'm not sure of too much these days, Kent."

His eyes were unwavering. "You can be sure of me."

He had to say that much. There was a limit to anyone's restraint. And he had waited so long to say anything at all to her.

"If you want to know how I honestly feel about your renting George's condo," he said, "I have to tell you that you'll make the most terrific neighbor I've ever had."

His voice was warm, his words flowed over Susan like a gentle balm, holding the promise of the healing she so badly needed. But there was heat to the balm, too, a delicious heat that began to spread through her, filling the spaces that had been cold and empty for so long.

Susan drew a deep breath and said, "Thank you."

Kent slowly rubbed his fingers along her chin. Her skin felt like rose petals.

He wished they were alone together, miles away from here, in a small and special place that no one else could find. He had waited for her for so long, wanted her for so long. His insides twisted with an ache that was much too familiar.

He gently released Susan's chin, and picked up his drink. He tried to concentrate on the glass and its contents. Unless he quickly fixated on something specific, he didn't see how he was going to keep from spilling out a saga of eight years of repression.

Though he wished he and Susan could simply bridge those eight years and start from the present, Kent was sure that wasn't possible. They needed to fill in the gap, for both their sakes. Before he could hope to spirit Susan away in search of a small bit of paradise, he had to make her understand what had happened to him—starting eight years ago—and why he'd behaved as he had.

She couldn't possibly know unless he told her how Elaine had rushed into his life. And how the romance that had led to their setting a wedding date had been like a continuing ride on a roller coaster.

Yes, he'd admit to Susan, he'd been dazzled by Elaine. But he had met Elaine at a time when he was especially vulnerable. Professionally, he was still in a learning stage. For such a long while, he had been devoting himself almost entirely to medicine.

The party where he and Elaine literally had bumped into each other was a rare social excursion for him just then. Elaine had been beautiful, exciting, and he was not carved of ice.

God, Susan would understand that, wouldn't she? He'd *let* himself become wildly infatuated with her twin, and capitulating to a heady sexual attraction had felt great. But by the time the wedding day approached, he'd not been without misgivings.

Yes, of course, he should have paid more attention to those misgivings. He was more than willing to admit that freely. But at the time, between the pressure of his grant work at the National Institutes of Health and getting ready to be married, he hadn't stopped to *think*.

Would that make sense to Susan?

Could he possibly explain how, when he'd met her the night before the wedding, he'd felt as if he'd been turned upside down? His emotions had become a mass of tangled confusion, making it impossibly difficult to sort through *anything*.

When he'd looked at Susan, then looked at Elaine, he'd felt as if he had been handed a two-sided mirror. He was seeing a woman reflected in each side of the mirror, and the women looked exactly alike. But, from the beginning, Kent had known instinctively that they were very different. It was the woman on the other side of the mirror who belonged in his life.

Regardless, he'd gone on the next day to make the biggest mistake of that life. He'd stood at the altar next to Elaine, and repeated the marriage vows the minister told him to say....

He winced, and Susan prodded, "Kent?"

Kent shook himself mentally, and managed to smile at her. "Sorry."

Susan hesitated, torn between curiosity over Kent's sudden self-preoccupation and her own natural reserve. Curiosity won. "Would it be too much to ask what you were thinking?"

She was sure that whatever he'd been thinking about involved her.

"I was wool-gathering," Kent admitted.

Susan waited for him to say more.

Finally he said slowly, "I wonder—how is it that so many years went by without our ever seeing each other, Susan?"

Susan wished she hadn't led into this. She said, "I went back to Paris right after... the wedding. At the time of the Oktoberfest in Germany I went to Stuttgart to visit friends. Army friends, who were stationed at Kelly Barracks. I ran into Glenn Evans... he was an Army brat, too. Years before, his father had been stationed at the Presidio in San Francisco when my father was. By the time we met again, Glenn himself was a captain, and he was stationed at Kelly. . . ."

She was deliberately vague. "One thing led to another."

"And you and Glenn got married?"

"Yes. On the spur of the moment, actually. We were married at Kelly Barracks. Friends arranged an on-the-spot military wedding. Glenn took a week's leave, and we went off to Heidelberg on a honeymoon.

"We were at Kelly for over two years after that. Then we went to London for two years. Glenn was attached to the embassy. We'd been in Georgia, at Fort Benning, for only a short while when . . . Elaine died."

Kent nodded. "I never did get the chronology quite straight."

That was true enough, though he distinctly remembered exactly when he'd heard about Susan's marriage. Elaine's parents had phoned from Washington one evening, a short while after he'd gotten home from the hospital.

He had lied that night, Kent remembered. He had been off duty, but he had told Elaine he was on call. He'd gone out by himself and gotten drunk, and had wound up sleeping on the living-room couch in another resident's apartment.

By then, of course, neither he nor Elaine had any illusions about where their marriage was going. Ironically, he'd been on the verge of asking her for a divorce. But once he learned that Susan was married, whether or not he got a divorce no longer seemed especially important.

Then, one day not long before she died, Elaine had brought up the subject of divorce herself. There was someone else, she said. Kent agreed that she should consult an attorney. But she had gone to Salzwald the weekend before she was to keep the appointment she made.

Three years ago, Kent thought. And the memory was still like a heavy stone.

Would it have been better if they'd had a child?

Probably not, he had to admit. Whatever had been between Elaine and himself had turned to ashes much too fast. A child would have suffered....

He suddenly asked Susan, "Did you want children?"

"Yes," she admitted. "And . . . I did get pregnant once. I had a miscarriage."

Kent reached for her hand, imagining how that must have hurt her. "I'm sorry," he said.

"I tell myself it was probably just as well."

He forced a smile. "You're young enough to have a dozen kids."

"Not quite. I'm thirty-one, Kent."

But of course Kent would know that, Susan reminded herself. Elaine also would be thirty-one, had she lived. And Kent? He was thirty-seven, if she remembered correctly.

The thought came. *Some of the best years of our lives still lie ahead.* But she wasn't going to deceive herself about their being able to spend those years together.

She wondered if Elaine would have enjoyed playing the role that seemed to have been meted out to her? The part of the ghost who wouldn't go away?

Susan switched gears abruptly.

"Kent," she said, "it's true that I came to Boston looking for information about Monet." *The truth,* she confessed to herself, *but not the whole truth.* "But I'm a bit overwhelmed by what I've fallen into, thanks to you."

She went on. "Having access to the Monet letters will probably be the biggest coup in my professional life. I'll be eternally grateful to you for having brought Joe and me together. But I just hope I can handle this, so your faith will be justified.''

"There's no need for you to justify anything." Kent's dark eyes were sparkling now. "I predict you'll do something magnificent with Joe's material."

The hostess came to the table and said, "Excuse me, Doctor. There is a telephone call for you."

Kent swore as he followed Madame. He had left strict instructions about calling him at the restaurant, which just about guaranteed this was an emergency.

When he returned to the table, Susan was glancing at the menu Madame had provided. It seemed to Kent that she was reading the same line over and over again.

He sat down and muttered, "Damn, I'm sorry. I have to make tracks for the CCU."

Susan smiled at him. "Don't look so guilty. It's not your fault."

Kent drew a deep breath. "Can we do this again?"

She said gently, "Of course we can do it again."

Kent looked at her beautiful, understanding face and felt as if a weight had been lifted from his shoulders. His spirit soared a little, and even that small exercise in freedom made him aware of how he'd been shackled, for so long.

His voice was husky as he urged, "Stick around and order some lunch, will you please? Or, I could ask Madame to choose something special for you."

"Kent, I'm not especially hungry."

"You *will* give me a guilt complex if you don't let Madame fuss over you a little—which she's certain to want to do when she learns I've abandoned you. Let her bring you some samples of the fabulous food they serve in this place. Then it will be time for you to meet with Joe. I'll be anxious to know how it goes with the two of you."

"I'm looking forward to this afternoon." Susan looked up at him, and added wistfully, "I wish you could be with us."

Why should such a simple statement make his heart sing?

How could he possibly manage to walk away from Susan right now?

"When do you plan to move into George's place?" he asked her.

She frowned slightly. "Although I have the key, I'm not sure. I haven't told Beth what I intend to do, and I don't want to be too abrupt. She's been a very generous hostess."

"Call me this evening and let me know, will you? And let me know how you and Joe make out? I should be home, unless I get stuck at the hospital."

Kent took his notepad out of his pocket and quickly scrawled down some numbers.

Handing Susan the slip of paper, he said, "This is my home number, which is unlisted. This is the hospital number, and this is my page number. The operator may ask who you are, just tell her I asked you to call me, then don't hang up. Sometimes it takes a while for me to answer my beeper. Susan..."

She tucked the slip with the phone numbers on it into her handbag. "Yes?"

"Don't forget to call, okay?"

Kent bent and brushed a kiss across her lips, then left before she could say anything.

Chapter Four

Susan hailed a taxi on Newbury Street and tried to straighten out her private world during the drive to Newton. Kent had jostled her off her axis again, though all he'd done was kiss her goodbye.

She corrected herself. No, that wasn't all Kent had done. He'd done a job on her just by the way he looked at her, and the way he spoke to her. Every glance he'd given her and every word he'd spoken had packed an emotional wallop.

She needed to be more objective about Kent, Susan warned herself, especially since they would be living in the same building. She knew she must try to do a better job of keeping her guard up when she was with him, since she could not be at peace either with Kent or with herself until she found out exactly what had happened at Salzwald and what his role had been.

She owed that much to Elaine.

A sudden sense of loss came over Susan that was all the sharper because it was unexpected. She had grieved for Elaine—it would have been inhuman not to. But lately she'd been thinking more and more of all they'd missed as sisters, let alone as twins.

She'd never been much of a believer in the occult. But she hated the phrase used in one of the anonymous letters about Elaine's soul being "shackled." That in itself would have impelled her to search out the author.

Outside Joe's house, the early-autumn sunlight highlighted his chrysanthemums. The sight of their bright colors helped Susan shake off a threatening gray mood.

She paid the cab driver, a little daunted by the tally on the meter. From now on, she decided, she'd better either settle for public transportation or rent a car. Otherwise, getting back and forth to Joe's would classify as a major expense.

Joe opened the door himself. He thrust out a welcoming hand, and, as Susan clasped it, she couldn't help but wish that a miracle might free this man from the wheelchair that held him prisoner. Again, she was struck by his vitality. It didn't seem right that he should be so chained.

She saw that Joe was scanning the curb. Her cab had driven off, and he asked, "How did you get out here?"

"I took a taxi."

Joe rolled his chair back a little, so Susan could get past him, and said, "I guess it didn't occur to either Kent or me that you'd need wheels." As he spoke, he led the way down the hall to the sun porch.

"I think I'll rent a car, but I want to get settled first," Susan told him. "Incidentally, I've sublet a condo in Kent's building."

"He hoped you'd do that."

So, at some point, Joe and Kent must have talked since the visit here yesterday afternoon.

The closeness between the two men had been apparent yesterday. But, Susan wondered, just how large a role did Joe Chase play in Kent's life? Was he like a surrogate father, or uncle, to Kent, maybe? Or more like an older brother?

Joe said, "Mrs. Bancroft went shopping. She said she needed to get a couple of things for our tea."

He waved Susan to a chair. "Now, about a car. I have a perfectly good sedan in the garage that you're more than welcome to use. It hasn't been driven much for a while. But I see to it that a mechanic friend of mine checks it out occasionally, so I know it's in good shape and ready to go."

"Joe," Susan protested, "I couldn't possibly take your car."

"I'm sure it would appreciate your tender loving care," Joe told her. "Everything needs to be used, Susan. Anyway, this is a second car. These days, I prefer the van. It's more comfortable for me and can even accommodate both me and my wheelchair when I want to travel that way," Joe confided. "Also, it has hand controls, which are easier for me now. So, if you'd deign to use my car, you wouldn't be depriving me of a thing."

Susan smiled. "The next thing I know, you'll be telling me I'd be doing you a favor by taking it."

"Well, that would pretty much be so."

She murmured helplessly, "I don't seem to be able to say no."

"Great, then that's settled. Now," Joe held out a key ring from which a single key dangled. "You'll need this. It unlocks the attic door.

"As I told you, the attic's the next thing to a bank vault. There's both a separate security system and fire alarm system. You'll find a small panel on the wall at the head of the attic stairs. You'll need to punch out the code numbers before you can unlock the door.''

Joe hesitated, then said, "This may sound melodramatic, but I'd like you to memorize the number combination I'm going to give you, and then destroy the paper it's written on.''

His smile was sheepish. "The line of work I was in tended to promote paranoia.''

Susan had to laugh. "I doubt you're paranoid, Joe," she assured him. "In fact, I would think that your attic security system is essential.''

"Considering the climate of today's world, you're probably right...more's the pity," Joe said. "I do have some original oils up in the attic that are pretty valuable. Plus the Monet sketches, the letters, and a few other odds and ends. As you'll soon see for yourself.''

Susan said slowly, "You're trusting me with a lot. I appreciate that confidence.''

"I'd trust you just from the little contact I've had with you, Susan. But the way Kent vouches for you adds a golden edge.''

"That's good to hear," Susan said softly.

She thought about Kent vouching for her, and the idea made her feel warm all over.

Susan was aware that Joe was watching her very closely, and she was sure she was giving away some of her feelings about his handsome cousin.

Joe Chase was sharp. She was learning that fast.

She was also realizing that Joe must know far more about Kent than anyone else she was apt to encounter. With the differences in their ages, he might even remember Kent as a child.

She wished she could ask him a thousand questions.

As it was, she said hesitantly, "Joe, after visiting you here yesterday, I was thinking of our first meeting at Kent and Elaine's wedding. I can't recall any of Kent's other relatives being there."

"There weren't any others, Susan."

"Are you saying you're all the family Kent has?"

Joe nodded. "Afraid so. And the same pretty much holds for me. On my father's side of the family, I have a few cousins, though none of them live in New England. But Kent is the last on my mother's side."

"How long ago did Kent's mother die, Joe?"

"Louise died when Kent was nine," Joe said soberly. "She was a beautiful woman. Kent takes after her in looks. Then," Joe volunteered, "when Kent was in med school, his father killed himself."

The shock was like a physical blow. "Kent's father *killed* himself?"

"Yes. It was one of the scandals of the year, here in Boston. A wealthy Beacon Hill banker committing suicide in his Louisburg Square mansion."

Joe sighed. "It was a hell of a time for Kent. He came home one winter afternoon to find that his father had shot himself in the head with his pearl-handled revolver. He was slumped over his desk, in the library. Kent was the first to find him."

"Dear God!" The vision that swam before her eyes made Susan feel sick.

"They'd never had much of a relationship," Joe said, "but, if anything, that made it even harder for Kent. He blamed himself for their lack of communication. He felt that if he'd been a better son to Arthur, he would have had some idea of what was apt to happen.

"I never agreed with that, and I think that after a time I convinced Kent, as much as anyone could, that there was nothing he could have done. Kent's twenty years younger than I am, Arthur was perhaps ten years older than me. He was a distant kind of person, very much a loner, especially after his wife died. I never felt I knew him.

"There are those who envy Kent," Joe continued. "He inherited wealth, he's exceptionally handsome, and now he's successful in his chosen field. I've heard some say that he was born with a platinum spoon in his mouth, and perhaps that's true to an extent. But his life has not been easy—he's had more than his share of tragedy."

Joe grinned, and admitted, "That's one reason I'm glad you've decided to stay around and work on my grandfather's letters. Kent would have my head for this, but I'm going to say it anyway. He needs you, Susan."

Susan didn't know how to answer that.

Alice had stumbled into Wonderland. Susan felt as if she'd stumbled into a giant-sized magic treasure chest.

Did Joe have any idea what he had here?

Each inch of the attic lured her to devote her attention to its particular space. Then, as she was studying one thing, something else would catch her eye, and she would move on. She was dazzled by the riches she was finding, and she hadn't even gotten to the carved wooden chest Joe had described that held the Monet letters.

She saw a Childe Hassam original and was enraptured. Monet was her favorite artist, but Hassam's *Boston Common at Twilight* was her favorite painting.

And—could she believe her eyes? There was a Cézanne, a Vuillard and a Sargent.

These paintings belonged in museums.

Susan cautiously lifted the lid of an old steamer trunk and saw that it was full of clothes. Rich green satin gleamed, and she carefully drew out an exquisite Victorian ball gown. The

person who wore it, she estimated, must have been just
about her size.

Another trunk held papers. Yet another, an assortment
of memorabilia—small objects, everything from a kaleido-
scope to some political campaign buttons.

Joe had insisted that nothing in the attic was off-limits to
her. He'd added that he would much appreciate it, in fact,
if she'd go through all of it, in due course, and then help him
determine what should be done with what he termed his
"various inheritances."

Their Monet project was, of course, a priority, they'd
both conceded. Now Susan somewhat reluctantly closed a
trunk lid—there was so much to look at—and concentrated
on finding the small wooden chest.

But, before she finished her search, Susan again was
sidetracked several times by many different things that
clamored for her attention. It was amazing, she thought
with a smile, how vociferous inanimate objects could be.
She fondled the spokes of a spinning wheel, chuckled at a
dress form that had been made for a very ample lady and
pictured a parrot in the ornate brass bird cage.

With each new object she came across, she wished more
and more that Kent were here to share her discoveries. She
felt sure he'd be every much as intrigued as she was. They
could laugh together over some of the things, grow nostal-
gic over others. This attic told the saga of not one but many
lives.

There was romance here, and love and joy, and also pain
and sorrow. A mix of the entire emotional gamut, to be experienced, studied, learned from . . .

Susan clamped a temporary lid on her wandering fancies
when, finally, she came to the carved wooden chest. But,
though she was sorely tempted, she didn't open it. Instead,

she carried it down to the second floor, after first stopping to activate the alarm system again.

The study in which Susan was to work was a delightful, high-ceilinged room with windows overlooking Joe's small garden. Susan set the chest on a chair, then took a little time to explore. There was everything she could possibly want for her project, she discovered. A state-of-the-art computer and printer, and an equally efficient copying machine, a liberal supply of paper, notepads, pens, pencils, boxes of tissue, even French and English dictionaries.

The bookshelves that lined one side of the room were partially filled, but there were plenty of empty spaces to hold books she would need in her research. There was even a comfortable-looking daybed in the corner, where she could snatch a nap now and then.

Joe had thought of everything. Susan could imagine him and Mrs. Bancroft putting their heads together, to make sure she wouldn't lack for anything. She saw an intercom, which she supposed would connect her with either Joe or Mrs. Bancroft, or even both of them. And, as a final touch, there was a box of chocolates.

On impulse, Susan opened the box and popped a succulent caramel into her mouth.

Kent's cousin, she decided, was fabulous.

A quality that must run in the family.

As she devoured the candy, Susan cast a slightly apprehensive eye at the small carved wooden chest. She was dying to open it. Yet she was almost afraid to discover what was inside.

It would be such a tremendous letdown if the letters actually weren't from Monet, or were merely copies of letters Monet had written. Or, if perhaps only a couple of them were from the great artist, and the rest a heap of miscellaneous correspondence.

Finally, Susan diagnosed her problem, or at least the major part of it. The simple truth was that she wanted to share the moment when she opened the chest and took out the first letter. Preferably with Kent. But his cousin would be the best possible substitute.

Joe was still on the sun porch, and he was reading. As Susan approached him, he whipped off a pair of dark-rimmed glasses, and put his book aside.

"A problem?" he asked.

"No." As Susan put the chest down on the coffee table, she added, "I do want to say, though, that there's nothing in the least paranoid about your wanting to keep that attic as secure as possible. Joe, do you realize what a treasure trove you have up there?"

"To tell you the truth," Joe admitted, "I'm not sure I do. I appreciate art, and nice old things, but I'm no expert about their value."

"Nice old things," Susan scoffed. "Joe, you have any number of things that are fascinating unto themselves—and valuable, as well. Plus some real museum pieces. And, I might add, vintage clothing some collectors caught up in nostalgia would kill for. There is one green satin dress..."

"Did you try it on?"

Susan's eyes widened. "Of course not."

"Don't be so taken aback, my dear. All I was going to say is that if the dress fits you, it's yours. For that matter, if it doesn't fit you, maybe you could have it altered, if you like it."

Susan said severely, "I can see that I'm going to have to watch you, and make sure your interests are protected."

Joe asked with a straight face, "Can you picture me ever wearing a Victorian satin dress, Susan?"

Susan burst out laughing. And the sound of her laughter was more heartening to Joe than anything he'd heard for a long time. He only wished that Kent were here to hear it too.

He said, "What about the letters, Susan? Do they live up to your expectations?"

"I haven't opened the chest yet," Susan confessed. She added, almost shyly, "I wanted someone to share the experience with me."

Joe was touched. He said softly, "Well, I'd be glad to try to be that someone."

"Joe, you *have* read the letters, haven't you?"

"Yes, but it's been quite a while. I read them not long after my grandfather died."

"All of them?"

"Yes, all of them. That's when I counted them."

Susan was hovering over the chest, obviously still hesitant about opening it, and Joe chuckled. "Susan," he asked, "just what do you expect to jump out when you lift the lid?"

Susan had to laugh. Still, her fingers trembled slightly as she opened the little chest, and then looked down at history.

She saw that Joe had neatly stacked the letters according to dates, and had separated them by years. Each year's correspondence was bound with a wide rubber band.

"They probably should be coordinated," Joe admitted. "As it is, I have Monet's letters grouped separately from my grandfather's."

Susan was gently lifting out a stack of letters and she nodded. "So I see."

The paper, she found, felt crisp and brittle, and the ink had faded from what she imagined had been blue, originally, to a dull sepia.

She took out the first letter and read Monet's salutation: *"Mon cher Henri, how very good to hear from you."*

She looked up at Joe in disbelief. "I feel as if I should pinch myself to make sure this is real," she confessed.

Joe watched her silently read the letter and was moved by her reverence.

Then, after a moment, she paused to ask, "Would you like me to read it aloud?"

Joe nodded, not quite trusting himself to speak.

He listened to the great artist's words, but they didn't fully register because Susan was capturing more of his attention just now than Monet could.

No wonder Kent loved her.

True, Kent had never voiced that sentiment in so many words. But that didn't make Joe doubt its veracity.

Again, he had the same gut feeling he'd had yesterday when Susan and Kent had been with him on this porch. Susan also loved Kent.

There were obstacles in their path. Joe, knowing Kent as he did, realized that. Yet he wished he could somehow convince Kent and Susan not to let looming problems keep them from each other. The time slot allotted to each individual was much too brief at best. He'd learned that the hard way, Joe thought ruefully. He didn't want to see the lesson repeated with Kent and Susan.

Maybe, Joe mused, he could be a kind of catalyst where they were concerned.

He scolded himself.

You are a romantic old idiot.

Joe muttered the words silently just as Susan stopped reading, and looked right at him.

She had such incredible eyes. A friend of Joe's had given him a tie slide made by the Navajos, silver, set with an especially fine piece of turquoise. Susan's eyes, he decided, were almost exactly the same color.

She said, "This letter was written in the winter of 1885. Monet was living in Giverny, and there were eight children in the household. Two of them were his, and six were the children of Alice Hoschede, who had moved in with him several years earlier.

"Her husband, Ernest, was Monet's financial supporter, but he went bankrupt in the late 1870s. That's when Alice and her children came to live with the Monets."

Susan went on. "Monet's wife, Camille, was still alive. She died a couple of years later. By then, Monet's work had begun to sell. He'd had dreadful money problems for so many years. It was a tremendous relief not to have to worry about finances any longer...."

She paused. "Am I boring you with all this?"

"No," Joe said. "But I was just thinking that you could probably write a book about Monet without consulting any references."

"Not really. I've studied a fair bit about Monet, that's all. So it's fantastic to read what he says about living in Giverny, and about his plans to travel around France and the Mediterranean coast to paint and paint and paint—which he did."

Susan sounded apologetic as she admitted, "I lose track of time when I get into something like this, Joe." She glanced at her watch, then muttered, "I can't believe it's so late. I've kept you much too long."

"Not at all," Joe protested.

"Well, I should be getting back to the Farraguts anyway."

It seemed to Joe that a shadow passed over Susan's face as she said, "I still have to tell my hostess that I've rented the condo. I only brought enough to Boston to fill a couple of suitcases, but in the morning I should pack up and move out...." She added, "Beth and Harvey mentioned that they know you."

"True, though it's been a while since I last saw them. Of course, the crowd they travel with is considerably younger than I am. Also, I lost track of a lot of people...."

Joe stared into space for a moment, and Susan felt sure he must be thinking about the accident that had put him in a wheelchair.

She didn't know what to say, but before she could say anything, Joe rallied, and suggested with his usual cheerfulness, "Unless you really have to be back in short order, please stay for a cup of tea. Otherwise, Mrs. Bancroft's apt to be crushed. I'm sure she's made some special kind of treat."

There was an intercom on the table at Joe's side. As he pushed the button to summon Mrs. Bancroft, he said, "There's one of these gadgets in your study."

"I noticed."

"Push the button once, and you'll reach me. Twice, and you'll reach Mrs. Bancroft. I promise you we'll be sparing about our reverse use of it. Though I'm not sure I can prevent Mrs. Bancroft's buzzing you when lunch is almost ready."

"Joe," Susan chided, "I am *not* going to impose on you for my lunches."

"Susan, what can I say to convince you that your lunching here would be anything but an imposition? I imagine you'll want to start work out here most mornings, unless something else demands your attention. So I see no reason at all why you shouldn't favor us with your presence at lunch when your schedule is otherwise free."

Susan shook her head despairingly. "What am I going to do with you?"

"Humor me," Joe said mischievously. "You'll find that the men in the Chase-Davenport clan love to be humored."

Susan relaxed as she shared tea and some special home-made pastries with Joe.

"If you keep feeding me like this, I won't be able to fit into my clothes," she complained.

He laughed. "I'd say that calls for me to say something gallant."

"Don't strain yourself," Susan teased.

"No problem. My guess is that you don't have to worry about your weight anyway, but even if you did, another ten pounds would only make what is already lovely even love-lier."

"You're outrageous, Joe."

"It runs in the family," Joe assured her solemnly.

"Does it?"

Joe gave her a mock frown. "Do you mean to tell me you've never noted the same quality in Kent?"

There was something she had to set straight, Susan decided. She said, "Kent and I don't actually know each other very well, Joe. Until the other day, I'd only seen him on two occasions—at his wedding, and at my sister's memorial service."

"I know that, Susan," Joe admitted, somewhat to Susan's surprise.

"If you wondered why I wasn't at the service for Elaine," he went on, "it was because I was in the hospital. I'd been in the hospital for nearly six months by then, and I still had quite a way to go. I just about lost count of the number of times they operated." He tapped the edge of his wheel-chair. "But the end result was that this came into my life."

He grimaced and said, "I don't usually talk about...this aspect of myself. But you wouldn't be human if you weren't curious, Susan. Especially since you met me when I could get around on my own two feet."

"Joe, please . . ." Susan began.

"No," Joe said. "I'd rather tell you my story myself. Then, at least, you'll have the facts as they should be."

He leaned back in the wheelchair, and said, "I guess you could say I was a daredevil when I was younger, and maybe that inclination lasted longer than it should have. I was motivated to get into as much danger as I could legally get into. Some other time, maybe I'll tell you why.

"Anyway . . . most of my career was spent with an extremely specialized and sophisticated—and highly secret—branch of the government. I was usually attached to an embassy staff, as have been members of the CIA, and other intelligence groups. A diplomatic status provided a good cover, though I was never under any illusion that it was infallible. Nothing is.

"I came upon information that still remains classified. A certain action needed to be taken. It's not overly dramatic to say that otherwise we might have been plunged into a third World War. I was given the job, though I, and everyone associated with me, knew I'd already been marked for assassination.

"My task was to complete a vital mission before the people who were after me got to me. And I did. But the escape plan that had been worked out backfired. I was intercepted and shot not once but three times. My assailants wanted to make sure they'd killed me, and fortunately for me I managed to do a good enough job of faking death so they thought they'd succeeded. As, I have to admit, they damned near did."

"Joe . . ."

"Don't look so stricken, my dear. I'm here. My backup people got to me. They reached me a little bit too late, that's all. And, yes, I'm damned glad I'm here. I have my bad days. Who doesn't? But mostly I think I've managed to adjust pretty well.''

Susan said slowly, "You are a very remarkable man, Joe Chase."

"I'd like to accept the compliment, but it wouldn't be honest," Joe told her. "I'm no more remarkable than anyone else, Susan. When the chips are down, most of us do what we have to do, that's all."

After Susan had left Joe, his words kept coming back to her, echoing again, and again, as if to warn her this was a lesson she too must learn.

It was dusk when Susan got back to Louisburg Square, and neither Beth nor Harvey was home.

"But they're expected for dinner," Martha told Susan.

Martha added, "Some mail came for you today that was forwarded from Washington, Mrs. Evans. I put it on the dresser up in your room."

It was a relief not to have to face Beth and Harvey immediately. As she climbed the stairs, Susan was remembering yesterday's tension, and she hoped they'd both gotten over whatever it was that had caused it, and were in better moods.

Twilight shadowed her room. Before she switched on a light, Susan went to the window to look out over Louisburg Square.

She wondered if Kent ever missed the beautiful house across the way in which he'd grown up, and to which he had taken Elaine as a bride. Then she remembered what Joe had told her. Kent, while in medical school, had gone home one day and found his father's body. His father had shot himself in the head....

Maybe after that, Kent had never really wanted to live in the Louisburg Square house at all.

She remembered that Kent had asked her to phone him and tell him how things had gone with Joe. It might be an idea, she thought, to try to place a call to him now. Though it was early, once Harvey and Beth were back, she'd probably be involved in a cocktail hour, and then dinner....

Susan switched on a lamp, then her eyes fell on the mail Martha had put on the dresser. She saw a long white envelope on top of a small pile of letters. And suddenly there was a bitter taste in her mouth.

She recoiled, not wanting to touch the envelope. And her fingers felt soiled as she ripped the flap open, then withdrew the single piece of paper.

Her skin crawled as she read the words, again typed in capital letters.

YOUR SISTER'S BLOOD STAINS KENT DAVENPORT'S HANDS. DO NOT LET HIM FOOL YOU. YOU MUST MAKE HIM PAY, OR YOU WILL BE AS GUILTY AS HE IS.

Susan felt as if an intolerable weight had crashed into her and was pressing the air out of her lungs. She sank onto the bed, and took a deep, gasping breath. The room swirled, then steadied.

How much more of this could she stand?

She was holding the piece of paper by its edges. She looked at it in revulsion, then opened the drawer where she'd hidden the other letters and took them out.

She compared the envelopes. They were all the same. All white Number Ten envelopes, identical to thousands of envelopes that could be purchased in stores almost everywhere.

This latest one, like the others, bore her Washington address. Like the others, it carried a Boston postmark.

She put the latest letter back in its envelope, and put all four envelopes back in the drawer, tucking them under her lingerie. Then she went into the bathroom, soaped her hands and washed them in scalding hot water, then rinsed them.

Susan kept repeating the soaping, washing and rinsing process over and over again. But her hands still didn't feel clean.

Chapter Five

She had to talk to someone.

She had to talk to Kent.

Susan found the slip of paper with the telephone numbers Kent had given her, sat down on the edge of the bed and pulled the extension phone on the bedside table toward her.

She dialed the hospital number. She gave Kent's name, and the page operator requested, "Hold, please."

Time passed, so much time that Susan nearly hung up, despite Kent's having told her earlier to stay on the line until he answered.

Her nerves already were frayed, and by the time she heard him say, "Dr. Davenport," she was so on edge she wondered if she'd be able to speak to him coherently.

She felt as if the anonymous letter writer were taunting her, accusing her of turning for consolation to the man who had caused her sister's death.

Kent said, "Hello? Operator, is there still a call on the line for me?"

"Kent, this is Susan." It was all Susan could do to speak.

"Susan! I didn't expect to hear from you so soon."

He sounded so... *normal.*

"Did I pick a bad time to call?" she asked.

"No time could be a bad time when it's you."

Susan wished she could let the warm tenderness she heard in Kent's voice wash over her without remembering the awful accusation in the latest letter.

"Susan?"

God, she had to say something, but she felt as if her throat were frozen.

"Y-yes?" Her teeth actually were chattering.

Kent's voice sharpened. "What's wrong, Susan?"

When she didn't immediately answer, he demanded, "Susan, what is it?"

She had to get hold of herself. It had been crazy to call him while she was still so rattled by the letter. She fought for self-control, and her voice was reasonably steady as she said, "Nothing's wrong, Kent."

"The hell there isn't."

She imagined she could see a frown knitting Kent's dark brows.

"Something's happened," he insisted. "Tell me what it is."

It was odd, but Kent's anxiety had the effect of calming her down. She said, "I wanted to tell you the afternoon with Joe was really great, that's all."

"Good." With a single word, Kent managed to convey that he didn't believe her.

"The things in his attic are unbelievable. Have you ever been up in Joe's attic?"

"No."

"We only read one of the Monet letters but it was wonderful, and there's a whole chestful of them. This is real treasure, Kent. I can't thank you enough for putting me in touch with Joe."

Words were coming more easily.

Kent said, "I still think you're keeping something back. What happened, Susan?"

Susan's skin prickled. Could Kent read her so easily, without even seeing her face?

"I thought you looked tired today." He sounded worried. "It might be a good idea for you to rest up for a few days before you get into this project with Joe."

Rest?

Susan nearly laughed. She could think of few things that would be more elusive right now than rest.

She said, "I'm fine, and I can't wait to get back to Joe's. But, Kent . . . he wants to lend me his car. And both he and Mrs. Bancroft insist that I have lunch at the house every day. I can't let Joe do all that for me."

"You're the best thing that's happened to Joe in a long time, Susan. Just as . . ."

Kent broke off, and Susan wondered if he'd been about to say she was also the best thing that had happened to him.

Could she believe him if he said that?

She was not about to be tested. "Excuse me," Kent said. "My beeper just went off. Don't hang up."

He came back on the phone to say reluctantly, "Looks like I'm wanted in the ER. And here I thought I was about to get out of this place."

He sounded so weary that Susan asked, "Has it been a rough day?"

"Yes. But the good part is that I think the patient who took me away from my lunch with you will make it."

Susan heard the gratification in Kent's voice, and she became acutely aware of something.

Kent doesn't destroy lives. He saves them.

She clung to the truth of that.

"Do you know when you're moving into George's place?" Kent asked.

She made a sudden decision.

"Tomorrow. Beth wasn't here when I got back from Joe's, so I haven't had the chance to tell her. But I will, as soon as I see her. I just hope she won't think I'm an ungrateful guest."

"I doubt she will."

Kent sighed. "Damn, they're beeping me again. I really have to go."

His voice softened. "I hope you'll tell me about whatever it was that upset you, Susan. Anyway, take care, will you? I'll try to catch up with you tomorrow."

Beth still wasn't home. But Susan found Harvey in the library, mixing a drink.

"Well, hey there," he greeted her. He held up the bottle he'd been pouring from. "How about joining me?"

"I wouldn't mind a glass of sherry."

"Consider it yours."

Harvey found the sherry, found a glass, and said, "There's no telling when we'll see Beth. She's up to her neck in this charity bazaar she's chairing. When Beth gets involved, she gets involved all the way." He paused. "Do you have any favorite causes, Susan?"

"Causes?" Susan echoed.

"Yeah. With Beth it's one thing after another. I sometimes wonder what Boston's various charities would do without her. She plunges, she goes overboard. Trouble is, she tries to drag other people in with her. She used to get annoyed as hell at Elaine because..."

Harvey broke off and looked as if he might just have said the wrong thing. But then he continued, "Not all of Beth's friends get enthusiastic about the same kind of things Beth does, and she can be very compulsive."

He prodded an ice cube in his glass, and watched it rotate. "I sound critical," he said, "but I don't mean to be. At least Beth keeps busy, I have to hand her that."

His mouth twisted in a wry smile. "Funny, isn't it, how life deals things out? Beth wanted children, and we never had any. Probably she wouldn't need to fill up time the way she does if we'd had kids. Maybe we should have adopted, but now it's a little late in the day."

"You and Beth are not that old, Harvey," Susan protested.

"I'm forty-four, and Beth is forty-two. For us I'd say that's too old."

Harvey concentrated on the ice cubes again, and commented, "Funny, neither you nor Elaine ever had a child."

"Yes," Susan agreed, and hoped he'd let it go at that.

She didn't want to tell Harvey that she had lost a child. Nor did she want to explain to him that Elaine never had wanted to have children.

They had been in their teens, and their father had been stationed at Fort Sheridan outside Chicago, she remembered, when Elaine had announced that she no longer had anything to worry about because she was on the Pill.

She had gone to a doctor in Chicago, and she advised Susan to follow her example. When Susan didn't, Elaine had become annoyed. Susan remembered her saying impatiently, "Well, if you get into trouble, you have nobody to blame but yourself."

Susan hadn't told her sister that she was still a virgin and not ready to give herself to a man. She'd stayed a virgin for quite a while longer, matter of fact. She'd felt that when she did give herself to someone, she wanted it to be right.

Finally, in art school, she'd surrendered, but unfortunately it hadn't been especially right. Neither had it been really right with Glenn. He had been demanding, and not a very considerate lover.

Susan pushed away the image of what it might be like to make love with Kent.

Harvey said suddenly, "How is it you never came to Boston for a visit all the time Elaine was living here on Louisburg Square?"

Susan wasn't ready with an answer.

She couldn't tell Harvey that the real reason she'd never visited the Davenport home was that she knew she couldn't bear seeing Elaine and Kent living under the same roof.

She settled for an explanation that was essentially the truth. "I was in Europe almost all of the time Elaine was in Boston."

"In some ways, it must be hard for you to be here now," Harvey said. "I admired the way you handled everything Saturday night, Susan. It must have been very difficult to walk into our drawing room, knowing you were going to put a lot of people in a state of shock for a few minutes."

Harvey looked up and met Susan's eyes.

"Sorry," he apologized. "It's a good thing Beth isn't here or she'd give me hell for being so gauche."

His glass was now empty, and he glanced at hers. "Another sherry?"

"Please."

As Harvey went over to the bar, Susan took advantage of the opportunity to study him. Harvey Farragut was not an especially good-looking man. He was fairly tall, but too thin. His reddish hair was thinning, and he had a redhead's pale, freckled skin. His eyes were very light blue, somewhat magnified by the glasses he wore.

He certainly would not stand out in a crowd, but he'd already proven himself to be one of the sharpest defense attorneys in New England. Though Elaine had not been much of a letter writer, Susan recalled a clipping her sister had sent a few years back, with a note in which she'd explained that Harvey Farragut was a neighbor.

The clipping involved a sensational Boston murder trial, which had made headlines all over the country. Harvey had represented the prominent man accused of having killed his wife in a singularly brutal fashion. Though the consensus was that the man was undeniably guilty, Harvey had masterminded a defense that resulted in his client's going free.

It would not do to underestimate Harvey Farragut, and she'd do well to remember that.

It would also be a wise idea to take advantage of that sharp mind of Harvey's. He had been with the group in the White Mountains when Elaine died. He might recall small but important details that a less trained person wouldn't notice.

Harvey handed Susan her second glass of sherry, then sat down again.

"I didn't intend to bring up Elaine," he confessed. "But I have to admit that when I'm with you, I keep thinking about her."

Was it that way with Kent, too?

Harvey's rueful grin was appealing. "There, I've done it again. Suppose we talk about the Red Sox. Are you a baseball fan, Susan?"

"No. But, Harvey..."

Just how should she put this to him?

Susan took the direct approach. "I *want* to talk about Elaine," she told him. "That's always a problem when someone dies, don't you think? People tend to clam up, they seem to be trying to pretend that the person who's gone never existed.

"Even my parents still can't talk very much about Elaine. They haven't yet worked their way through their grief. And as for me . . . I really haven't anyone to talk to about her, Harvey, and there are so many questions that trouble me."

"Questions?"

"I've never known *exactly* what happened. And that makes dealing with her death all the harder."

Harvey said slowly, "I'm not sure anyone knows exactly what happened, Susan."

"But you were there, at that place in the White Mountains."

He nodded. "Salzwald. Yeah, I was there."

"Who else was there, Harvey?"

"In our crowd? The Donavans, the Whitfields, the Benedicts, Kent and Elaine, and Beth and myself," Harvey said. "The Kellys were coming, they sometimes join up with our crowd. But Gina Kelly came down with the flu at the last minute."

"Your group often went to Salzwald, didn't it?"

"Sometimes we went skiing up there. But mainly we got together over the Columbus Day weekend. That's a very popular time. The foliage is usually at peak."

"You went there as a group?"

"We traveled separately, if that's what you're asking, but we stayed at the same place. The Schloss. It's a resort complex outside of town, right at the base of Mount Schloss.

"There's a big central lodge," Harvey explained, "and a number of chalets scattered around the grounds. Some of the chalets are big enough to accommodate six people, some

take four. That last time, Beth and I were with the Donavans and the Whitfields, and Kent and Elaine were with the
Benedicts."

"That last time?"

"We haven't been back to Salzwald since Elaine died,
Susan."

Harvey tossed down the rest of his drink, then got up and
headed for the bar again. As he measured Scotch into a shot
glass, he said, "We used to drive up to Salzwald on Friday.
We'd usually leave after work. That way, we'd all get there
in time to have a late dinner together.

"Saturday morning, it was each man for himself. Some
of us are experienced rock climbers. Others like to follow
some relatively easy trails up Mount Schloss, and still others just like to lie around and do nothing.

"There's a road that goes more than halfway up the
mountain and ends at a picnic grove. It's a beautiful setting, a clearing right in the middle of a pine forest. No matter what any of us was doing earlier, we'd all rendezvous at
the grove in the early afternoon. They'd fix a spread for us
at the lodge, and a couple of our guys who'd felt like being
lazy and had stayed behind would drive it up.

"The last time..." Harvey stopped for a minute, then said
unhappily, "Hell, this is all history, Susan. We should let the
past stay in the past."

"That's something I can't do until I've filled in a few
missing pieces, Harvey."

"I don't know that I can help you." Harvey admitted.
"I've never filled in all the pieces for myself."

Harvey concentrated on his drink. Then he said, "That
last time at Salzwald, I had a hell of a head cold. So I decided to stay at the lodge, until it was time to drive the lunch
up the mountain.

"We always had plenty of wine and beer as well as hard stuff with us. Once I got up to the grove, I drank my share. I said I was pushing fluids, because of my cold.

"The others weren't exactly stinting, either. By the time we finished lunch, I'd say none of us was feeling any pain. It was a nice day, still plenty of warmth to the sun. We always brought along some sleeping bags. That afternoon some of us, me included, stretched out and snoozed. Others wandered off along the different trails, or did whatever they wanted to do."

"What about Elaine?"

Harvey pursed his lips, then said, "I wish I could be more precise, Susan. The last I remember seeing of Elaine, she was starting up the trail that goes to Castle Ledge. I think she was by herself."

"How far is Castle Ledge from the grove, Harvey? Is it higher up the mountain, or..."

"Yeah, the ledge is higher up. But I wouldn't say it's more than maybe three hundred feet from the grove. The path twists through a mix of pines and rocky terrain, but it's a fairly easy trek.

"The ledge is a big flat expanse of solid granite. It juts out. You get a really great view of the valley, as well as of the surrounding mountains." Harvey's voice lowered. "I guess you do know that Elaine fell from Castle Ledge."

Susan shuddered. "Yes."

"There's a sheer drop of several hundred feet from the ledge down to Castle Lake." Harvey looked like a man seeing terrible visions. "That time of year," he continued, "it starts getting dark early, up in the mountains. The daylight was fading fast by the time everyone came to and started to get their acts together. That's when we realized Elaine was missing.

"We'd packed up the picnic things. We all intended to cram into the large van we'd borrowed from The Schloss to transport lunch, and ride back.

"When we didn't see Elaine, we started calling her. When there wasn't any answer, we started shouting her name. When she still didn't show up or yell back, we began to worry. We broke up into parties of two or three, and went looking for her.

"Pretty soon it was too dark to see, and we didn't have flashlights with us. Finally we figured that Elaine must have decided to go back to The Schloss by herself, so we all piled into the van and drove down the mountain. But she wasn't at the lodge.

"We contacted the management, and some of the lodge personnel joined us to search the grounds. When we still couldn't find Elaine, we called the state police."

Harvey leaned forward, his glass empty again, but he didn't stop to refill it. He said, "The state cops brought floodlights. Some of us went with them to search the area at the base of the mountain."

Susan saw that he was gripping his glass so tightly his knuckles were white.

"Oh, Christ," he said. "This is hard to talk about. It was dark, it was getting cold, it was hell. Then we found Elaine in a thicket back of a path that leads to a narrow stretch of sand and stones bordering Castle Lake.

"She was so broken up. So broken up, Susan. Thank God her face wasn't . . . marred. Except there was dried blood on her forehead, and the skin on her hands looked like it had been shredded.

"Kent pushed ahead of the cops and went to her. He put his arms around her and started to lift her up, and her head lolled at a crazy angle. Then Kent said, 'Her neck's broken.' God . . . I'll never forget the expression on his face."

Harvey leaned back. He looked exhausted as he said, "Even the state cops made way for Kent. A couple of the vans from The Schloss had driven some of the searchers over to the scene. Kent took Elaine over to one of the vans, and he tried to lay her out on the back seat. He had a hard time handling her arms and legs. Later, the medical examiner said she'd been dead for a while."

Susan fought a vicious surge of nausea.

Harvey was staring straight ahead, his face expressionless. "We made a procession back to The Schloss, with the state police cruisers in the lead, and the van with Elaine's body in it right behind them, and then the rest of us.

"Kent was in the van with Elaine, one of the state cops was driving. When we got to the lodge, Kent just sat there. The cops took Elaine's body over to a kind of barn near the main lodge building. There was no way to keep what had happened from the other guests. I know there were people watching what was going on, but to tell you the truth I was hardly aware of them. We were all in a state of shock."

"What about Kent?"

"I don't think there's any doubt Kent was in a state of shock. He took it very hard."

"You know," Harvey said after a minute, "you're right when you say people often try to shut off talking about someone who's died. That's the way it's been with our crowd. I think we've all bottled up the events of that weekend. It was so goddamn terrible we've locked it inside ourselves, and I think it's done a job on each of us. That's why I'm willing to go along with this idea of a reunion."

"A reunion?"

"At the party the other night it was mentioned that this upcoming Columbus Day weekend will mark the third anniversary of Elaine's death. Someone said we should go up to Salzwald and honor her memory."

"Who made that suggestion?" Susan asked quickly.

"I'm not sure. I think it was either Lilian Whitfield or Heddy Donavan, but I couldn't swear to it. Right away, everyone started elaborating on the idea. They came up with a plan to go up on Mount Schloss and have a picnic as we always did. Then to drink a champagne toast to Elaine, and toss the empty bottles over Castle Ledge."

Susan stared at Harvey, horrified. "My God, that's macabre!"

"I thought so at first," Harvey agreed. "But the more I think of it the more it doesn't seem like such a bad idea."

"How can you possibly say that?"

"Because we need to come to terms with what happened. The experience was hell for all of us. We need to vent our feelings about it. As it is, Elaine's death is still like a cancer that's been eating away at us for the past three years."

Harvey's eyes, framed by his gold-rimmed glasses, looked enormous.

"I think you should go with us, Susan," he said.

Susan stared at him, horrified. "Harvey, there's no way I could do that."

"Well, I'd say you've made it pretty plain that you haven't worked through Elaine's death any more than the rest of us have."

"That may be true. But that doesn't mean I could possibly go along with what you're planning."

"Think about it," Harvey said. Then he grimaced. "Forgive me, Susan. I've no right to suggest what you should or shouldn't do. My problem is that I keep feeling I know you much better than I do. When I'm with you, I have this crazy feeling Elaine's come back to life."

Beth's arrival was a welcome interruption.

She swept into the room, stunning in a bright red suit with a matching cape. As she tossed the cape over the back of a chair, she said, "Fix me a martini, will you, Harvey?"

She turned to Susan. "I had no idea I'd be so late. People!" Beth made a face. "It will be a miracle if we even *have* a bazaar. My committee members don't seem to be able to agree about even the smallest detail."

Beth took the drink Harvey handed her, then complained, "What a boring, boring day. I hope you found something interesting to do, Susan."

"I did."

"Lucky you."

Harvey said, "I've been telling Susan about our plans for the Columbus Day weekend, Beth."

"Harvey," Beth protested, "I told you I didn't think we should bring that up to Susan. At least not until we're sure we're going."

"I thought we *were* sure."

"Well, I'm certainly not sure *I'm* going, even if the others go. I couldn't quite believe my ears when Clark Benedict came up with the idea."

"It was one of you girls who came up with the idea," Harvey told Beth.

She shrugged. "As I recall, it was Clark, but it doesn't really matter, does it? We've less than two weeks to the Columbus Day weekend, anyway. The foliage is supposed to be excellent this year, which means that there'll be more of a crowd than ever. We don't even know if The Schloss would have room for us."

"They have room," Harvey said.

There was an edge to Beth's voice. "And how do you know that, Harvey?"

"I had my secretary call Klaus Bergstrom this afternoon and ask him. Klaus assured her there is always room for our crowd."

"Well, how *decent* of him. Klaus Bergstrom's the manager at The Schloss, Susan. Naturally he'd welcome us. Our bar bill alone probably pays his salary for a month. But as far as our going up there over Columbus Day...I don't know,'' Beth admitted. "I just don't know. But certainly there's one thing for sure. No one would expect you to join us, Susan.''

Wouldn't they? Susan wondered.

Chapter Six

"But there's no need for you to rent a condo." Beth really seemed distressed. "Susan, you can stay here as long as you like. Harvey and I just rattle around by ourselves in this huge house."

Beth, holding the latest Stephen King novel, was again propped up in bed against an array of pale green and ivory pillows.

Earlier in the evening, Susan had tried to latch onto a right moment in which to tell Beth about renting the condo. But there hadn't been one, either during dinner or, later, as she, Beth and Harvey watched an old World War II movie on TV.

Finally she'd decided to wait till morning to talk to Beth.

Once in her room again, she'd been too restless to settle down. She knew there was no way she could fall asleep without reading for a while first, and she'd finished the paperback mystery she'd brought from Washington.

After a time, she decided to go downstairs and borrow a book from the Farragut library. Then, as she started down the hall, she saw a sliver of light under Beth's door.

She'd made an impromptu decision, knocked and began apologetically, "Beth, if I won't be disturbing you, there's something I want to tell you about."

She had expected Beth to make a perfunctory protest, out of politeness. She hadn't expected to be urged to stay.

Now she said, "I'm flattered, Beth." She smiled. "I definitely think I should leave while you feel as you do. This way I won't wear out my welcome. After all, I've been here since last Thursday."

"You could never wear out your welcome," Beth insisted. "And you've only been here five days. I expected you to stay for at least a couple of weeks."

"I thought I heard voices," Harvey said from the doorway. Wearing blue pajamas and a maroon wool robe, he edged into the room and asked, "What are you girls up to?"

"Susan has rented a condo, and she thinks she should move tomorrow." Beth pouted slightly as she told him that. She appealed, "Tell her, Harvey, that there's no need for her to do that."

"Of course there isn't," Harvey agreed. There was a cynical edge to his smile. "Have you tired of us so quickly, Susan?"

Was Harvey also going to make this difficult?

Susan said, "The fact is, Harvey—as I've been trying to explain to Beth—it looks as if I'm going to be involved in a writing project that will take a lot more time than I'd expected to spend in Boston.

"I understand good rentals aren't easy to come by, so when I had a chance to sublet a condo in the Back Bay, I thought I should take it."

Harvey nodded, and to Susan's relief said, "That makes sense." Then he added, "Where exactly in the Back Bay, Susan?"

There was no way to evade this particular issue. "On Bay State Road," Susan said. "This is a studio apartment in Kent Davenport's building. A friend of Kent's owns it. He's going to be away for a while."

"Well," Beth said, "that makes the whole thing more understandable."

Beth wagged an accusing finger. "You should simply have *said,*" she reproved.

She sank back against her pillows again, and added, "At least you won't be very far away. We'll have plenty of chances to get together. Incidentally, I forgot to tell you that Mandy Benedict called before I went out this afternoon. The Benedicts would like us for cocktails Friday. Around six, Mandy said. You'll be able to make it, won't you, Susan?"

She *had* to make it.

"Yes," Susan nodded.

"Good. I'll call Mandy in the morning."

There were rows of leather-bound classics on the library shelves. Many of them were books Susan had read in school, long ago. She settled for Hawthorne's *The House of Seven Gables*, and was almost to the foot of the stairs when Harvey hailed her.

He was coming from the direction of the kitchen, carrying a glass of milk.

As he caught up with her, he said, "I'm sorry you're leaving, Susan. Beth and I have both enjoyed having you here."

"Well, you haven't seen the last of me, I assure you," Susan promised. "And I do want to say that you and Beth have been great hosts."

"If you like," Harvey volunteered, "I can drop you by Bay State Road on my way to the office in the morning."

"Wouldn't that be out of your way?"

"Not at all. Would nine be too early for you?"

"Nine would be fine."

"Beth won't be up, but that's probably just as well," Harvey said. "She's one of those people who gets teary if she hears the word *goodbye*. Do you have much stuff to take with you?"

"Just two suitcases."

"You've got yourself a chauffeur, lady."

Harvey followed Susan to the foot of the stairs, but there he halted. She glanced down when she reached the top, and he was still standing in the hall, looking up at her.

There were shadows in the hall, some of them slanting across Harvey's face so that she couldn't see his expression clearly. But what disturbed her was that he'd stood there watching her every step of the way as she'd mounted the stairs.

Harvey had said that he felt he knew her better than he actually did, because she looked so much like Elaine.

That brought up an obvious question.

Just how well had Harvey Farragut known Elaine?

Before she started down the corridor to her room, Susan looked down at him again. Harvey was still watching her, and he raised his glass in a mock salute.

The old elevator ascended slowly, groaning a little along the way. Morning aches and pains, Susan thought with a smile. Daisy Crandall had assured her that the elevator was safe.

Harvey Farragut had insisted on carrying her suitcases as far as the elevator, but there he'd left her. Now Susan lugged the bags out into the fourth floor corridor, and took the key to George Bartlett's condo out of her handbag. Then, as she neared the door, she froze.

A long white envelope protruded into the corridor, looking stark and white against the pale green carpeting.

Susan suddenly felt sick.

She actually averted her eyes as she inserted the key in the lock. She dragged both her suitcases into the big studio room without looking at the envelope again. But then she had to turn back, stoop down and pick it up. And she saw the printing in the left-hand corner.

She sagged as she read, "Kent L. Davenport, M.D." and saw Kent's office address printed under his name. Then she realized that even the *feel* of this envelope was different. The paper was of a much better quality.

She sat down, because her legs were wobbly, and drew forth a sheet of Kent's office stationery. He used a pen with black ink, she discovered, and his writing was fairly large, slightly slanted, distinctive. He had written:

Welcome. I've put a special bottle of champagne in my fridge, and I hope you'll share it with me later so I can celebrate having you as a neighbor.

I should be home by six. If I'm detained, I'll call you at Joe's. Otherwise, come knock on my door, will you? One floor down, one door to the right.

One floor down, one door to the right.
Kent was going to be so close.
Too close?

It was nearly eleven when Mrs. Bancroft opened Joe's front door in response to Susan's knock.

She watched the cab that Susan had taken from Boston pull away from the curb, and murmured, "Oh, dear. Mr.

Chase *said* you should have taken the Pontiac when you left here yesterday."

"I honestly don't know what to do about that, Mrs. Bancroft," Susan confided. "It just doesn't seem right to take Joe's car."

"It would please him."

Mrs. Bancroft sounded as if pleasing Joe Chase were the most important thing in the world.

Well, maybe it was.

A little while later, Susan accepted the car keys from Joe.

"Mrs. Bancroft took it for a spin this morning, and she says it works fine," Joe said, obviously pleased by this whole transaction. "You might like a trial run yourself, though."

"I'm sure the car's fine," Susan said. "I was more worried about finding a parking place around the condo. But I checked with the manager before I came out here—just in case you talked me into this, Joe."

Joe grinned, as she continued, "She said parking's at a premium, but the tenants have reserved spaces along an alley at the side of the building. All I need is a sticker so I won't be towed, and she'll give me one as soon as I get back."

"Great," Joe approved, and Susan agreed with him.

Her transportation and parking problems had been easily settled. As she climbed the stairs to Joe's attic to get the chest with the Monet letters, Susan only wished she could solve some of the other difficulties that were plaguing her half so effortlessly.

The anonymous letters were always there, like dark shadows in the back corners of her mind.

And then . . . there was Kent.

When all was said and done, she really knew so very little about him.

Kent, the letters, being here in Boston, and meeting Elaine's friends, had all stirred thoughts and memories of Elaine that she had managed to submerge until now.

The memories were not all negative—though, unhappily, too many of them were. But there were good times to be recalled, too, and as she walked through Joe's attic—which was of itself so redolent of nostalgia—Susan tried to concentrate on them. She thought about the Christmases and shared birthdays, when there had been so much excitement. She and Elaine had never had to squabble over gifts. They'd always been given exactly the same things.

Even there, though, Elaine's restless nature had usually gained the upper hand. Toys, games, clothing—nothing Susan could think of had ever been able to capture Elaine's interest and enthusiasm for very long, whereas Susan still had her beloved old teddy bear in her Washington apartment.

To Elaine, had marriage been like everything else in her life? Susan wondered. Was it possible that Elaine just hadn't had it in her to make a long-term commitment, especially to someone like Kent who was so deeply immersed in his career. Elaine would have hated having to take second place to medicine.

Could Elaine have been genuinely unhappy in her marriage? So unhappy, that possibly things had reached a climax that weekend at Salzwald?

Elaine had never been able to stand being tied down...to anyone or anything. Could she have become so desperate that she'd *jumped* from Castle Ledge?

If that were the case, and if Kent had been the cause of her misery, perhaps he *was* as guilty of her death as if he'd pushed her himself.

Susan felt as if she were carrying a double burden as she toted the wooden chest down to the study.

She put the chest down on an oak worktable, and once again wished she'd known her twin better. Neither of them, she thought sadly, had ever given enough to the other.

Susan sighed. Then, following a sudden impulse, she buzzed the intercom and Joe answered.

"I don't want to be a pest," she told him. "But I've been pondering about how much of this you'd like to get into with me?"

"Could you spell that out?" Joe asked her.

"I guess that, for starters, I'm wondering if you would like to read the letters with me?"

Joe chuckled. "I thought you'd never ask."

Susan and Joe spent the time before lunchtime putting the letters Monet had written Henry Chase and the letters Henry Chase had written Monet into chronological order.

Mrs. Bancroft served them on the sun porch. Once she'd taken the dishes away, Joe suggested, "Suppose I play Monet and you play my grandfather. How would that be?"

Susan giggled. "You really don't look much like Monet, Joe, but all right. I'll buy that."

"You certainly don't look like my grandfather," Joe retorted, and was pleased to see Susan grin.

She didn't smile enough, he thought.

He wished he knew exactly what had motivated her to come to Boston at this particular time. He didn't doubt her genuine interest in Monet, yet he couldn't quite believe that she'd trekked north only to touch base with someone at the Museum of Fine Arts who was an expert on the illustrious French artist.

He was a strong believer in hunches, especially his own, he had to admit. And he had a strong hunch that Susan's real reason for being here had very little to do with art. She had more than the Impressionists on her mind.

Would Kent know what was bothering her so much?

As Joe watched Susan carefully put the letters back into the chest in the right order, he pondered that question and came to a quick answer. If Kent knew, he would have told him. Lately, Kent had not only been sharing confidences with him, but had also enlisted his help.

Now the latest problem to be solved was what to do about the upcoming Columbus Day weekend.

Joe frowned as he thought of Kent's call last night. Kent had been upset, and Joe was damned if he could blame him.

It astonished him that Heddy Donavan actually had been so tactless as to call Kent and invite him to make a trip to the scene of Elaine's death over the holiday weekend, with the group who'd been at Salzwald when Elaine died.

Kent had admitted that the invitation had shaken him, shaken him badly. But, he'd told Joe, at least he'd had the presence of mind not to refuse it outright.

He'd told Heddy he'd get back to her.

Now Joe stared at the fall sunlight speckling his garden fence. Before *anyone* went back to Salzwald, he needed to do some in-depth thinking.

Susan looked across at him, and asked, "Ready, Monet?"

"*Mais, oui.*"

"Since we've already read Monet's first letter to your grandfather, suppose we begin by my reading the first letter your grandfather wrote Monet? Then we can take it from there."

Joe nodded, "Sounds good to me."

But, as Susan started to read, the words his grandfather had written long ago slid right over Joe's head.

As he listened to Susan, as he watched her, he became a little bit mesmerized by her. And that, he soon realized, was because she reminded him of Megan.

The old, familiar pain twisted. Susan didn't really look like Megan, but she had that same haunting beauty that came not merely from physical perfection, but from the invisible qualities that mattered most.

Joe was sure that Susan was as generous and giving as Megan had been. If she loved, she would not stint with her love, and she would not expect as much as she gave. But if her love were returned in equal measure, her devotion would be without reserve. If Susan truly loved, she would love forever.

If only he had realized that about Megan in time....

Susan finished the letter. Fortunately, Joe heard her say, "Yours very truly, Henry," and so he was ready for her.

He gave her a wicked grin, picked up the second of Monet's letters, and asked, "Do you want this with or without a French accent?"

Joe was again rewarded by the silvery sound of Susan's laugh.

The time passed so quickly. Susan commented on that as the late-afternoon shadows slanted across the sun porch, then mused, "I suppose that's the way it always is when you're doing something you really like to do."

"I intend to take that as a personal compliment," Joe told her.

"Please do. You deserve it. Joe, it was kind of you to share your afternoon with me."

Joe said quietly, "If it would be agreeable to you, I'd like to go right on doing this with you, Susan. I've enjoyed every minute."

"Well," Susan said, with an impish gleam in her turquoise eyes, "you make a terrific Monet. Now, if only you could paint..."

* * *

One floor down, one door to the right.

Susan raised the antique door knocker centered with an elaborately monogrammed *D,* and let it clang.

She was suffering from a bad case of stage fright. At least she guessed that was as good a name as any for the fluttering sensation in her chest that made her feel as if she needed to take a few deep breaths.

Kent opened the door and for a moment just stared at her.

Was he seeing a ghost? Susan wondered. Or, whenever he looked at her, did Kent feel as if he were witnessing Elaine's resurrection?

"I wasn't sure you'd be able to make it on such short notice," he said. And then he smiled.

His smile was like warm honey sent to flow through Susan's veins. She forgot about everything except being here, being with Kent. The shadows lifted, the ghosts vanished. She took this moment and made it hers; it became a small space in time that no one could ever take away from her.

Kent said very softly, "Welcome to my *casita.* It's wonderful to have you here."

He stood aside, so she could go into his living room. She walked slowly, intensely aware of him just behind her as she let her senses absorb the surroundings.

This was where he lived. Susan's eyes traveled around the room, and she liked everything she saw. Kent's living room was not quite as big as her studio, but it had the same high ceilings, a wood-burning fireplace, and a solid row of windows that overlooked the river.

Susan saw bookcases and comfortable chairs, a long, low couch, and some choice antiques that must, she thought, have come from his house on Louisburg Square.

She crossed to the windows and looked out on the view already familiar to her. Across the river, the lights in Cambridge twinkled through a deep blue darkness. Below them, traffic streamed along Storrow Drive. There was enough moonlight so that the Charles, in between, shimmered.

Kent, at Susan's shoulder, said, "I never get tired of the view. Sometimes I just stand here and look out and lose track of time. I think about the people driving along down there, rushing like hell to get somewhere. I wonder who they are and where they're going, and how this day treated them. Do you ever ask yourself questions like that?"

"All the time," Susan confessed. "Especially when I go by houses at night, and see lights in the windows. I wonder about the people inside. Who they are, what they're doing..."

Kent laughed. "Maybe we're a couple of frustrated Peeping Toms."

Susan loved the sound of his laugh. She loved being so close to him. He smelled good, and she would have sworn that she could feel his body heat.

She closed her eyes, a little shocked by the sudden invasion of a need that was like a wave propelled on an incoming tide.

Kent said huskily, "Time to open the champagne."

The champagne bottle was nested in ice in a silver bucket. The bucket sat on an old oak sea chest that now served as a cocktail table.

Kent popped the cork, then handed Susan a tulip-shaped glass. "To the Monet project," he toasted. "How did it go today?"

"Marvelously," Susan said. "You should hear the phony French accent your cousin puts on sometimes when he's playing Monet."

"Joe's having a terrific time with you."

"He told you that?"

Kent hesitated only slightly, then said, "Yes. He called a little while ago."

Kent hated the change of mood, yet there were a couple of questions he had to put to Susan. He asked, "Were Harvey and Beth agreeable to your making the move?"

"Beth did want me to stay," Susan admitted.

"What about Harvey?"

"He backed up Beth, but I'd say he's more practical. Also, he was kind enough to drive me over here this morning with my suitcases."

"Were there any comments about your renting a condo in the same building I live in?"

"Oh . . . Beth was a little bit coy about it. Why?"

Susan looked puzzled, and Kent couldn't blame her. It was difficult to ask one question after another without turning a conversation into an interrogation.

He said casually, "No particular reason," and topped Susan's glass with more champagne.

Susan didn't let him off so easily. "I don't think you'd ask something like that without a reason, Kent," she told him.

"Well . . . I think we both have to realize we may be the subjects of some speculation," Kent allowed.

"Speculation?"

"The crowd the Farraguts travel with love to speculate, and it doesn't take much to get them going."

Susan said slowly, "They're your crowd, too, are they not?"

He supposed he could have expected that.

"I suppose they were once, in a way," he conceded. "I've known most of them a fairly long time. But I've never been much of a party animal. And most of them are."

"Well," Susan said, "speaking of parties...Beth told me the Benedicts are having a cocktail party this Friday, and I guess I'm to be the guest of honor. I imagine you'll be invited."

Kent nodded. "I already have been. Mandy Benedict called this morning and left a message with my secretary."

"Are you going?"

"Yes," he said, and tried to make light of it. "If only to make sure you have a proper escort . . . that is, if you'd like to go with me, of course."

Yes, he would be going to the Benedicts' party, but certainly not because he wanted to, Kent thought grimly, as he left Susan to pop a tray of hors d'oeuvres in the oven.

There was no way he could refuse an invitation to the Benedicts, the Donavans, the Farraguts, the Whitfields, or any of their crowd, no matter how he felt about accepting.

Probably there'd be no chance of escaping the trip back to Salzwald over Columbus Day, either, though the mere thought of going sickened him.

But how could he risk not being there?

Kent slid the hot appetizers onto a platter, and tried to shake the depression that was settling over him as he went back to the living room.

He was damned if he was going to let himself get into a funk that might ruin Susan's first visit to his home.

He munched a canapé as he asked Susan, "Are Joe's letters interesting?"

"Fascinating. Did I tell you that Joe reads the letters Monet wrote, and I read the ones from his grandfather?"

"I suspected as much when you mentioned the phony French accent. What would it take to get the two of you to tape the readings? I think they should be preserved for posterity."

"You wouldn't if you heard us."

Susan looked around, and admitted, "I was snooping while you were out of the room. You have so many lovely things, Kent. I like your inkwell collection, and the mechanical toy banks. Did they come from Louisburg Square?"

"Some of them did. Others I've picked up, from time to time."

"It must have been difficult to decide what to keep and what to let go when you sold the house."

Kent shrugged. "It was a major consolidation, yes, but I didn't find weeding that difficult. I just wanted to be sure that I donated things that had real value to the right places. I think I did that."

"Have you ever regretted selling the house?"

"God, no. I'd never felt as free as I did when I walked out for the last time. This is a good place to come back to, when I've finished work. Maybe some day I'll want to move on. But for now this is fine."

He asked, "What about you, Susan? Do you like the place you live in?"

"Well enough," Susan said. "After the divorce, I went back to Washington and rented a furnished apartment in Georgetown. It's in a lovely old house, and my landlords have become friends. But, so far, I haven't done much to make it really mine."

"You want to move on?"

"I don't know," Susan admitted.

"Is there anyone else, Susan?"

Susan's thoughts had been straying, and for a minute she didn't understand him. Then, before she could answer, he rephrased the question.

"Since Glenn . . . is there someone else?"

"No," she said. And, of course, she could not elaborate, could not say it all.

There isn't anyone else, and there never could be. Because, for eight long years, there has been only you.

Chapter Seven

They were going to be late for the Benedicts' cocktail party. In fact, if Kent didn't soon appear they were going to be very late.

Susan had checked the bedroom clock at least a dozen times, and she was damned if she'd go look at it again.

Kent, she thought, could at least have called when he knew he was going to be delayed, or he could have had someone else make the call for him. She hadn't wanted to be the first at the party—not that there was any danger of that happening now—but she also didn't want to be the last.

This affair *was* being given in her honor, after all....

Finally, Susan heard the knock she'd been waiting for.

When she opened the door, Kent looked down at her and merely said, "Sorry."

No real apology, no contrition.

Well...though she felt she deserved an explanation, Susan was not about to ask him for one.

He was wearing a dark suit, a dark tie and a white shirt. He looked startlingly handsome, but extremely austere. He seemed like a total stranger, and Susan was confused. She had felt so close to him in his apartment Tuesday night, as they'd shared champagne and canapés and conversation. He'd thrown another log on the fire a couple of times as they talked about all kinds of things. Impersonal things, though—shared enthusiasms involving movies and music and food and even the weather. Susan had discovered that they both liked to go for long walks in the rain, and didn't like fried eggs without a liberal sprinkling of red-hot sauce.

Kent had heated up some clam chowder, so she'd shared a late supper with him, too. And, all the while, she was so conscious of wanting to share much more.

She gave Kent credit for the control that had kept them from doing what she was sure they both yearned to do. She, certainly, had wanted to be in his arms, and to finally find out what making love could be like when it was right. As the evening had progressed, she wasn't sure she could have prevented that happening, on her own. It was Kent who had kept the brakes on.

His good-night kiss had been gentle. A promise, Susan thought, as she went back upstairs. Now she wondered.

Since Tuesday, they hadn't seen each other, and they'd talked on the phone only once. Kent had called her at Joe's today to say that it looked as if he'd have no problem getting away.

Something must have happened to alter that scenario. So, why didn't he tell her what it was?

He picked up her coat and held it for her. She thought perhaps he'd make a comment about the way she looked, but he didn't.

Susan knew exactly what her mirror told her. It had been telling her the same story for years. Early on, the knowledge that God had been kind to Elaine and her had crossed her mind, and in turn had established the fact that she'd had nothing to do with the way she was put together. As a result, she wasn't vain about her appearance. But, tonight she could have done with a compliment.

She'd wanted to really look good... for Kent. So she had elected to wear a simple, beautifully designed dress, made of an exquisite, gleaming fabric that blended blues and greens and turquoise.

She considered it the most becoming dress she'd ever had. She'd also taken special pains with her makeup, and her hair. As a result, Kent's seeming indifference rankled, and she stood silently at his side as the elevator wheezed its way to the first floor.

She felt as if she would have gotten as much response from him if she'd worn a burlap sack.

What was the matter with him tonight?

As soon as they pulled into Bay State Road, they were deep into rush-hour traffic. That made Kent's silence understandable, but didn't alleviate the tension that shared the front seat of the Porsche with them.

They'd gone several blocks when he suddenly pulled to the right, and slid the Porsche into what was probably the only vacant parking space in a long city block.

"This is absolutely insane," he snapped.

To Susan's surprise, he leaned back and closed his eyes. She saw weariness she hadn't noticed before stamped on his handsome face, and couldn't halt the sudden flow of both caring and concern.

"Damn it," Kent grated. "They're a bunch of ghouls." He added, with a savagery that surprised her, "You should have told the whole bunch of them that you're too tied up in your work to socialize. There's absolutely no reason for you to get involved with those people, Susan."

How could she answer that?

Susan thought of the anonymous letters. In those letters, Kent was the accused. Perhaps someday she could show the accusing words to him, but certainly not now. First, she had to find out what had motivated them. And her one chance of doing that, she reminded herself yet again, was to cultivate a relationship with Elaine's closest Boston friends.

Maybe doing that wouldn't work. But it was the best she could do, unless—or until—she came up with a better idea.

There was no way she could explain to Kent how much she needed to become involved with the people he was talking about. And she deplored having to keep that knowledge from him. What she and Kent needed was an open channel of communication, not this.

Her sigh was deep and ragged, and Kent quickly sat up, his dark eyes intent as they scanned her face.

"Susan, I'm sorry," he said. "I really am sorry. I freely admit that the last thing in God's world I want to do is to go to Mandy Benedict's party. But that doesn't mean I should let my feelings dampen your pleasure."

Her pleasure!

Kent's lips twisted in a sad attempt at a smile. "I have a confession to make," he told her. "I was holed up in my condo for over an hour. I damned near called you. I thought about faking a virus, and asking you to come down and take care of me. Or, to ask you to skip this party for my sake. I could think of a dozen other wonderful things we could have done with this time. But then I knew I couldn't back out. This is your party...."

"My party?" Susan echoed, and heard the bitterness in her own voice.

There was an odd expression in Kent's eyes. "You don't want to go, either, do you?" he asked her.

"No." Susan discovered she wasn't able to be less than honest with him.

"Then—" Kent couldn't entirely suppress his irritation "—may I ask just why you accepted? You could have come up with some kind of an excuse."

"No. That wasn't possible."

"Why not?"

"I suppose I feel that I—that I owe it to Elaine to do this."

Susan had never, *ever* intended to say anything like that.

Kent looked at her as if she'd lost her mind. "Why the hell would you think that?" he demanded.

"It's hard to explain, Kent."

"Try," he suggested.

Susan stared at a corner street lamp. She tried to focus on the light, to let it absorb her so that she could become objective enough to clear her mind.

If she was careful, could she say enough to Kent so that perhaps he'd understand, even a little bit, what she was talking about? Could she do that without taking the risk of telling him too much?

"All those people knew Elaine," she began.

"So?"

"Kent, when I met them at the Farraguts' party last Saturday..."

"Yes?"

"I reminded them of her, I know that."

"You *were* identical twins. So, you reminded them of her. Are you going to keep seeing them so that perhaps they'll begin to believe Elaine never really died? Is that what you want?"

Kent drew in a long breath, let it out, then said, "You're acting like a person who's laboring under some kind of guilt. What possible guilt could you have where Elaine's concerned, Susan?''

"I should have been closer to her."

"You think so?" Kent's laugh was short and caustic. "Why not turn that around? Maybe she should have been closer to you."

"I lost track of her so completely when she moved to Boston."

"You were living on the opposite side of the world, remember? She could have made contact, if she'd wanted to. Any damned time the mood struck her, she could have hopped a Concorde to London when you were there. Or flown to Germany. Why should the burden be yours, Susan?''

Susan's words came in a whisper. "Perhaps because she's dead."

"Oh, yes," Kent said. "She's dead. Is that really why you want to be around her friends? Do you like the idea that when they look at you, they may think they're seeing a ghost? Especially if they've had too much to drink, and that's a given with most of them."

Susan cringed, then saw Kent bury his head in his hands. After a moment, he groaned, "Oh, God, Susan... forgive me... Forgive me, will you? That was such a rotten thing to say.

"Susan—" he could not have sounded more miserable "—I know I've been going about this in a hell of a strange way. I don't blame you if you don't believe what I'm about to say to you. But all I want is to protect you. I want to save you from the hurt and grief these people are apt to heap on you, mostly because of their own problems and hangups. As for anything else . . ."

"Please let it go, Kent."

Kent looked at her, started to speak, then didn't.

After a minute, he started the engine up again, and swung out into traffic. After another minute, Susan said, "Drop me off at the Benedicts', if you like. There's no need for you to come to the party. I'll make an excuse for you."

"No," Kent said.

"There's no need for you to come," she repeated.

"There's every need," Kent said, and didn't elaborate.

The Benedicts lived in a beautiful Colonial house on a street lined with beautiful homes, spaced well apart. The maid who opened the door for Susan and Kent wore a trim black uniform with a crisp white apron. Another maid stood behind her, ready to take their coats.

There were party sounds in the background. Susan heard music, and voices pitched higher than usual as people talked over the throb of the stereo music.

She was dismayed. She had expected this to be a small affair, with just a few people who'd been close to Elaine as the other guests.

She glanced at Kent, and he gave her a smile laced with cynicism.

"Did you expect an intimate little get-together?" he asked, keeping his voice low enough so only she could hear. "That's not the Benedict style. Mandy comes from a family with money, but Clark made it up the hard way," Kent explained. "Now he heads the most successful insurance agency in Boston. One of the reasons he keeps several jumps ahead of the competition is that he never loses the chance to take advantage of an opportunity. Hosting any kind of a party is an opportunity where Clark's concerned, and Mandy's a natural social butterfly. The more the merrier."

Still speaking for Susan's ears only, Kent said, "I guarantee you that some of Clark's most valuable clients are presently guzzling his excellent liquor and putting away his pâté and beluga. Before they get out of here, they'll be convinced, if they aren't already, that he's the greatest guy around. When he suggests that they should up their company policies for one of a dozen possible reasons, all he'll have to do is hand them his pen."

Kent took Susan's arm and guided her toward the sound of the revelry. Ahead of them, Susan saw a big room, lighted by elaborate crystal chandeliers.

She felt as if the crystals were winking at her, as if to tell her this whole thing was a big joke. She could go along with that, but the problem was that she didn't find the joke very funny. There was no way she was going to find out any more than she already knew about Elaine's death, or the letter writer, in a setting like this.

"Chin up," Kent said unexpectedly, and before he let go of her arm, he kneaded her tensed muscles ever so gently.

"Relax," he urged, and the tenderness in his voice was almost more unnerving to Susan than his earlier aloofness had been. "We'll get through this."

We'll get through this.

Mandy Benedict swooped down on them. Mandy was not an especially pretty woman, but she had gorgeous long black hair, vivid green eyes and an excellent figure, dramatically displayed by her emerald silk dress.

"Finally, you guys," she said. She gave Susan a hug, then turned to Kent and favored him with a warm embrace.

Kent gently disengaged himself, and Mandy giggled.

"I know, you think Clark'll get jealous," she teased. "Let's face it. Clark has *always* been jealous of you, darling."

Before Kent could answer that, Mandy turned and faced her guests. She was holding a glass half-full of champagne, and she lifted it high.

"Hey, everyone," she called out. "Time for a toast. The guest of honor has arrived. May I present Susan Evans? I think all of you know Kent Davenport."

Most of the people had stopped talking as soon as Mandy said, "Hey." Now the silence became so total that when someone coughed, it sounded like a sonic boom.

God knows how many pairs of eyes were focused on her. Susan wanted to squirm. Probably most of these people had known Elaine. Now she wondered how many of them were looking at *her*, but imagining that they were seeing her twin sister.

She became aware of a single pair of eyes that somehow emerged from all the others. She found herself focusing on Harvey Farragut. His gold-rimmed glasses failed to hide an expression of such intense agony it made Susan catch her breath.

She was relieved when Clark Benedict loomed up at her side. Clark was a big, hearty man, with a quick smile and small, sharp hazel eyes.

He boomed, "Susan, you look fantastic," and then kissed her on the cheek as if he'd known her for years.

That broke the ice. Sound began to swirl again, people began to move. Susan became separated from Kent as she was introduced to everyone, or almost everyone.

Beth Farragut caught up with her before long, and promptly scolded, "You haven't called me all week long."

"I know," Susan admitted guiltily.

Beth wagged a slim finger. "Naughty," she chided.

"Beth, I'm sorry," Susan said, and she was. "This week has flown by, and I've spent most of my time getting into my writing project."

That was true. She'd been driving out to Joe's house earlier each morning, and getting back to the condo later each afternoon. Yesterday, in fact, Joe had persuaded her to stay to dinner, and had regaled her with stories about some of his career exploits that were no longer classified.

She discovered that she could—almost—relax when she was with Joe. He was not exactly a surrogate father, but more like a beloved uncle. Also, each day brought new revelations about art, and Monet. The letters were so entertaining, and the Monet sketches absolutely fantastic.

She said to Beth, "Maybe you and I can have lunch together one day next week, and I'll fill you in about what I'm doing."

"Well," Beth said with a smile, "since I'm dying of curiosity, I'd really like that. Any day but...let's see...Tuesday or Thursday. I have committee meetings those days that will include lunch."

"I'll call you," Susan promised.

Beth nodded, then lowered her voice. "Susan," she asked, "have you really *looked* at that skirt Lilian is wearing? If you haven't, now's your chance. She's over there, talking to Dennis Ciano."

Susan glanced in the direction Beth was indicating and saw Lilian Whitfield talking to a stocky, middle-aged man.

Susan remembered that while she was staying at the Farraguts, Beth had mentioned that Lilian Whitfield had been a high-fashion model in New York a few years back.

"Then she married Bert," Beth had said. "Albert Lodge Whitfield the Third. Big Boston Brahman money that neither fire, flood nor famine could ever make a dent in. Lilian still models for some of the charity fashion shows here in Boston...."

Lilian still looked like a high-fashion model, Susan thought. She was tall and very slim. Her hair was blond, and had obviously been cut by someone who wasn't merely a hairdresser, but an artist. She had the kind of facial bones that gave a woman a Katharine Hepburn-ish, classical sort of beauty. But the skirt in question wasn't what Susan would have expected Lilian to be wearing.

Lilian was such a sophisticated type, but her costume would have done her well at a Western rodeo. Her blue shirt was man-tailored. Her skirt was full, brushed her ankles, and featured a large, splashy design of desert sky, sand and cactus.

"Hand-painted silk," Beth whispered. "She got it at Neiman's. I should say she ordered it through Neiman's. It was painted especially for her, and she paid seven thousand dollars for it. Can you imagine that? *Seven thousand dollars.*"

Beth sounded so outraged that Susan had to smile. But she also had to admit, "No, I can't."

"With people starving," Beth said virtuously.

Heddy Donavan worked her way past a couple standing near Beth and Susan just in time to hear Beth's last remark.

"Who's starving?" Heddy asked ingenuously. "If that's your problem, there's some sensational food in the dining room. I intend to ask Mandy who her caterer is."

"I was talking about Lilian's skirt," Beth said.

Heddy glanced toward Lilian and admitted, "It was the first thing I noticed when I walked in here tonight. Gorgeous, isn't it? Not that most of us could wear it. It takes someone tall and skinny."

Susan held back a smile. Heddy was trying to hide her envy, and that gave her an appealingly human touch. Heddy had curly brown hair, big gray eyes, and was not very tall, but she couldn't be called petite. She had to be at least twenty pounds overweight, Susan thought, though she camouflaged her plumpness quite skillfully with the clothes she wore. Tonight's outfit was a dark cranberry-red skirt, with a loose matching overblouse.

Her eyes still on Lilian Whitfield, Heddy said, "I think Phil has a thing going for her."

"Are you talking about Phil, your husband?" Beth shook her head. "Come on, Heddy, she'd never be Phil's type."

"No? Tastes change, Beth. Phil used to call me his private pillow. Now I think he feels I'm more like a whole mattress. And there's nothing so new about the switch. I felt for a long time that Phil had his eye on Elaine—if not more than that. She wasn't as skinny as Lilian, but she certainly was slim and gorgeous. And I don't think she was exactly immune to Phil, either. She . . ."

Heddy looked at Susan in consternation, and she sounded genuinely horrified as she gasped, "Susan, I'm sorry."

"Heddy, don't be," Susan insisted. Then she added something she'd had no intention of saying. It just came out. "For all I know, you could be right. I daresay both you and Beth knew my sister a lot better than I ever did. So you've a right to your opinions of her."

Heddy and Beth stared at her, speechless. Then Kent Davenport stepped into the silent void, saying, "Don't you think it's about time you had a drink, Susan? I snagged a glass of champagne for you."

Was Kent psychic? Susan wondered. Had she been sending out a subliminal cry for help?

Heddy and Beth went in different directions, and Kent and Susan were alone in the small alcove where she'd stood with the other two women just a minute ago.

"What was that all about?" Kent asked. "Beth and Heddy looked as if you'd thrown them both a curve."

"Maybe I did," Susan admitted. And decided that since she'd gone that far, she'd go a little farther.

"The subject of Elaine came up, and I told them they'd probably known her better than I ever did. Which happens to be the truth."

Kent didn't answer, and Susan glanced up at him. His face was inscrutable.

"It's true, you know," she persisted. "Way back, Elaine and I drifted apart. Lately, I've been wondering why. There's supposed to be something so special between twins, particularly identical twins. I can only think that either the ingredient was missing, where Elaine and I were concerned, or that we were never lucky enough to find it. I never knew her."

Even as she spoke, Susan wondered why she felt so impelled to confess this to Kent. She repeated, "I never really knew her. I keep thinking about that, and it hurts, Kent."

He nodded. "I know. I realized long ago that you didn't really know Elaine, Susan. But, for that matter, neither did I."

Despite the mob at the party, she'd touched base this evening with Heddy Donavan and Beth Farragut, as well as with Mandy and Clark Benedict, Susan reflected, as Kent drove down Beacon Street toward the Back Bay. Also, she'd had brief encounters with both Phil Donavan and Bert Whitfield, and she'd had a couple of words with Lilian in passing.

Harvey had kept his distance. Perhaps he was as conscious as she was of her witnessing that anguished expression on his face. She still couldn't put it out of her mind.

Kent, staring at the road ahead of them, said, "I have to admit I was surprised when you accepted Heddy Donavan's invitation for brunch Sunday, Susan. The day after tomorrow? That's pretty short notice. You could certainly have found some acceptable excuse. Or are you just a stickler for punishment?"

He added, "I thought maybe you'd gotten enough of the crowd tonight."

Susan sidestepped that, and asked, "Are you going to the brunch, Kent?"

"Yes," he admitted reluctantly. "Though it means I'll have to persuade one of my partners to switch days-off with me. I'm supposed to be on call."

When she didn't answer, Kent said, "If you like, I'll pick you up at noon on Sunday. The Donavans live in one of those high rises overlooking the harbor, so we won't have far to go."

"Kent, I don't want you to feel you have to take me."

"Why wouldn't I want to take you?" Kent shrugged. "Anyway, by now they all know that we live in the same building. Wouldn't it seem logical for me to give you a ride?"

"I suppose so."

Kent pulled up in front of the house on Bay State Road. Susan had thought that he'd take her along while he parked. Then the two of them could have walked around to the front door together. But evidently he intended this to be parting time, and she suddenly felt at a loss.

She and Kent hadn't actually quarreled, but there had been friction between them earlier, and there was again now. Yet, at the party, he'd been warm and understanding for the most part.

Now it seemed to her that Kent was putting her on an emotional roller coaster, and it was getting harder and harder to accept the variety of the rides. One moment she could feel so close to him, but then the next moment he could so suddenly distance himself. The changes were confusing. Who was the real Kent?

Susan rubbed her forehead. Usually she didn't suffer from headaches, but lately she'd discovered what stress and tension could do to a person. Just a couple of days ago, she'd bought a large bottle of aspirin.

Kent said roughly, "You look done in, damn it. Are you sleeping well these days?"

"Not really," she had to admit.

He frowned. "I don't keep any sleeping pills around. But tomorrow I can write you a prescription for a mild sedative that might help. Just leave a message at my office if you want me to do that."

What Susan really wanted was for Kent to take her in his arms and hold her very close to him. If that triggered other responses, she wasn't going to pull back. Tonight they needed each other, she thought. And they were two adults, way past the age of consent. Why should they let anything or anyone stand in their way?

Susan imagined she heard the echo of ghostly laughter.

Nevertheless, she turned toward Kent, determined to ask him to stop by her place for a nightcap. But she saw that he was pushing the button that unlocked the door on her side of the car. The gesture was so explicit, the words she had been about to speak froze in her throat.

She muttered, "Thanks," as she slipped out of the car, then she heard the Porsche engine catch as she went up the steps to the front door.

Intending to be in her condo by the time Kent had finished parking his car, Susan walked around to the front of the house. But, as she passed the row of mailboxes in the tiny foyer, she couldn't fail to see that there was mail in her box.

Before she even got out the mailbox key and opened the narrow glass door, she had a terrible premonition about what she was going to find.

Still, it was a shock when she saw the long white envelope, which had been crumpled a little so that it would fit into the small space.

She stood stock-still, unable to bring herself to reach out for it.

She was still staring at the envelope as Kent came into the foyer.

Chapter Eight

Kent looked from Susan's stricken face to the envelope and felt sure he knew what she was seeing.

He reached past her, grabbed the envelope and straightened it out. One glance told him that this was exactly what he had expected it would be. The spacing of the capital letters in the name and address was the same. The computer font used in the printing was the same. The postmark was the same. The cheap, Number Ten envelope was the same.

Everything about this envelope was much too familiar to Kent.

He glanced at Susan and saw the stark fear in her eyes. Then he realized, to his horror, that the fear was directed at him.

His instinct was to reach for her, to touch her, so he gripped her arm. His intention was to reassure her. When she shrank from him, the pain of her rejection was so searing that his fingers clutched more tightly.

She flinched, her eyes widening and then darting around, as if in search of an escape route.

Kent watched her and doubted if anything in his life would ever have the power to hurt him more than this.

He was so shaken by Susan's reaction that he felt as if he were about to spin out of control. It took effort to speak at all, and his voice sounded harsh as he said, "Let's go up to your place."

"No."

Susan began to struggle, and she was considerably stronger than Kent would have expected her to be. As she fought to get away from him, the ache inside him began to change to anger.

How could she imagine he would ever hurt her?

"For God's sake," he rasped. "Just what do you think I'm about to do to you?"

She didn't answer him.

They were still standing in the small foyer between the front and inner doors. Kent was afraid that if he let go of Susan, she would bolt. So he held on to her as he unlocked the inner door, and then propelled her toward it.

"Come on," he said. And then added, almost desperately, "I've been getting some very strange letters, Susan, and they come in envelopes just like this one. My guess is that they're from the same person."

The question exploded from Susan. "You know who it is?"

"No. But I damned well intend to find out."

Susan gave him a strange look, then said, "Let me go, please, Kent."

Reluctantly, Kent released her arm. He still wondered what she might do, and it was a tremendous relief when she headed down the hall to the elevator.

Kent followed her, his hurt and anger beginning to mix with resentment.

He knew that Susan had recognized the envelope. The way she'd looked at it had made that obvious. So, it was equally obvious that this wasn't the first letter of its kind she'd received.

If the same person who'd been writing to him was also writing to Susan, she'd been on the receiving end of a lot of verbal poison. But how could she have allowed that poison to work against *him?*

The thought that she might have made Kent boil.

It infuriated him that she'd evidently accepted whatever she'd read, even believed it. It outraged him that she hadn't even given him the chance to deny whatever it was he stood accused of.

That was so blatantly unfair.

If her letters were anything like his letters, how could she believe the garbage, the filth, the anonymous author had spewed?

How could Susan connect him with anything, *anything* that was written in those letters?

Kent's mouth was tight and grim as he pushed the elevator button. Outwardly he was stony-faced as he stood next to Susan as the elevator slowly creaked upward. Inwardly, he felt as if a giant had grabbed his chest and was twisting it.

They were both silent as they got off the elevator at the fourth floor, and Susan opened the door to the studio. She had forgotten to leave on any lights, and Kent waited in the doorway while she pushed a switch.

When he saw her face, his anger began to subside, despite himself. She looked so vulnerable. She looked as if she were going through hell, and was holding herself together by sheer force of will.

It would be a lot easier to hang on to the hurt and resentment if he didn't love her so much, Kent thought ruefully. As it was, he wanted, more than anything in God's world, to take her in his arms and comfort her. He wanted to convince her that she could trust him. He wanted her to know how much she meant to him. . . .

But those were things he could neither say nor do right now. Susan still had her guard up. She was keeping a cautious distance from him. It nearly killed Kent to think she felt she had to do that. But he pushed aside his own trauma, because it was so urgent that he regain her confidence.

Keeping his tone low, he said, "How many letters have there been, Susan?"

He saw the dreadful suspicion still in her eyes as she asked, "What makes you think there have been more than one?"

"Your reaction when you saw the envelope," Kent told her wearily. "You *knew* what you were about to find."

When she didn't answer, Kent turned, and headed for the door. He was on the threshold when he heard her voice.

"Please," she implored, and he swung around.

"Kent . . . where are you going?"

"Down to my place," Kent said. "I want to get something. I'll be back in a few minutes . . . if that's okay with you."

She nodded, and Kent took that to mean her answer was affirmative.

When the door closed behind Kent, Susan sagged. She felt as if her last ounce of strength had seeped out of her.

She sat down on the couch and buried her head in her hands. She rocked back and forth, miserable. She felt so ashamed. She had hurt Kent. She had hurt him so dreadfully she wondered if he'd ever forgive her.

She couldn't blame him if he didn't. How could she ever make up to him for displaying such a lack of trust?

She couldn't believe just the sight of that envelope had affected her so dramatically. Upset her so much that she'd stabbed the man she loved with her silent accusation as surely as if she'd used a knife on him.

Now the envelope lay on the coffee table where Kent had tossed it, and Susan made no move to pick it up.

They would open it together, she decided. Maybe that would show Kent that she did trust him, that she believed in him. And maybe she could somehow find a way to show him how deeply she regretted the way she'd just acted.

Dear God, how could she possibly have been suspicious of Kent Davenport, for even a minute?

She loved him with all her heart. And that heart told her to trust him, utterly and completely.

Susan pressed her fingers against her aching temples, and wished that Kent would come back. She wanted him here. She needed him here.

She needed to make him understand why seeing the envelope had been such a shock. What had hit her so hard was spotting the address on it. It hadn't been forwarded from Washington. It had been addressed to her here, on Bay State Road. She'd gone cold at the thought that the writer knew exactly where she lived, could even be keeping watch over her.

Then she'd remembered the terrible accusations against Kent. And suddenly everything had telescoped.

She'd become completely irrational. Though it didn't excuse the way she'd treated Kent, she knew it would be valid to blame the way she'd fallen apart on lack of sleep, anxiety, worry. And, as well, the tension created by wondering, as she circulated among her sister's friends, if any of them knew something about Elaine's death they weren't telling. Or, if one of them was writing the letters.

She shouldn't have let herself become so jolted, regardless, Susan chided herself. From the beginning, she had known that Boston was the pivotal point, where the letters were concerned. That's why she'd come here, after all. It had stood to reason from the start that the author lived in or near Boston.

But now there was more. The author was close, very close. The chances seemed higher than ever that the author had been at Salzwald when Elaine died. And, at the Benedicts' party tonight.

So near, but so very far.

Time passed, and Susan began to think that Kent wasn't coming back. Nor could she blame him.

She owed him an apology.

But then he arrived, carrying a nearly full bottle of Scotch in one hand, and some familiar-looking white envelopes in the other.

"Sorry I took so long," he told Susan. "The phone was ringing when I walked through the door, and it was the hospital."

"Do you have to go in?"

Susan hoped that he didn't have to leave on a mission that might keep him away for hours. She wanted the chance to try to make retribution. She needed, so much, to have things right between them.

He said, "No, the resident has everything under control. He just wanted to ask me a couple of questions."

He held out the bottle of Scotch, and said, "I took the liberty of bringing this along. I could use a drink. Would you care to join me?"

She nodded. "Yes."

She led the way to the kitchenette, and took a couple of glasses out of the cabinet. She produced ice cubes. Kent mixed their drinks.

Neither of them said much, and it was an uneasy silence. Back in the living room, she saw that Kent had placed his stack of letters next to the envelope on the coffee table.

He sat down, thrust out his long legs and nodded toward the letters. "You can read those if you like."

"Tell me about them first, will you please?"

"I got the first letter not long after Elaine died," Kent said. "They've been coming ever since. Sometimes they came as often as once a week. Other times, there may be a gap of a couple of months. Lately, the tempo has been picking up."

He paused, then asked, "What about you?"

"This is the fifth letter I've gotten," Susan said. "The first three have come each year just before the anniversary of Elaine's death. The fourth one broke that pattern. It was written to my Washington address, then forwarded while I was at the Farraguts. My landlords in Georgetown are taking care of my mail for me. Now there's this one," she added slowly, "So, you're right. The tempo has picked up."

Susan glanced at the envelope on the coffee table, still unopened. "I guess you noticed," she said. "This one was addressed to Bay State Road."

"Yes, I did notice."

Kent asked, "Did you go to the police with any of the earlier letters, Susan?"

"No. It never occurred to me," she admitted. "Did you go to the police about yours?"

He shook his head. "It did occur to me, but instead I consulted Joe. He has talked to friends of his in the Boston Police Department. There's very little to trace. So far, anyway. I imagine the same's true of the letters you've been getting.''

Kent gestured toward the letter she'd just received. "Hadn't you better open it?"

"Yes . . . though I'm sure it's going to say more of the same."

"Perhaps you'd rather read the letters I've received first?"

"I don't want to read your letters, Kent. There's no need. I can imagine the kind of things they must say."

Susan forced herself to pick up the long white envelope, and she slit it open with her fingernail.

She withdrew the single sheet of paper, and read:

GUILT, BLACKER THAN DEATH, SURROUNDS YOU. AND DANGER. KENT DAVENPORT'S FINGERS ARE STAINED WITH YOUR SISTER'S BLOOD. HE MUST BE PUNISHED!

Without saying a word, she held the letter out to Kent.

When he finished reading, Kent was tempted to crunch the damned letter in his fist, then touch a match to the crumpled paper.

He picked up the envelope, and scanned it. A Boston postmark, as usual; he'd already checked out the postmark, and knew that all the letters had been mailed from the same downtown post office.

He turned the envelope over, then back again, giving it as close an inspection as could be given anything without a microscope. There was nothing to provide any sort of clue, let alone give any identification.

Kent picked up one of his letters and compared both the envelope and the letter itself with the one Susan had just received. The spacing of the capital letters was the same, and the type was a Courier Bold that was a standard font on most word processors.

He put the letters back on the coffee table, grateful that Susan hadn't wanted to read his. He suspected that this was her way of showing him that she trusted him, regardless of her earlier attitude, and he appreciated that. But he hadn't wanted her to read the verbal garbage that had been heaped on him by the letter writer for the better part of three years.

From the beginning, his letters had been littered with profanity. The worst kind of obscenities were scattered through each venomous sentence.

As it was...Kent had held out on her, though he felt no guilt over having done so. He had left the last letter he'd received in the desk down in his condo. He hadn't wanted Susan to see that one, not just because of its tone but because the writer had sworn that if Kent himself didn't "pay the price," Susan would.

That was the first threat that had been made against Susan.

Now Kent stole a glance at Susan, and he thought she looked better. She was calmer, and—thank God—she no longer seemed apprehensive about him.

He asked, "Have all the letters you've gotten mentioned me, Susan?"

"No. Just the later ones."

"Then when you got the first one that mentioned me, why didn't you call me? Why didn't you get in touch?"

"I couldn't," she admitted.

"Why, for God's sake?"

"Kent, I couldn't simply dial your number and tell you—like a bolt out of the blue—that I was getting letters making terrible accusations against you. But when that did happen, I knew I was going to have to do something about it."

"And that's when you decided you'd better come to Boston?"

"Yes."

"What did you think you could do here?"

"Start," Susan said. "I had to begin somewhere. Beginning with people who'd known Elaine seemed my best course."

"People aside from me, I take it."

She couldn't look at him. "Yes." She went on, hurrying the words. "That's why I got in touch with Beth Farragut. I think I must have mentioned to you that when I met her at Elaine's memorial service she told me I was more than welcome to come for a visit anytime."

"And so that's why you're so anxious to go to the parties these people want to give for you. You're hoping to find out something?"

"Yes."

"That makes two of us," Kent said. Then he hesitated. He didn't want to frighten her, but on the other hand he didn't want her to take any risks.

He asked, "Who have you told about the letters?"

She looked up in surprise. "No one. You're the first."

That was a relief.

"Where have you kept them, Susan?"

"In Washington, I kept them in a locked drawer in my desk. At the Farraguts', I kept them in the dresser, under some of my lingerie. That's where I put them here, too."

Kent burst out laughing. "Susan, Susan," he chided. "Don't you know that's a classic hiding place for women?"

"I'm not up on subterfuge, Kent."

"I hope you never have to be, sweetheart. And these are not exactly something a thief is apt to be looking for. Even so..."

Sweetheart.

To Susan, that single word leaped out of everything else Kent was saying, and sang.

Neither of them was hungry. And this was not a night made for love. They had been through the wrong kind of emotional whirlwind, they knew that. There had been too much shock and fear and suspicion on Susan's part, too much hurt and anger and resentment on Kent's, for which she could not blame him.

But now Kent seemed to have put that behind him as he said, "Since tomorrow is Saturday, what have you planned?"

"I intend to make it a regular working day. In other words, I'm going out to Joe's as usual. That was fine with him. He doesn't have anything special on, so we thought we'd read some more of the Monet letters." She smiled wryly. "Letters. I seem to be surrounded by letters. But how different they can be!"

"Let's hope that soon there won't be any more of the kind you got tonight," Kent said. And wished that might be true. But he was afraid that neither he nor Susan was home-free where the anonymous letter writer was concerned.

He said, "I'll drive out to Newton with you in the morning, Susan."

"Don't you have to be at the hospital?"

"I'm on call, but I'll only have to go in if there's an emergency." Kent smiled faintly. "Sometimes I luck out. Anyway, Newton's not that far off base."

"Bring your letters with you," he counseled. "Joe, remember, has had a hundred times more experience with this kind of thing than you and I will ever have. Maybe the three of us can put our heads together and come up with something."

* * *

A chill rain was falling Saturday. Joe awaited Kent and Susan in his living room, where a fire burned on the hearth.

Joe put on his dark-rimmed glasses and read Susan's letters not once, but three times. Each reading was slower than the last. He frowned slightly as he studied the words, sometimes returning to one of the earlier letters to make comparisons.

Finally he said, "All right, I'll give you an off-the-cuff opinion, for what it's worth. I'd say the pressure on the person who's writing these things is intensifying. Just let the continuity flow, as you read, and you can feel the buildup.

"I'm neither a psychiatrist nor a psychologist," Joe went on, "but I'm still willing to make the guess that this person has progressed to the point of a genuine psychosis, or is awfully close to it. In other words, they're in the grip of a real paranoia."

Joe leaned back. "I think we're dealing with someone who is either already dangerous, or could easily become so. Also, though neither of you may like to hear this, I suspect that what's been happening here in Boston between Susan and yourself, Kent, probably has only aggravated the situation."

Kent looked startled. "What's that supposed to mean?"

"Before I get into that, let me buzz Mrs. Bancroft and ask her to make us some coffee," Joe suggested, and did so. Then he said, "Now, let me put a couple of questions to you two. You met again for the first time at the Farraguts', didn't you?"

Kent nodded. "At the cocktail party they gave for Susan a week ago tonight. I got tied up with an emergency case so I arrived late."

"Was everyone who'd been at Salzwald three years ago there?"

"Yes."

"Refresh my memory and name them for me, will you, Kent?"

"Well," Kent said slowly. "Harvey and Beth Farragut were there. And Mandy and Clark Benedict. Then there were Phil and Heddy Donavan, Bert and Lilian Whitfield. And, myself, of course."

"I know you and I have gone over this before. I wish I could alter the opinion I gave you then, because I know you don't like it. But I can't. It seems to me one of them must be writing these letters."

"I can't disagree with you," Kent admitted. "It's just that it would be hard enough to think a stranger was singling you out for something like this. But it's infinitely worse to suspect that it's someone you know. I've always thought that *friend* is a word most of us use too lightly. On the other hand, I've known these people a long time. They're more than acquaintances. Certainly I've never felt that I had an enemy among them. So... why would one of them do this, Joe?"

"I wish I knew. The human mind is incredibly complex," Joe said. "Hell, Kent, you're a doctor. You know that."

"I handle the heart, not the brain, Joe."

Then Kent smiled wryly and admitted, "I did one psychiatry rotation when I was in med school, and I didn't like it. I put in six weeks at a state hospital, and I have to admit it depressed the hell out of me because I didn't feel I was getting anywhere in my attempts to reach the patients. I tried my damnedest to figure out how to help them, and all I got for my efforts was considerable frustration.

"I felt helpless then, and I feel helpless now. I know how hard it is to get to someone who is hiding something very deep, very dark...."

Kent broke off and looked at Susan. He said abruptly, "I think you should go back to Washington."

Susan was staggered. That was the last thing she had expected to hear.

Before she could say anything, Joe pointed out, "Washington isn't that far away, Kent. No place is. I'd rather have Susan here, where we can keep an eye on her."

"That's just it," Kent retorted. "You and I can't guard Susan twenty-four hours a day and—"

Susan broke in, "Please, guys. Susan's a big girl, remember? She can take turns guarding herself."

Mrs. Bancroft appeared, with coffee and a tray of French crullers. There was an intermission of sorts while they drank and nibbled silently. Then Kent, who had been frowning all the while, said, "Joe, let me ask you something. Do you think the letters have all been leading up to this rendezvous at Salzwald over the Columbus Day weekend?"

"I think so, yes," Joe said. "That may not have been the original intention, but I think that as time has passed, this person's need for some kind of a confrontation has intensified. Salzwald certainly is the obvious place, especially now that the plans for the reunion are going forward. But that doesn't mean that we can be positive something won't happen between now and Columbus Day to trigger that erratic mind we're talking about.

"I think, as I've already indicated, that Susan's coming to Boston has had an effect. Forgive me for saying this, Susan, but it's possible that you look so much like Elaine that you're evoking some very painful memories. Or maybe the motivation is jealousy, hate, and is directed at Kent, not at you. You could merely be a kind of decoy. Kent could be the real target."

"Joe," Susan protested. "You make me feel as if I should have stayed in Washington."

"No," Joe said quickly. "Let me tell you right now that I definitely don't think you should have stayed in Washington. This has been brewing for three years. Sooner or later, writing letters isn't going to be enough for this person. They're going to have to do something, precipitate something.

"In my opinion, the sooner that happens the better. The longer it goes on, the more dangerous the situation will become. Our letter writer is getting sicker, not better, remember.

"So...since you've asked my advice, I'm going to give it to you," Joe decided. "For now, Kent, what you and Susan both need to do, is to play the letter writer's game."

Kent raised his eyebrows. "And just how would you suggest we go about doing that?"

"Accept any and all invitations from the people who were at Salzwald, but maybe don't always go together," Joe advised. "Create an atmosphere that will throw this person off guard, because you won't be behaving as you're expected to behave. Make him start guessing.

"An as example, you might go to the Donavans' brunch tomorrow by yourself, Susan. You trek along later, Kent. You can always say that you had to stop by the hospital to see a patient.

"If other invitations are forthcoming between now and the Columbus Day weekend, accept them. Go together next time, but don't get along too well. Don't do anything so blatant as having an argument on the scene, but maybe convey that you'd had one just before you arrived.

"As I've said, the tempo has picked up since Susan has been in Boston, and moved into your building. I find that significant, though I admit I still don't fully understand the significance. But I think it might be as well, when you're out in public, if the two of you convey the impression that you definitely are not having a love affair.''

Susan nearly choked on her coffee, and she didn't dare look at Kent. She felt as if her face were flaming.

Joe Chase, she decided, was a sly old fox.

''Now,'' Joe suggested urbanely, ''why don't we read a couple of very different letters for Kent's benefit, Susan? I, of course, will be Monet.''

Chapter Nine

Heddy Donavan peered over Susan's shoulder.

"Where's Kent?" she asked.

Susan smiled, and shrugged. "I don't know. I thought he might already be here."

Was it her imagination? Susan wondered. Or was there really a nervous edge to Heddy's laugh?

Heddy admitted, "I guess I assumed the two of you would come together."

Heddy's husband joined them.

"Welcome, Susan." Phil drew her toward him in what she was coming to think of as the traditional New England hug, but instead of kissing her on the cheek, he kissed her on the mouth. A light kiss, but squarely on target.

Glancing over Phil's shoulder, Susan saw a strange expression on Heddy's face.

Heddy had said the other evening at the Benedicts' that she suspected Phil had been interested in Elaine at one time.

Was Heddy wondering now if that interest might be transferred to Elaine's look-alike?

Phil was fairly tall, dark, and quite good-looking. It was easy to see why Heddy, who evidently constantly struggled with a weight problem, might be jealous.

Now Phil glanced toward the door, which was still open. "Where's Kent?" he asked.

Susan smiled. "That's what Heddy just asked me. People, I don't keep tabs on Kent."

"Good for you," Phil approved. Then, with exaggerated gallantry, he said, "Allow me," and took Susan's arm with a flourish.

Susan felt that he was pressing her a bit closer to his side than he needed to, but she refrained from pulling away. She was remembering Joe's instructions, and one of them had been, "Go along with whatever happens—as much as you feel you can, of course."

Phil's tone was low and intimate, and his lips were definitely too close to her ear, Susan thought, as he said, "It's great to have you here. You brighten up the scene on a dull day."

"Thanks," Susan murmured, and she was glad when they came in view of the living room and the assembled guests.

Phil released her, and her attention was momentarily drawn to the window wall at the end of the large, square room. There was a spectacular vista of Boston Harbor, and Logan Airport, she thought, must be just across the way. She watched a jet that had just taken off soar skyward.

"What an absolutely magnificent view," she exclaimed.

"We like it," Phil Donavan agreed casually.

He clapped his hands, and made an announcement. "Here she is, ladies and gentlemen. Susan, I think you know most of these people, and you'll soon get to know the rest."

Susan became the center of attention, and she was still too much in the spotlight to suit her when Kent arrived, almost half an hour later.

Kent greeted her pleasantly, but there was nothing special about his, "Hi there, Susan."

After a while, though, he sauntered toward her, a mimosa in hand.

Susan was chatting with the Whitfields, and a couple she had never met before. Kent joined the group, and kept up his end of the conversation. The talk was general, and nothing was said about any excursions to the White Mountains.

The Benedicts had been on the scene when Susan arrived. The Farraguts were late. Again, Susan had the feeling that Harvey was avoiding her, and that bothered her. But she knew she was in danger of becoming overly speculative about all of these people. That could be true of this disturbing feeling about Harvey.

Beth, certainly, was friendly, and reminded Susan that they still needed to set a date for lunch.

"If you're free Tuesday, it might be a good time," Beth said. "We're not having the Tuesday committee meeting this week."

"Let me call you tomorrow," Susan temporized.

"All right. This is an absolutely terrific apartment, isn't it?" Beth commented. "Sometimes I wish I could persuade Harvey to sell the house so we could get something like this. Let me show you around."

"Would Heddy mind?"

"Of course not."

The Donavan apartment, in contrast to both the Farragut and Benedict homes, was starkly contemporary. The walls were uniformly white, the decor black and white, with a bright primary color splashed here and there.

No heirlooms here, no antiques, Susan saw. There were abstract paintings, some very modern sculptures, and no bookcases at all, at least none she could see. Evidently the Donavans weren't big on reading.

One of the bedrooms did depart from the color scheme. Though as contemporary in furnishings as the rest of the rooms, it was a study in pink and white, and there was a white baby grand piano in one corner.

"This is Tricia's," Beth explained. "Phil and Heddy's daughter. She's away at school in Virginia."

"How old is she?"

"Fifteen, if I remember rightly."

"She must be quite a musician."

Beth smiled. "Her parents think so. None of the rest of us have heard her play."

As they finished their tour, then went back to the living room to join the others, Susan continued to be surprised by the contrast in the Donavan, Farragut and Benedict homes.

She could imagine this being Lilian Whitfield's apartment—it looked like the kind of place an ex-high-fashion model might live in. But she would have expected Heddy Donavan to choose a more traditional background.

Maybe the decor was Phil's idea.

The brunch guests began to depart by the middle of the afternoon. And the moment came when Susan felt that she, too, could leave without having shortchanged her hostess.

She sought Heddy out to say goodbye, and found her in the front hall talking to Kent.

Heddy seemed very intent on what she was saying. She broke off when she saw Susan, switched on a polite smile and asked with the proper tone of regret, "Must you go so soon?"

"Yes, but it has been a lovely party, Heddy. Thank you so much. I . . ."

"There you are."

Lilian Whitfield swept up to Susan, as stunning as a model on a *Vogue* cover in a black suit that looked as if it had been especially designed for her.

"I was afraid you might have left," she told Susan. "I wanted to ask you if you'd be free for dinner Wednesday night?"

"You, too, of course, Kent." Lilian added. "Why don't you bring Susan?"

Not wanting to let Lilian foil Joe's plan for them, Susan said quickly, "I'd love to come, Lilian. But why don't I just fend for myself? You're apt to be tied up, aren't you, Kent?"

Was that overplaying it?

"As it happens, I'm off Wednesday night," Kent said smoothly. "So, I'd be glad to be your escort, Susan."

"Settled," Lilian announced. "Sevenish, all right?"

Susan nodded, thanked Heddy again and left.

She was still waiting for the elevator when Kent loomed up beside her.

She frowned at him, and hissed, "Was it wise to make such a hasty exit?"

Kent laughed. "Sweetheart, we haven't fallen into a spy story. Besides, there's no one around. The rest of them won't leave until they've drained the last of the mimosas."

"Cynic," Susan accused, but her pulse was thumping a little faster than usual. This was the second time Kent had used that term of endearment to her. . . .

Kent pushed the elevator button, then chuckled as they began a smooth descent. "Not much like our house, is it?" he commented.

Our house.

Hearing that phrase shot a bolt of emotional current through Susan, the voltage mixed with what she frankly recognized as wishful thinking.

As they stepped into the afternoon sunlight, Kent said, "I think you and I deserve a break."

She looked up at him, curious. "What kind of a break?"

"We both need to relax, to put this whole miserable mess out of our minds for a little while."

He smiled down at her, and the effect on Susan was like being touched with a magic wand.

"Tell you what," he suggested. "Let's drive over to the North End. If I'm lucky enough to find a parking place, we can have some coffee and cannoli in my favorite little Italian restaurant."

"Do you mean to say you're hungry after eating all that brunch food?" Susan asked him.

"You're damned right I'm hungry," Kent informed her. He nodded toward the Donavan's building, now behind them. "I was as uptight as you were. Heddy's gourmet delicacies tasted like sawdust."

"No one would have known you were uptight."

"Professional expertise. Incidentally, you were doing a pretty good camouflage job yourself. But now we're reprieved till we show up at the Whitfields'." Kent grinned. "Anyway, I can usually go for cannoli and espresso on top of a six-course dinner."

Kent's luck held. He found a parking space. Then, as they started down a narrow street toward the restaurant, he reached for Susan's hand.

They clasped fingers as they walked, pausing now and then to look over the contents of a shop window. Earlier, the day had been gray and cloudy, but now the October sun kissed Susan's cheeks. She caught a wonderful whiff of fresh-baked bread, and she discovered that everything in the world looked different. Even the sky was a new shade of blue.

Susan felt as if she were about sixteen years old again, madly in love, and without a care in the world. And she decided that for the space of this unexpected hiatus, she was going to let herself believe that nothing mattered except strolling hand-in-hand with Kent.

The restaurant was just big enough to accommodate a few square tables, covered with red-checked cloths. Baskets of hanging plants almost obliterated the front window. Gold-framed paintings—mostly varying vistas of the Bay of Naples—dominated the walls. The air was redolent of a tantalizing mix of garlic, herbs and spices.

Kent sniffed, and said, "There's no way I can settle for a cannoli."

The proprietor came over to wait on them personally. Kent seemed to be well-known in at least some of Boston's restaurant circles, Susan thought, remembering the French café on Newbury Street.

Now Kent said, "Luigi, as a starter, how about an antipasto for two?"

"An antipasto?" Luigi's thick eyebrows merged as he scowled fiercely. "*Per piacere,* let me concoct for you and the *signorina* a platter of delicacies as close to heaven as anything you will ever eat. And, of course, some wine as my great-grandfather made it in the old country."

"Of course," Kent agreed seriously, and then he sat back and grinned at Susan.

She loved him. Oh, dear God, how she loved him. She let herself bask in the warmth of his dark eyes, and the tightness inside her began to uncurl, making room for desire to fill its place. It insinuated itself into every pore in her body.

It penetrated every atom of her. And the insidiousness of its invasion threatened to become overwhelming.

You couldn't go to bed with a man in the middle of an Italian restaurant, Susan told herself, then nearly burst out laughing.

Kent saw merriment spark her beautiful turquoise eyes, and, at least for now, the dark cloud that had been hanging over him for so long lifted.

The crystal clarity that took its place became a miracle.

Kent looked at Susan and told himself he was going to seize this time with her, this day, this hour. He was going to live each minute as if it were his last.

He had gone without her for too damned long.

He poured from the carafe of red wine Luigi had brought them, clicked his glass with Susan's and toasted, *"Salute e amore."*

"Grazie," Susan retorted impishly. "And the same to you."

An answer came so close to Kent's lips. He nearly bent toward Susan, nearly said, "I love you."

Maybe it was as well, he thought later, that Luigi arrived at that precise moment with his platter of celestial antipasto.

They ate, they talked, they drank wine. Then they talked some more. They finished their repast with cannoli and cups of strong, scorching hot espresso.

They wandered out of the little restaurant into a night where the sky was sprinkled with stars, and the dazzling white moon was lopsided. They stopped in a little corner bakery that was still open, and Kent insisted on buying Susan a box of almond macaroons to take back to Bay State Road.

Farther down the street Susan saw a pair of silver fili-greed earrings in a shop window, and she exclaimed over them. But the shop was closed.

Kent wrote a mental note to himself. He would come back to the North End as soon as he could and buy her those earrings.

Too soon, much too soon, they came to the place where Kent had parked the Porsche. And as they drove back to Bay State Road, Susan could feel some of the magic begin to drift away. Home, unfortunately, would bring with it the need to face reality.

But, as she and Kent walked from the parking lot to the front entrance of their building, Susan knew that actually all the desire, the need and wanting were still there between them. The fires had been banked a little, that was all.

Would Kent want to rekindle them?

Kent looked preoccupied as he unlocked the front door. Once inside, Susan glanced toward her mailbox apprehensively. Though it was Sunday, which of course meant that there had been no mail delivery, she was still afraid that when she looked through the glass, she'd see a long white envelope. But the box was empty.

As the elevator wheezed its way upstairs, Kent said, "I need to stop by my place and check the answering machine. Then how about putting on a couple of layers of warm clothing so I can show you something?"

"What?" Susan asked.

"Don't you like surprises?" he teased.

"Yes, but I wouldn't mind a clue."

He laughed, then asked, "Did Daisy tell you all the tenants have equal rights to the roof?"

"The roof?"

"That's right. There's a kind of roof garden on top of this building with tables and chairs and a barbecue, which is great in summer. But mostly there's a view, which on a night like this will be fantastic. You may even be able to polish up the moon, and pick a couple of stars. Want to try?"

"I think you've talked me into it."

"Then give me a couple of minutes," Kent said, as the elevator stopped at his floor. And warned, "Be sure you put on something warm."

Susan got a heavy sweater out of the closet, and a lined jacket. Then she put some Mozart on the stereo as she settled back to wait for Kent.

When they went up on the roof, would they be able to escape into the same wonderland they'd been in earlier? Could they really polish up the moon and pick some stars?

She thought so.

But time passed, and with it some of her joy and excitement.

Kent was taking too long. And, when the phone finally rang, she could have foretold what he was going to tell her.

He was needed at the hospital. He was on his way out the door. And there was no telling when he'd be back.

Susan was thankful that she had Joe's house to go to Monday morning. She badly needed diversion.

Joe was waiting for her on the sun porch. Mrs. Bancroft brought coffee, and fresh-baked scones. But before they addressed the subject of the late Oscar Claude Monet, Joe asked, "How did it go at the Donavans' yesterday?"

"I'm not sure," Susan admitted. "The problem is, the more I think about it the less sure I am. When Beth gave that first party for me, it seemed to me she had half of Boston there. At the Benedicts', Clark was entertaining his clients and business associates as well as friends. The Donavans' condo was packed yesterday. The people who were at Salzwald were somewhat lost in the shuffle, Joe."

"Regardless—did anything come across to you?" Joe persisted.

Susan nodded slowly. "I think I have to say yes to that. But I'm afraid I can't be specific. What's come across so far is mostly a matter of feelings. Vibes, I guess you could say."

"Don't downplay intuition," Joe said quickly. "I have the greatest respect for gut feelings, Susan. So share your vibes, will you?"

"Well . . . I'd say that Harvey Farragut is avoiding me."

Susan told Joe about the expression she'd surprised on Harvey's face at the Benedicts' party, and how he'd scarcely come near her at the Donavans' yesterday.

"Heddy Donavan definitely expected Kent to be with me," she added. "I also got the impression that it wasn't me she wanted there anyway, despite her reason for giving the brunch. It was Kent she wanted to see. When it came time to leave, I interrupted her talking to Kent, and for a couple of seconds she let her annoyance show."

Susan went on, "Then, when Lilian Whitfield came up to Kent, she didn't give him what I call the usual New England hug. It was a genuine embrace, Joe." Susan paused and laughed. "Joe, I sound like such a gossipy snoop."

"Everything you've seen, everything you're telling me, is important," Joe said. "What about Beth Farragut?"

"I would say that Beth was keeping a close eye on Harvey both at the Benedicts' and at the Donavans', but that may be because he was drinking too much.

"As for the Donavans . . . Heddy has a few chips on her shoulder, I'd say, and she's jealous of Phil. And, not without reason, I suspect. Phil is quite . . . friendly.

"Also," she went on, "Heddy said at the Benedicts' the other night that she thinks Phil was in love with Elaine."

She passed over that quickly, and said, "When it comes to the Benedicts . . . I'm not sure where Mandy stands. And,

I suppose that goes for Clark, too. He's very outgoing, hearty. Always cordial, but those sharp little eyes of his bother me. I don't think he misses much. My God, Joe, I do sound like a gossip.''

Joe grinned. ''You're doing just fine. When's the next get-together, Susan?''

''Dinner at the Whitfields' Wednesday night,'' Susan said. ''And, since Lilian came right out and asked Kent to escort me, we're going to have to go together, unless his work ties him up.''

''Might as well go together at this point, I guess.'' Joe sighed. ''I wish we'd had a head start on this, Susan. Then I might have advised you not to move into Kent's condo, in order to negate the appearance that there's anything between the two of you.''

''Joe...there hasn't been anything between Kent and me.''

''Susan, my dear, you don't have to make any explanations to me.''

Joe folded his hands, pressed his fingertips together and gazed out at the morning sun flooding his little garden.

He said carefully, ''Sometimes it isn't so much what *is* as what appears to be. Do you follow me on that?''

''I think perhaps I do, Joe, but I wouldn't mind your spelling it out a bit.''

''Well, you know the old saw about appearances being deceptive? That's certainly true, yet most of us judge primarily on appearance because often that's all we have to go on.''

Joe was feeling his way on this. He didn't want to come out and tell Susan flatly that to anyone with half an observing eye, she and Kent appeared to be in love with each other. On the other hand, that was something he couldn't afford to skip over.

"I'm still trying to figure out what's in the mind of the coward who's writing those letters," he said. "And, yes, Susan, people who write anonymous letters are cowards. I'm grasping at straws," he admitted, "or else I would face up to the fact that Elaine's friends already see you and Kent as a couple."

Susan stared at him, and said tightly, "But Kent and I are not a couple, Joe."

Joe wasn't going to argue that with her. He said, "Again, it's how things seem, not necessarily how they are, Susan. I think if you could poll those people and get honest answers out of them, you'd find they've teamed you with Kent, which maybe was subconscious at first. And, understandable, I have to admit."

Joe hated to say this, but it had to be said. "You do look so much like Elaine."

Susan heard that, and felt sick. She got up and walked over to the window and stood with her back to Joe.

The flowers were so bright in his little garden, and her mood was so dark.

Joe had just put his finger precisely on the core of the problem between Kent and herself—a problem that would possibly linger even if they found out who was writing the letters, and put a stop to them.

With Kent, as well as with all of these people who had been Elaine's friends—even with Joe—she would always walk in Elaine's shadow.

Joe said gently, "Susan."

Hot tears stung Susan's eyes, and right now she couldn't turn around and face Joe.

"I knew your sister," he said.

That did it. Susan swung around, brushing angrily at the tears on her cheeks as she confronted Joe.

"I suppose every time you look at me you have to stop and remind yourself that I'm not Elaine," she accused him.

"No," he said, his sympathy for her showing in his bright blue eyes. "At Kent's wedding, I naturally noticed the resemblance between you and your twin. But that was eight years ago, Susan."

Joe went on, "I've always felt that a person's life story is written in his face. As the plot progresses, there are subtle changes, usually to do with character—or the lack of it— more than with age. I could see differences between you and Elaine even eight years ago. And I think that if you and Elaine were to stand side by side today, no one would have any problem telling you apart."

"Except Kent," Susan said thickly.

"Ah, Susan, that's not so. Kent would have less of a problem than anyone else. Kent saw you for yourself the first time he ever looked at you."

Before Susan could dwell on that statement, Joe said briskly, "Enough. Suppose we go on with what Monet was doing in the early 1890s."

It was a relief to get back to the world of Claude Monet, and Joe's grandfather.

The year was 1892, and Monet wrote Henry that he had finally married Alice Hoschede, who, for fourteen years, had been living in his household with her six children.

Earlier, some of his work had been taken on traveling exhibitions in the United States. But, though a few paintings had sold, the shows had not been considered much of a commercial success.

It was at a show in Paris, given jointly with Rodin, that Monet finally had achieved what he referred to wryly as, "a measure of acceptance."

He told Henry that he was beginning to realize the value of working in one's studio, as well as outdoors, in order to refine impressions he'd made on the scene. He was doing a series of paintings of the Rouen Cathedral, and he sent Henry a sketch of one of them.

Susan shook her head. "Every time we come across something like this, I have to start believing all over again," she confessed. "Monet worked on that Rouen series for two years. He was trying different techniques, different brush strokes. Even the palette of colors he was using was somewhat new for him. Joe, this may be one of the most valuable sketches you have."

Joe was pleased to see Susan losing herself in what he had come to think of as "their" work. It kept her mind off the anonymous letters and the people with whom she'd had to become involved, and he thought for the moment she'd had enough of both.

Also, he didn't want to convey his growing concern to her, and it was difficult not to do that.

He had dealt with psychos before, far more often than he would ever have wanted to. He knew how easily threats could be triggered into violence, and he was convinced that the person writing those letters to Susan and Kent was a true paranoiac.

He wished he could have persuaded Susan to move into his house before she sublet George Bartlett's condo. Wheelchair-bound or not, he would trust himself to ensure her safety more than he would anyone, with the possible exception of Kent.

Kent had a couple of strikes against him, though. The demands of his profession forced him away from Bay State Road at odd hours.

The building had good security, true. Also, Joe reminded himself, neither he nor Kent could watch over Susan twenty-four hours a day....

Susan accused, "Joe, you haven't been listening."

"I agree with you about the cathedral sketch," Joe said promptly.

"I'd changed subjects," Susan informed him. "Beth Farragut has been wanting to have lunch with me, and she suggested tomorrow. What would you think of that? I need to call her."

"Susan, my dear, you're not working for me, you know," Joe protested.

"Yes, I know, but you and I have achieved a certain momentum, and I don't want to break it. I thought it might be a good idea to meet with Beth, though. We can make it an early lunch. Then maybe we can work a bit later than we usually do."

"Perhaps we can prevail upon Kent to join us for dinner," Joe suggested, and was both pleased and amused when Susan's cheeks became flushed with a soft peach color.

She said, "I also wanted to ask you if you'd mind my giving Beth an idea of what we're doing. I know she's curious."

"Use your discretion, Susan. Personally, I can't think you'd be giving away any trade secrets."

"No," Susan agreed. "In fact, maybe if Beth spreads the word a bit, it may reach the ears of an interested publisher."

"That's fine with me."

Joe thought about Beth Farragut. He was just as suspicious of her as he was of the rest of the crowd. Still, he could imagine few places where Susan would be much safer than in a downtown Boston restaurant at the lunch hour.

Chapter Ten

Susan and Beth lunched in the small tearoom at Neiman Marcus, where there was a fashion show in progress.

The setting was not exactly conducive to in-depth conversation, but Susan thought that was just as well. Right now she wanted to say as little as possible about herself and what was going on in her life—whether to Beth, or anyone else.

Beth seemed content to do most of the talking, anyway. And none of what she'd had to say so far was personal. She had gotten herself involved in a fashion show for charity, to be held in the spring, she told Susan.

"I just don't seem to be able to say no, when it's something for a worthwhile cause," she said rather dolefully. "That's one reason I wanted to lunch at Neiman's today. It's never too early to start planning, and I'd heard their models were very good."

Beth insisted that as a final indulgence, they splurge with meringues topped with fresh raspberries and whipped cream. It was while they were spooning up the last of the dessert that she finally focused on Susan.

"Tell me," she urged, "just what is this project you're working on with Joe Chase?"

"Joe's grandfather carried on a lengthy correspondence with Claude Monet that began over a century ago," Susan said. "Joe's sharing the letters with me, and we hope to get a book out of them."

"Monet—he's the very artist you came to Boston to study, isn't he?" Beth queried. She marveled, "That's really a remarkable twist. Or did you know that Joe had the letters?"

"I had no idea."

"Lilian Whitfield has an original Monet in her bedroom," Beth volunteered. "You'll have to see it tomorrow night. She persuaded Bert to buy it for her for their tenth anniversary. Nice gift, wouldn't you say? But, of course, Bert is absolutely besotted with Lilian, he'd do anything to hold her. And I've heard that at moments Lilian is pretty hard to hold."

Beth nodded toward a tall, blond model who was displaying a stunning costume designed for cruise wear. "Looks rather like Lilian, doesn't she?"

Susan thought the model did look quite a bit like Lilian Whitfield might have, a dozen or so years ago.

"Well," Beth said, "I have a thousand things to do, so I guess I'd better be on my way. I need to stop and buy a lipstick while I'm here in Neiman's. Susan..."

A change in Beth's tone alerted Susan. Over Beth's protests, Susan had insisted that they share the tab for their lunch, and she was taking a couple of bills out of her wallet.

She looked up to find Beth's eyes fixed on her face, and to see that Beth looked extremely serious.

Beth lowered her voice as she said, "There's something I have to ask you."

What could this be?

Susan fought back one of the knots of apprehension that formed much too easily these days, and invited, "Well, ask away."

"Susan, you didn't decide to sublease the condo in Kent's building because of Harvey, did you?"

The question staggered Susan. "Of course not," she said quickly.

"I know that must have sounded odd," Beth admitted. "But . . . I had to know, Susan. I've been afraid the reason you wanted to leave our house in such a hurry was that Harvey was making things . . . unpleasant for you."

"Unpleasant? Harvey was an excellent host, Beth. I would say he's been anything but unpleasant to me."

"Well, perhaps I used the wrong word," Beth conceded. "It's difficult to come right out and ask the question. To put it bluntly, I wondered if you moved out because Harvey had tried to come on to you."

Susan had a sudden vision of the tormented expression she'd seen on Harvey Farragut's face.

She'd wondered at the time—and often since—what had caused that kind of pain. She wondered again now.

She started to protest that Harvey had been unfailingly polite to her. But Beth spoke first.

"I know that was out of line of me," Beth admitted. "Susan, please forgive me. I honestly didn't mean to put you on the spot. I suppose all marriages have their ups and downs. Harvey's and mine has been on the down side for a while."

"I'm sorry, Beth."

Beth shrugged. "We've been together a long time, we'll work it out. Meantime...I'm really sorry I brought this up. I've enjoyed having lunch, just the two of us. Let's do it again soon, all right?"

"I'd like that, Beth."

As they walked down the staircase to the main floor, Susan stole a glance at Beth. She was a very pretty woman, was exquisitely dressed, and most people would have said that Beth Farragut had everything anyone could want. But this was not the first time Susan had sensed Beth's discontent.

What was it Harvey had said to her, that night they shared a drink and conversation before Beth got home?

If they'd had children, it might have been different . . .

Susan couldn't help but think how different her own life would have been if the child she'd carried had lived.

Going to Joe's was almost like going home, these days. Both Joe and Mrs. Bancroft pampered her outrageously, and probably she should protest more, Susan supposed. But she loved the warmth, the caring and affection she felt when she was in Joe's house.

As they sipped some herbal tea that afternoon, she told Joe about lunch with Beth, and the last-minute turn in the conversation.

When she'd finished, he said thoughtfully, "Beth sounds like a woman who plunges into all sorts of causes because she's trying to escape from her own unhappiness, or loneliness, or both. Not unusual. From what I know of the others, the same thing probably could be said of them.

"For example, Lilian Whitfield was in the limelight when she was a high-fashion model, and often when people become used to applause, it's like soul food to them. Take it away, and they can feel very empty. The Whitfields don't have children, do they?"

"As I understand it, this is Bert's second marriage, and he has a son and daughter by the first one. They're both grown—well, college age, anyway," Susan said.

"Seems to me Heddy Donavan had a baby somewhere along the line," Joe reflected. "Years ago."

"A daughter," Susan said. "She's away in a private girl's school."

"And the Benedicts don't have kids, do they?"

"No."

"Well, what we're saying is that none of these women have in-house family ties to demand their time and attention. No children to care for—none at home, anyway. No elderly parents to look after. A lot of free time, plenty of money. It sounds ideal, but it isn't."

Susan nodded. "Yes. I'm beginning to see that."

"As for the men—Clark Benedict, from what I've heard of him, is an overachiever. He married into money, and he appears to constantly feel the need to prove himself. Bert Whitfield inherited a couple of fortunes—all he has to do is show up at a board meeting now and then."

Joe frowned, then continued, "Harvey, of course, is a very successful lawyer, and he also inherited money. I think Phil Donavan had political ambitions at one time, but he seems to have dropped them. He's not wanting for old family cash, either.

"To go back to Harvey...*did* he make a pass at you when you were staying in Louisburg Square, Susan?"

"No," Susan said. She admitted, "Phil Donavan came a lot closer to doing that at the brunch Sunday."

Joe didn't comment, and after a few minutes they went back to the Monet letters.

Each one, Susan found, was more fascinating than the last.

It was late afternoon when Susan read aloud a letter Joe's grandfather had written to Monet, telling him how much he'd enjoyed the visit he'd made to the artist's home in Giverny, a few weeks earlier. Henry Chase had written:

There is such life in your household, such color and vitality. Here, in a Boston winter, my surroundings seem cold and bleak and monochromatic in contrast, and my life parallels them. There are times when I long for France as much as if I had been born there. Moments when I yearn to smear rich, wonderful pigments on a palette, and to smell linseed oil and turpentine.

I wonder if I will ever paint again? Probably not, I fear. The family business is not conducive to creativity. Now I am paying my dues for the priceless escape that will forever remain the most precious time in my life.

Susan put down the letter and moaned, "That's so sad."
Kent, standing in the doorway, observed, "You two look as if you've been to a funeral."
Susan was so startled she dropped the letter. Several sheets of paper fluttered to the floor before she could reach out for them.
Kent crossed the room, knelt, gently retrieved the pages and handed them to her.
Susan was used to looking up into his eyes. Now she looked down into them, imagined she was seeing banked fires, and the flame that suddenly flared deep inside her was a heated mix of pain and passion.
It hurt terribly to want someone so much...when you couldn't have them. Yet at the same time, to feel as she was feeling now was the very essence of life. She was vibrant all over, so terribly and so wonderfully alive.

Kent's hands touched hers as he handed her Henry Chase's letter. Susan felt a sweet hot ache spread through her loins. She saw Kent swallow hard, then he got to his feet and asked curiously, "What was so sad?"

"My grandfather's life, because he gave up what he loved to do for the sake of the family's prosperity," Joe explained.

Joe looked around him. "If Henry had settled for disinheritance and the life of a struggling artist, I wouldn't be sitting here today, I suppose. And I certainly wouldn't have what you've been telling me is a fortune in artwork, Susan, because almost all of the paintings you've seen in the attic were Henry's.

"I suppose that's why I've always kept them apart from the other family things," Joe confessed. "When I was just a teenager, I found a diary that Henry had kept, and from then on he was a very special person to me. I guess I wanted to keep the things that meant so much to him together. When they go to the Museum of Fine Arts, I'd like to provide a sufficient endowment so there will be a small corner named after him."

"Do you still have the diary, Joe?" Susan asked.

"Yes, and I intend to show it to you."

"But you never knew Henry?"

"No, unfortunately. Henry didn't marry until quite late in life. My mother was his youngest child. My sister, who was quite a bit older than I was, remembered seeing him when she was a little girl. But I wasn't much more than a baby when he died. Now . . . well, as I read these letters with you, I'm getting to know him and to like him, Susan."

"Yes, I feel the same way," Susan said.

Joe admitted ruefully, "I find it hard to think that I, and quite a few who've gone before me, profited by his sacrifice."

"Hadn't you ever read the letters before, Joe?" Kent asked.

"Not this way. I'd skimmed them, and promised myself one day I'd sit down and read them carefully, but the day just never came. Who knows? But for Susan, maybe it never would have."

Joe paused to ask, "May I concoct a drink for you, Kent?"

"No," Kent said, "I'm not on call, but I'm still driving, so I guess I'll have to settle for a club soda."

"My pleasure," said Joe, and began to propel his wheelchair in the direction of the kitchen.

Kent waited until Joe was out of sight, then he went over to Susan, and clasped her hands.

"Come here," he urged.

Puzzled, she let him draw her to her feet. Then she was startled as he pulled her toward him so abruptly she nearly lost her balance.

"You've been on my mind every minute," he groaned. "I walk down a corridor, and I think I'm seeing you. I take a case history, and I think I'm hearing your voice." He attempted a smile. "I don't know whether to call in another cardiologist on consultation, or get myself a good psychiatrist."

His voice lowered, became husky. "Oh, God," he said. "I want you so much. But, almost more, I wish I could do something so you'd never look sad again, the way you did just now."

"Kent," she protested, "I only looked sad because Joe and I were reading his grandfather's letter and . . ."

"I know, I know. I also know I can't protect you from life, and that means tears as well as laughter. But, I want so much to make you happy, Susan. Do you think I'll ever have the chance to make you happy?"

Susan looked up at Kent, and thought he had to be the handsomest man in the world. But what she saw in his face went beyond his good looks. Life had forged character that showed. He had suffered, and the suffering had left little lines that wouldn't go away. But there were also laugh lines edging his eyes, and an inner warmth that glowed at moments like this one.

He had strength and integrity. It was easy to see why he was so successful in his profession. There was a quiet confidence combined with his strength. A patient would know that he could trust his life to Kent.

So, Susan knew, could she.

Susan moved even closer to him, and threw her arms around his neck. She lifted her face to his, and her lips parted ever so slightly. Kent bent, and slowly outlined their curve with the tip of his tongue. Then he filled in the outline slowly, sensuously, before he lowered his mouth to hers.

Their kiss went on and on and on. As it deepened, their bodies spoke a voiceless language that communicated more eloquently than words. They might have become welded together forever, Susan thought, had they not both heard the slight squish of the wheels of Joe's chair. Then Joe came back to the sun porch, bearing a tray of beverages on his lap.

Kent relieved him of the burden, and Susan thought that Kent's hand was shaking slightly as he picked up his glass.

She, certainly, was trembling inside. It was so curious. Certainly their desire for each other had been unfulfilled; yet she was strangely satisfied.

For a few minutes, without speaking at all, she and Kent had said more to each other than they'd ever said before.

Kent and Susan followed each other home that night, parked their cars, then walked side by side around the building and up the steps to the front entrance.

As Kent unlocked the door, he said, "Shall we try to make it to the roof this time? Last time I looked, the moon was still up there, and I think the stars seem pretty secure."

Was a trip to the roof garden to be a preamble to love?

Susan smiled. She'd buy that.

But then, as she automatically glanced toward her mailbox, her smile froze.

There was a long white envelope in her mailbox, and an identical one in Kent's.

Kent saw the color drain out of Susan's face, saw the letter in his mailbox and swore.

Why, in God's name, was this happening? Especially to Susan, who'd had absolutely nothing to do with Elaine's death....

It was one thing to try to punish *him*. But it was sadistic, incredibly cruel, to include Susan.

"We'll take these upstairs," Kent snapped, and decided that "upstairs," in this instance, should be her place.

The elevator seemed to take forever to reach the fourth floor. Susan handed Kent her key. He saw how shaken she was and bit his lip in anger and frustration as he opened the door.

"It's chilly in here," Kent muttered. "Shall we use up some of George's firewood?"

Susan nodded without answering, and Kent got a fire going. But even the bright orange flames licking at the chimney bricks, and the soft glow of the lamps around the room, failed to take the chill out of the atmosphere.

Kent glanced at the two letters, which he had placed side by side on the coffee table. He'd never experienced real hatred, but he knew that the anger he felt toward whomever had written those letters came close.

He sat down on the couch, and tore open the envelope with his name on it. As he read, he was actually nauseated for a couple of seconds before he got a grip on himself.

This letter was the vilest of all. It suggested that terrible things would be done to Susan, unless he did penance by being loyal to Elaine's memory. And that translated as his remaining celibate. Otherwise, what was threatened was the outpouring of a very sick mind.

Kent felt there was no way he could let Susan see this letter, and he was tempted to throw it in the fireplace and let the flames consume it. But he knew he couldn't do that.

Joe would need to read this.

Kent folded the letter and stuck it in his pocket.

Susan asked, "Aren't you going to show it to me?"

Kent shook his head vehemently. "No."

"Kent . . ."

"I am not about to let you see this, Susan."

"Kent, I am not a child."

"That has nothing to do with it."

"I don't need this kind of protection from you."

"If there were a stark-raving lunatic loose, would you expect me to turn you over to him?"

"This is only a letter, Kent."

"Yes, I know it's only a letter, Susan. No," Kent corrected that. "It's a hell of a lot more than a letter. It's the distillation of hate." He added wearily, "It would accomplish nothing for you to see it. Now, open yours, will you?"

She made no move toward the envelope. She said, "I suppose I'm expected to let you read mine."

Kent's self-control snapped. "For God's sake," he snarled, "don't make things any worse than they are." He sat back and held out the letter addressed to her.

"Go ahead," he urged her. "Read the damned thing, will you, and give it back to me. I'm going to take both these letters out to Joe."

"Tonight?"

"Yes, tonight. Joe stays up late."

Susan said levelly, "I'm going to read my letter, Kent. But then, unless you let me read yours, I will throw it in the fireplace and let it burn up."

Kent ran a hand through his hair, rumpling it. "That would be pretty damned stupid," he grated. "Joe needs everything we've got and even then I don't see how the hell he's going to make sense out of any of this."

"I don't like the thought of being 'spared,' Kent."

As a response, he merely glared at her.

When Susan saw that he wasn't going to say anymore, she added, "It can't be that bad."

"It's that bad." And it was, Kent thought. But then he looked at Susan's face and knew he was going to get nowhere with her.

All right, she wasn't a child. She was a very intelligent woman. But could he be blamed for wanting to keep something so ugly from her . . . when he loved her so much?

Kent pulled the letter from his pocket and tossed it at Susan. She held it for a moment, closing her eyes as if she were gearing herself for an ordeal. Then she opened it.

Kent watched her face go ashen as she read. She turned to him, her turquoise eyes shock-filled. "My God," she moaned, "this person is so *sick!*"

"That's what I was attempting to tell you."

Susan clasped her hands in front of her, and expelled a deep sigh. Then she urged, "Go ahead. Open the other letter. We might as well read it together."

The crude black words leaped out at them:

YOU ARE NOT HEARING ME, AND THAT IS FOOLISH. HE IS EVIL, DO YOU NOT SEE THAT? KENT DAVENPORT IS A TOOL OF SATAN. WHY ARE YOU SO BLIND? MAY YOUR SISTER HAUNT YOU UNTIL YOU ARE IN HELL. WHICH MAY BE SOON, SOON, SOON.

Susan said shakily, "Well, that's mild in comparison to what you got."

"Yes." Kent's eyes looked like ebony coals.

He stood and said, "I'd better get on out to Joe's."

"Shall I call and tell him you're coming?"

"You might do that, yes."

At the door, he said, "Be sure to keep the bolt on, and the chain as well." He smiled ruefully. "I was about to say to be sure not to let anyone in unless you knew them. But this time around, the problem is that you'd undoubtedly be seeing a familiar face. So..." Kent sighed. "Be careful, please," he begged. "Be very damned careful, will you? I don't think I could handle it if anything happened to you."

It was 1890. Claude Monet was sixty, and he wrote Henry Chase that he had started what he intended to be an extensive series of paintings of his water garden in Giverny.

The paintings would feature water lilies, especially those in a small pond over which arched a Japanese-style footbridge. He intended, Monet wrote, to paint the pond and the pool over and over again, for there were almost limitless variations of light and color to be revealed.

"This will be an extension of my earlier haystack paintings, and those of the cathedral at Rouen," he explained to Henry.

He added that he was sending Henry a sketch, to give a clearer idea of what he planned....

As she read that, Susan looked across at Joe and said, "Do you mind if I say again that I keep thinking I must be dreaming?"

Joe chuckled. "It delights my soul that you're so enthusiastic about this," he admitted.

"Our book will be cherished by art lovers everywhere," Susan promised.

"I like the sound of that."

Joe also liked the fact that Susan seemed completely diverted by the Monet letters, for a little while anyway. When she'd arrived at his place a couple of hours earlier, she'd looked as if she'd had a very bad night's sleep.

Kent had stayed with him very late, last night. They'd done a lot of talking, a lot of conjecturing.

At lunch, Joe had asked Susan, "Did you see Kent after he got back from here?"

"No. He slipped a note under my door before he went out this morning."

How she wished he'd knocked, instead . . . or had wakened her last night, regardless of the hour.

"He said he had to do a cardioversion—I believe he called it—at the hospital, quite early this morning. Oh, Joe, finding those letters when we got back last night was so horrible."

Joe said, "If it helps at all, I don't think this is going to last much longer."

"Till Salzwald, is that it?" she asked.

"Yes, I think so. I can't help but believe that everything will climax then."

"That's a frightening idea, Joe."

"Not as frightening as thinking the letter writing could go on," Joe told her. "The writer is very close to the edge, in my opinion."

"I trust your opinion," Susan said. "But it makes me so terribly afraid. Not for myself, but for Kent. This person hates Kent so violently, Joe."

"Perhaps," Joe said, and didn't elaborate.

Lunch over, Joe suggested to Susan that she go upstairs and rest for a while.

She shook her head. "I couldn't."

"Then," Joe said, "I'll do the reading till you fall asleep."

He wished she *would* fall asleep, because she was operating too much on nerves. She desperately needed to unwind. But Joe knew that reading the Monet letters was probably the best therapy she could have right now.

Through the afternoon, Joe read the words of both his grandfather and Claude Monet—sometimes faking a French accent to coax a smile out of Susan—until by the time twilight shadows crept across the sun porch, he was hoarse.

Chapter Eleven

Joe knew he should wake Susan up, but he hated to. Nature was providing her with the best possible medicine for someone under stress. As it was, she needed a much bigger dose of it than she was apt to get.

The Whitfields lived in Marblehead. Joe did some mental clockwork. Susan needed time to drive back into Boston, change into something fairly fancy, he supposed, and then team up with Kent for the trip to the North Shore.

He decided reluctantly that he would have to bring her back to reality.

He spoke her name a couple of times before she stirred. Then he watched, amused, as she sat up and blinked in disbelief when she saw him.

"I thought I was home in bed," she confessed. "Do you mean to say I've just taken a *nap?* I never take naps."

Susan glanced at her wristwatch. "I can't believe it's so late. Joe, you shouldn't have let me crash like that."

"On the contrary, you'll be better able to face the evening," Joe said. "And don't push yourself. You have plenty of time."

He watched Susan gather up her coat and handbag, then went to the front door with her.

"There really isn't any need to hurry. So, don't break any speed limits," he cautioned, and had to laugh at himself. He was behaving like a father.

Joe indulged in just a little bit of wistfulness.

How wonderful it would be to have a daughter like Susan.

Susan waved goodbye to him, and, once again, felt grateful to Kent for having brought Joe Chase into her life. She wondered if Joe realized how much both she and Kent needed him right now. He represented stability. He was akin to their guardian angel, she thought whimsically. But she still wished he hadn't let her sleep so long.

There was a fair bit of traffic. Still, once she'd reached Bay State Road and parked, Susan realized that Joe had been right. There really was no need to hurry. She could even indulge in a nice, hot bath and still have plenty of time to get ready for the dinner party.

The phone was ringing as Susan walked into the studio. She crossed the room and picked up the receiver, and was sure she was about to hear Kent's voice. Chances were he'd been detained, or maybe he was tied up on a case and wouldn't be able to make tonight's date at all.

But it wasn't Kent she heard. It was Harvey Farragut.

"Susan, could I drop by? I need to see you." Harvey asked, once he'd identified himself. "I need to talk to you."

A visit from Harvey, who'd acted so strange the last couple of times they'd met?

"Are you talking about now?" Susan asked, dismayed.

"Yes. I know it's last minute, but I've been trying to connect with you all afternoon."

"I just got in, Harvey. And I have to be in Marblehead at seven."

"I know," Harvey said. "So do I. But I won't keep you long." He added, "My office isn't far from your place. I could be there in ten minutes."

Susan's mind went into overdrive. "Harvey, I'm racing the clock as it is. Anyway, we'll be seeing each other at the Whitfields' in just a little while. We can find a chance to talk then."

"You, me and a few dozen other people," Harvey said bitterly. "You don't think Lilian Whitfield ever gives small parties, do you? Any more than Beth or Mandy Benedict do, if they can help it. Susan, there wouldn't be a prayer of my getting you alone at the Whitfields.

"Look," he said, "I told Beth I'd be late today, so she's going on ahead with the Donavans. I can wait while you change, we can talk while you change. Then you can drive out to Marblehead with me."

"Kent Davenport's taking me," Susan said. "When Lilian invited us, she suggested we come together."

Now why had she felt the need to explain that to Harvey?

"Well," he said, "it shouldn't be too late a night. Suppose I come by your place afterward?"

The response came automatically. "I don't think that would be wise, Harvey."

"Frankly, I don't give a damn about being wise right now, Susan, and I'm pressured for time. I'd say we could get together tomorrow for breakfast or lunch or whatever the hell, but I have to fly down to New York on business. I have an early-morning flight, and I won't be back until Friday afternoon. Then there'll be just enough time to turn around and drive to Salzwald."

Harvey said abruptly, "Wait a minute, will you please?"

Susan could hear him talking to someone else, and then he came back on the phone to say, "My secretary's telling me a call I've been waiting for from L.A. has just come through. I'll have to catch up with you later, Susan."

Susan, puzzled by this whole exchange, heard the receiver click.

She was tempted to call Joe and tell me about this odd conversation with Harvey, but the clock was ticking away relentlessly.

Susan headed for the bathroom, showered, and had just finished dressing when Kent knocked on her door.

The Whitfields' waterfront Marblehead estate was impressive. As Kent drove down the long driveway and pulled up in front of a turreted stone mansion, Susan said, "Whew! It could double as a Scottish castle."

"Yes," Kent agreed. "And it also offers a panoramic view from every window. Nice, eh?"

"Very nice."

"Bert bought this place when he and Lilian got married," Kent said. "That must be about a dozen years ago, if I remember right. I wasn't very far along in my residency. Bert asked me to be an usher at the wedding, and I was surprised."

"Why?"

"We weren't in the same peer group. Bert's quite a bit older than I am—his age falls somewhere between mine and Joe's." Kent shrugged. "The difference didn't matter, but I thought Bert would have a slew of Harvard classmates he'd choose over me. It made me wonder if he had any close friends. I still wonder. He's a difficult person to figure out."

"I know he has children by a previous marriage," Susan said. "Did his first wife die?"

"No, she divorced him, and by Boston Brahman standards it was a messy divorce. Bert didn't want it, which meant that there were some headlines splashed around. She made some nasty accusations against Bert."

"Such as?"

"She claimed that he had some pretty weird habits. The case wound up with her agreeing to a cash settlement that was more than most people make in five lifetimes. Fortunately, Bert could afford it."

"Where is the first Mrs. Whitfield now?"

"She married an Englishman with a title. I think she used some of Bert's money to help restore her new husband's castle. The kids are at college here in the States."

Kent surrendered his car to an attendant and clasped Susan's arm as they walked up shallow steps to the mansion's ornate entrance. A butler in full livery admitted them to a baronial entrance hall that looked as if it belonged on a movie set.

Bert and Lilian Whitfield stood side by side as they received their guests.

Lilian, tall and willowy, wore a stunning ivory dress that set off her blond beauty. Bert was wearing a dark blue business suit, a striped shirt, and a tie whose knot was slightly askew. He was a slight man, a couple of inches shorter than Lilian, and he was pale—pale eyes, pale hair, pale skin.

Appearance-wise, he would have been lost in even a small crowd, Susan thought, whereas Lilian would stand out anywhere. She could see why Bert would be "besotted" with Lilian, to use Beth's phrase.

Susan greeted Lilian, then moved on to Bert. He was talking to another guest, and she waited her turn.

The other guest moved on, and Bert, a somewhat fixed smile on his face, thrust out his hand. But then he stopped short and peered at Susan.

"Elaine." He breathed the name. "My God, it *is* you."

There were other people coming up behind Susan and Kent, and Susan heard someone gasp. She halted, momentarily frozen into place. She couldn't believe that Bert Whitfield would have made such a slip deliberately. On the other hand, it didn't seem possible that he could be so unthinking.

"Bert!" Lilian's tone was low, but furious.

Bert glanced at Lilian, and then back to Susan. His confusion seemed genuine. But then he blinked, and managed a faint, embarrassed smile as he muttered, "Sorry. I'm terribly sorry. Welcome, Susan."

Susan felt Kent clutch her arm again, and he propelled her toward the drawing room, where a combo was playing soft music, and black-clad waiters were busily serving drinks.

"The bastard," Kent fumed. "What the hell can he have been thinking of?"

Elaine, Susan thought. Bert had been thinking of Elaine. Susan had come upon him unexpectedly, and he had glanced up quickly, and it was her twin who'd registered in his mind.

Was that the way it was with Kent? With him, was it simply a matter of his being able to camouflage his reactions better than Bert Whitfield could?

Susan fought back a wave of depression. Lately, she'd finally begun to feel that when Kent was with her, he really was with *her*. And she'd been so thankful. One of the greatest obstacles in their path—for her, anyway—had been the fear that when she was with him, she would never be able to free herself of Elaine's shadow.

Now all the old doubts started to surface again.

"Susan!" Kent's tone was sharp, and Susan saw that his dark brows were knit in a frown.

"Do you want to cut out of here?" he asked her. "You'd be justified."

"No," she said. "Oh, I want to cut out. There's nothing I'd rather do. But I need to stay here."

"Do you?" Kent looked around. "Lilian's outdone herself. Half of Boston must be here. I doubt either of us will have the chance to learn anything helpful through casual conversation.

"As for Bert—I still can't believe what I heard. What could have possessed him to say such a thing?" Kent scowled. "How the hell could anyone confuse you with Elaine?" he demanded. "They might get mixed up for a second, but a second at the most. Once anyone really *looked* at you, there's no resemblance. No resemblance at all. And Bert has certainly seen enough of you to know the difference."

Susan's heart began to sing.

It might be crazy, but a bad *faux pas* on her host's part was making her feel happier than she could remember feeling in a long, long time. . . .

Lilian and Bert Whitfield abandoned their two-person receiving line not long after Susan and Kent arrived and joined their guests.

The combo played on, and waiters passed around succulent hors d'oeuvres as well as drinks. Then dinner was served in a dining room as baronial as the entrance hall. Afterward, there was dancing, on a long, glass-enclosed porch overlooking the water.

Susan danced the first dance with Kent, but midway through it Bert Whitfield cut in.

She saw Kent hesitate and was afraid he was about to refuse to turn her over to Bert. But then he stepped back, and Bert Whitfield put his arm around her.

Kent was not an especially good dancer. But, Susan discovered, Bert Whitfield was.

Under different circumstances, dancing with Bert would have been enjoyable, because she loved to dance. Under these circumstances, she couldn't wait for the music to stop so she could get away from him.

Then Bert said softly, "I figured I'd better cut in. I felt pretty sure that if I asked you to dance, you'd refuse. Susan, if it's any help, I feel like such a damned fool."

"Bert, please. It was a slip of the tongue, I realize that."

"An unforgivably stupid slip," Bert said. "I'm not offering this as an excuse," he went on, "but it may help you understand what happened. Now and then I suffer from migraines. One started coming on this afternoon. I took more medication than I should have, because I wanted to be in halfway decent shape for Lilian's dinner party. Then," Bert confessed, "like an idiot I had a couple of drinks. I was pretty fuzzy, and when I saw you..."

He sounded so contrite that Susan felt sorry for him.

She said, "I understand, Bert. You don't have to say any more. Also...identical twins get used to having people confuse them. I can't tell you how many times in earlier years I was confused with Elaine, or she with me."

"I can appreciate that. I'm sure you must have been hard to tell apart when you were younger. But people develop different personalities as they grow older, and that shows in their faces. You're not like Elaine, I knew that the night I met you at the Farraguts'. So..."

Bert sighed, and said, "It's hard to explain how I felt, for a minute there. Like I was having a very strange vision..." He added slowly, "Your sister wove quite a spell over this group of ours, Susan."

"What kind of spell?"

"Different sorcery on different people. She was..."

Kent tapped on Bert's shoulder. Bert released Susan, stepped up, and, politely formal, said, "Thank you, Susan."

The combo began to play a waltz, and as she swayed in Kent's arms, Susan said, "Your timing was terrible."

Kent's left eyebrow quirked. "Was, or is? I admit I'm not the world's greatest dancer."

"Was," Susan said. "I think Bert may have been about to tell me something important."

"Well, maybe we should devise some sort of code. You waggle your right thumb, and that's a signal for me to butt out."

"Kent, this is serious," Susan protested.

"And you're so beautiful I'm having respiratory problems. Excuse me, but sometimes when I'm with you it's a bit difficult for me to set my mind on anything but you. We won't even get into what happens to my heart."

He drew her closer. Susan pillowed her head on his shoulder. And just then she didn't care if the people around them thought they looked like two people in love.

Dancing with Phil Donavan was just about what Susan would have expected it to be. He was suggestive, in a clever way. She suspected that a woman would only have to latch onto one of Phil's lines, and he'd take it from there.

As they moved around the floor, she decided to try to get some advantage out of a rather uncomfortable situation. She felt as if Joe were looking over her shoulder, and thought wryly that he'd approve. Nevertheless, it took courage and some self-revving-up to ask the question.

"Phil, do I remind you of Elaine?"

"I heard about Bert's greeting," Phil said. "Is that still bothering you? Don't confuse Bert with the rest of us, Susan. He's a case unto himself."

She took another plunge. "That doesn't really answer my question."

"You really want to know if you remind me of Elaine."

"Yes."

Susan felt as if Phil's eyes were boring right through her, and they were cool.

"Why do you want to know?" he asked. "Because Bert's gaffe nicked your self-confidence? Or because you're curious about how well I knew your sister?" Then Phil laughed. "Suppose I say I knew her well enough. Would that suffice?"

He didn't seem to expect an answer, so Susan didn't give him one. They danced the rest of the dance in silence. When it was over, they parted silently. Then the music started up again, and Susan looked around for Kent. But she couldn't spot him. So when Clark Benedict approached, there was nothing to do but to dance with him when he asked her.

Almost immediately, he brought up the subject of Bert Whitfield's unfortunate slip.

"Sometimes you wonder what planet Bert's living on," Clark said. "But even for him that was quite a blunder."

Susan took another plunge. "I think enough has been said about Bert's mistake," she told Clark. "I realize I must remind you people of Elaine. I imagine that must sometimes be hard for all of you. It must bring back a lot of memories."

"Well, yeah," Clark admitted. "I guess I'd have to say it does. But that flash of recognition only lasts a couple of seconds, when someone first sees you. It doesn't take much time around you to know that you're very different from your sister, Susan."

"Could you elaborate on that?"

"I could." There was a hard note in Clark's voice. "But I'm not crazy about speaking ill of the dead."

The blunt statement carried a shock wave with it. Jolted, Susan suddenly pictured her twin plunging hundreds of feet from a rocky ledge to the shore of a mountain lake.

Elaine's last seconds must have been sheer hell. God knows what kind of terror she had experienced.

How long did it take a person to black out, in a fall like that? Had Elaine's mind been working right to the end? Had she been able to think? Even more, how much had she *felt?*

Elaine hadn't deserved to die like that.

Susan's voice trembled as she said to Clark, "I think you've already spoken ill of the dead."

"Then I'm sorry," Clark said abruptly. And the combo stopped playing.

Kent still hadn't appeared when Harvey Farragut came over to ask Susan to dance.

Harvey wasn't drunk, but he wasn't steady, either. He staggered slightly as they moved onto the dance floor.

Fortunately, the combo was playing a piece with a slow beat. Even then, Harvey shuffled more than he danced, and Susan had a hard time trying to follow him.

After a moment, he said, "Nice."

He repeated, "Nice. You're nice. Listen, Susan . . ."

"Yes?"

"I still need to talk to you."

"Perhaps after you get back from New York, Harvey."

Harvey shook his head. "Nope. That would be too late. I need to talk to you before I go."

"Talk to me now, why don't you?"

"No chance," Harvey mumbled. "Davenport's heading this way, and he's going to cut in."

Susan groaned. Again, Kent couldn't have chosen a worse moment, and once they were circling the floor, she told him so.

"Here you *disappeared,* and then the very minute . . ."

Kent growled, "I didn't disappear, for one thing. I've kept an eye on you, I just stayed in the background. Then I decided I'd better come to your rescue. It looked like Harvey was walking all over your feet. Am I right in assuming he's had his usual too many?"

"I suppose so. But he was still perfectly coherent."

"Well," Kent said, "right now you're going to have to put up with *me* walking all over your feet. And I'm coherent, too."

He tugged her closer. Susan nestled her head against him again, and didn't protest.

Kent said, "I think we've paid our dues. Why don't we cut out of here?"

Susan smiled. "I wondered when you'd ask."

"Let's slink out to the hall, and see if the maid can unearth our coats."

"I should say good-night to Lilian...."

"For once, let etiquette take a hike, will you?" Kent urged. "You can call her tomorrow."

They were just stepping into the hall when Beth Farragut caught up with them.

"Are you two leaving?" Beth protested. "The night's young, and so are you."

"I have to be at the hospital early tomorrow," Kent said. "And Susan's working, too."

"Well, let me borrow Susan for a couple of minutes. You can wait around that long, can't you, Kent?" Beth added mysteriously, "There's something I must show you, Susan."

Beth led the way up a long curving staircase, then down a wide corridor into one of the largest bedrooms Susan had ever seen.

"Voilà!" Beth announced triumphantly, and Susan saw the painting hanging over the bed.

"You told me Lilian owned a Monet, and I'd actually forgotten," she admitted.

"Well, I'm sure you've had plenty of other things on your mind." Beth moved closer to the painting. "Gorgeous, isn't it? And so perfect in here."

Lilian's room was decorated in pale gray, pale blue, and creamy white, and Monet's painting perfectly matched that color scheme. Or, Susan thought, probably it was the other way around. Lilian had probably decorated her room to blend with the painting.

"A sailing regatta at Argenteuil," she said.

She looked at the choppy white water, the pale sails on boats that were being buffeted by a stiff wind, and the sky, a mass of swirling clouds. "This is very much like a Monet I've seen in Paris, at the Musée d'Orsay," she told Beth.

"Can you imagine what Bert must have paid for it?"

"A fair bit, I would say."

In Susan's opinion, paintings by Monet were without price; but she wasn't sure that Beth really would relate to what she meant by that.

Beth glanced toward the bedroom door. Then, to Susan's surprise, she went over and closed it.

"I don't want anyone to walk in on us," she explained. "Susan I have to speak to you."

Beth, too?

"A while ago, Lilian cornered Mandy and Heddy and me," Beth said. "We talked it over, and even though I don't really agree with them, they insist I know you better than they do. So, they asked me to ask you."

"Ask me what, Beth?"

"They want you to come to Salzwald this weekend, Susan. They feel that this trip is to be a memorial to Elaine, and they think you should be there.

"Now," Beth went on, "I'm still not so sure about that, myself. I can't help but think that being there would stir up a lot of sad memories for you. Matter of fact, I wish this idea had never been drummed up."

"I agree," Susan said. "It seems to me that it will be a difficult weekend for everyone."

Beth walked over to a large, gold-framed mirror and peered at her reflection. She smoothed her lipstick with her little finger, then said, "I think I made my position clear when you were at the house, and Harvey brought up the idea."

"Yes," Susan agreed. "Yes, you did."

"Well, regardless of that, it goes without saying that you should have the chance to make up your own mind. But there is a slight problem," Beth went on. "Accommodations are at a premium up in the mountains at foliage time. Our crowd has reservations at The Schloss, and of course they know us very well up there. I'm sure that if I call tomorrow they will find a place for both you and Kent. But I need your decision as soon as possible."

"Did you say for me and *Kent?*"

"Yes. I think Heddy contacted Kent, but he never got back to her. Do you know what he plans to do?"

"No."

"Then talk it over with him, will you, Susan? And give me a call first thing in the morning so I'll know what to do."

Beth hesitated, then admitted, "I think everyone expects Kent to be there. And he should be, don't you think?"

Susan sighed. "I don't know. If you think going to Salz-

wald would be difficult for me, how do you imagine it would
be for Kent?''

"Very hard, I would imagine. But he may feel it's something he has to do, now that everyone's decided to go
through with this. Anyway, talk to him, will you?" Beth
repeated.

Beth glanced in the mirror again. "I think I'll pay a visit
to the powder room before I go back downstairs," she said.
"Don't forget to call me, all right?"

Susan nodded, then lingered after Beth had left, to take
another look at the Monet.

It was a peaceful painting, though Monet had chosen a
cloudy, windy day to commit the regatta at Argenteuil to
canvas. Looking at it made Susan think of Monet's letters
to Henry Chase, and she wished she were away from the
Whitfields' house and back at Joe's, reading with him.
Those hours she spent with Joe and his grandfather and
Monet were so remarkably untroubled.

But, tomorrow, they would have to suffer some interfer-
ence. She and Joe would have to talk about her going to
Salzwald. And about Kent's going, too. She found the idea
of the macabre pilgrimage as repugnant as ever, and she
didn't want to have any part of it. But she knew she had to
be there. And so did Kent.

Joe was right. The morbid excursion was closely connected to the anonymous letters.

Susan wished she knew which one of the group had first
brought up the idea of making the trip. There seemed to be
considerable confusion about that....

The person who'd planted the seed was clever. Very
clever.

Susan suddenly wished she could huddle with Joe right
then and get his input. She wanted his help in attempting to

analyze the different conversations she'd had tonight, the various things that had happened.

But, even more important, she needed to go over all of this with Kent. Tonight, once they were back on Bay State Road.

Chapter Twelve

"You asked me what I think of it. All right, I think it's the most outrageous thing I've ever heard."

Kent was furious. "It's macabre," he flared, as he paced up and down Susan's studio. "It's sick. It's also in rotten taste. I don't know why the hell you didn't tell Beth there's no way you would consider going to Salzwald this weekend."

Susan never had seen Kent so angry. He'd been irritated enough earlier by Bert's ill-chosen remark at the dinner party. But now he was downright volatile.

It had been nearly midnight when they got back from Marblehead, and they were both tired. She knew it was a bad time to bring up a serious issue. But she didn't see how there could be another, better time to talk to him about their going to Salzwald, since Beth would be expecting to hear from her tomorrow.

As they rode up in the elevator together, she'd told Kent only that she needed to discuss something with him that couldn't wait. Weary though he was, he'd immediately agreed to come to her place.

From then on, things had gone downhill.

Now Kent glared at her as he demanded, "Exactly what are we supposed to do? Share a chalet so that everyone in the whole damned crowd can snicker up their sleeves? And get some vicarious kicks by imagining what might be going on between the two of us? Thanks but no thanks."

Susan tried to hang on to her patience as she told him, "All Beth said was that if I got back to her soon enough, she thought she still could get accommodations for us at The Schloss."

"Decent of her," Kent snarled. "Damned decent of her. I suppose she'll also supply oversize handkerchiefs for everyone when they go up on the mountain Saturday."

Susan winced. She wouldn't have believed he could be so caustic.

"Tell me, Susan," Kent snapped, biting off each word, "just what *is* everyone supposed to do Saturday? Congregate at Castle Ledge and let Phil or Harvey or Clark or Bert deliver a eulogy?"

He strode to the window, and stood with his back to Susan. Over his shoulder, he said, "I admit it might be damned interesting to hear what any one of those four would have to say about Elaine. I'm sure that at least one of them— maybe all of them, for that matter—had a lot more to do with her than I did."

Susan shrank from the raw bitterness she heard in his voice . . . and from her shock at what he'd said.

Kent swung around, and stared at her, appalled. "I'm sorry," he said. "Dear God, I'm sorry. For a minute, I forgot she was your sister."

He came and knelt beside her, and reached for her hands. But she wrenched her fingers away as he tried to clasp them, and averted her gaze.

"You hated her," she accused.

Kent didn't say anything.

"You *hated* her," she repeated. "I've wondered if you ever really loved her, but..."

"You wondered?" he queried. "You might have guessed, don't you think? Don't you remember my wedding day as well as I do? How long do you think it took me to know what a mistake I'd made?"

"That didn't mean you had to hate her."

"I didn't hate her... then."

"But... later?"

Kent stood, then went over to the other side of the room and sat down on the couch. He leaned forward and clasped his hands, his face dark and brooding.

"Oh, yes," he said. "Oh, yes, there were certainly times when I hated Elaine later. But not enough to wish her dead.

"If you think I picked up enough of a guilt burden three years ago to make me feel I had to atone for what happened to Elaine, you're dead wrong. I didn't write anonymous letters to motivate you to come to Boston, so I could do penance. God, do you think I also wrote those venomous letters to myself?"

Susan's throat ached so much she didn't think she could speak. She forced out her question. "How do I know what you did?"

Kent's voice was deadly quiet. "Do you really have to ask that, Susan?"

He stood, the terrible blankness on his face making Susan flinch. His lack of expression was far worse than if he'd glared at her. And the cold control in his voice was more terrifying than if he'd sworn at her. His coldness was harder to handle than his fury.

She'd hurt him, and this, she saw, was the way he reacted—he withdrew. Just now he was as remote as if he were a thousand miles away.

"It's late," he said, still showing no emotion at all. "You're very tired, and so am I. Are you going to Joe's in the morning?"

Susan nodded.

"I'll call you there if I get a chance. Meantime, fill Joe in on your conversation with Beth—and anything else that happened at the Whitfields'—will you please?"

Kent was speaking to her as if she were a stranger.

Susan murmured. "Yes."

"I'm sure you'll find Joe will agree that under no condition should you go to Salzwald," he said emotionlessly. "I hope you'll listen to him."

She had hurt him so deeply.

Kent fixed himself a Scotch and water, and looked across the river at the lights along Memorial Drive in Cambridge. He ached all over—mentally, physically, emotionally, and spiritually.

He loved her so much. And what she'd just said hurt doubly, because he'd felt closer and closer to her with each passing day. He'd thought that they'd begun to know each other in ways that went beyond the physical attraction that had been so overwhelming, right from the beginning.

Now he had to wonder if he knew Susan at all.

How could she possibly think he'd had anything to do with letters that had to be the product of a deranged mind?

The answer came fast. She couldn't, if their relationship meant even a fraction as much to her as it did to him.

Their relationship?

Kent's laugh was short and bitter. What relationship?

He'd held back with Susan, every step of the way.

The letters had resurrected Elaine in such a terrible way. And once he discovered that Susan, too, was a victim of the anonymous writer, a sixth sense had warned him that there was no way he could hope Susan would trust him fully until that writer was exposed.

Kent remembered, vividly, the horror in Susan's eyes—momentarily directed at him—when she'd seen that long white envelope in her mailbox. That memory had helped him stay in control at moments when his body was being a traitor to him.

Even so, though he'd done his damnedest, there had been moments lately when he couldn't entirely hold back. Nevertheless, he'd managed remarkably well, Kent thought wryly. It had taken more fortitude than he would have believed he possessed to refrain from making love to Susan. Especially when he could see in her eyes that she wanted him just as much as he wanted her.

Meantime, with Joe's help, and the help of those friends of Joe's who were with the Boston police, everything had been done that could be done to try to track down the letter writer. Finding such a person wasn't easy. Even after the number of possible suspects had been reduced to relatively few people, they'd still been unable to zero in on a single individual.

They had nothing to go on. Not even fingerprints. Whoever was writing the letters was clever and cautious.

The watching and the waiting had been bad enough. At each of these parties he and Susan had gone to, his nerves had been strained by the need to maintain a constant alertness. And then, tonight, he'd made the ultimate mistake. He'd admitted to Susan that there had been moments when he had hated her twin.

How could he get past that one?

All along, of course, he'd known that sometime he would have to talk to Susan about Elaine. That was another obstacle that would have to be cleared from their path. And he'd wondered, so many times, just what he could say to her that would make her understand.

Finally he'd decided he could only hope that when the moment came, the right words would come with it.

Kent downed the rest of the Scotch and wondered if he would have gone through with the wedding eight years ago, if he could have gotten a glimpse of the future. And he knew the answer would have to be *yes*.

He couldn't have walked away from the woman he'd asked to be his wife. He couldn't have forgiven himself for making a fool of Elaine at the last minute. So he'd said his vows. And tried to tell himself that the person who stood with him at the altar would possess the same, wonderful qualities he'd sensed so quickly and intuitively in her identical twin.

But she hadn't.

Kent headed for the kitchen to put his glass in the sink just as someone began knocking on his door.

He glanced at the mantel clock. It was almost two in the morning.

The thought crossed his mind that maybe the letter writer had come to confront him in person. In which case, he'd better be prepared.

Kent crossed the room carefully, moving silently, and peered through the tiny Judas window cut into the door.

He saw Susan's lovely face magnified by the lens in the little peephole.

He flung the door open, and first noticed that she'd been crying. Then he saw that she was wearing a heavy turtleneck sweater with a warm jacket zippered over it, dark wool slacks, and sneakers.

The urge to protect her overrode everything else.

"Where do you think you're going?" he asked gently.

Her voice sounded small and timid. "I thought it might be a good time to go up on the roof."

"On the *roof?*"

"Yes. We never seem to quite make it up there, but I thought that maybe we could now. There's a big moon and the...the stars look like they've been polished." Susan stumbled over the words.

Kent stared at her for a minute, and then he very nearly smiled. She looked like a small frightened child as she waited for his answer.

"Wait a sec," he told her. "I'll get a sweater and a flashlight."

Susan watched him head for his bedroom, and sagged with relief. She'd been so afraid he was going to refuse her, and she couldn't have blamed him.

When Kent rejoined her, he'd tugged on a bulky dark red sweater, tousling his hair in the process. Also, a faint stubble covered his chin. A few more hours, and he'd need a shave. Right now he looked human, Susan thought. And almost approachable.

He led them along the corridor to a door that opened onto the rather rickety back stairs that led to the roof. At the top of the flight, they stepped into a large open area bathed in silver and shadows.

Kent took Susan's arm, and guided her past groupings of chairs and tables and picnic benches to a ledge that came to her waist. She took a sharp breath, dazzled by the city lights, the moon, and the stars.

Kent, still holding her arm, said, "The world's at your feet, and everything's right in the heavens. I wish I could give it all to you, Susan."

He paused, and then let himself say it.

"I love you."

Susan's eyes shimmered with tears.

His voice was husky. "I've loved you for such a long time. I can't wait any longer to tell you."

Susan pressed her head against his shoulder, and her voice was muffled.

Kent stroked her hair, and heard her say, "Oh, dear God, Kent, I love you so much. And I've loved you for such a long time, too." Her voice broke. "I'm sorry, I'm so very sorry for what I said."

"I know." Kent held her close. "We've both been on edge. Neither of us can be blamed for losing it now and then."

Susan nodded vigorously. "It's been so terrible," she said. "And it still is. But regardless of all that, there's something you have to know. I trust you completely. I believe in you with all my heart and soul. After you left, all I could think about was *you*. I'd trust you with my life, Kent."

Kent felt tears sting *his* eyes, and it was a very unusual feeling for him.

He felt as if he'd been living through a cold, cold winter that had frozen so much of him for such a long time. Now the hard, frozen core inside him began to melt. New warmth flowed through his veins, chasing out the ice, and he felt *alive*.

His heart overflowed with love for Susan, and with it the knowledge that nothing, *nothing* any longer stood between them. Neither the letters with their ugly insinuations, nor anything else.

Right now, their souls were touching. They were soaring far above the merely physical.

Kent smiled into the darkness.

God knows, there was plenty of the physical left between them, too. Kent's need for Susan surged, and with it his arousal.

He moved back a little, and cupped her face between his hands. He touched his lips to hers, and put some of his soul into his kiss. It was a long and lingering kiss, deep as the thrust of his tongue when he gently pried her lips apart, and invaded her sweet, moist mouth.

Their bodies communicated, and Kent took time for only a single, deep breath before he claimed Susan's lips again. This time he nibbled, demanded, and her response was like a flame darting between the two of them, burning them both with a seductive fire.

Kent whispered, "Sweetheart, now that we've had our dose of moonlight and magic, how about going down to my place?"

He bypassed the living room, and took Susan to his bedroom. Silver radiance spilled through the windows, as he gently lowered her to his bed.

Kent stretched out alongside her, drawing her toward him. Pressed against him, Susan felt his hardness, and a wonderful ache began to throb deep inside her.

She clasped Kent's head, pressed her fingers into his dark velvet hair, then drew him close so that his mouth would mesh with hers. She nibbled, sucked, and felt a stab of desire so sharp it staggered her.

She let her body language speak as she rubbed against Kent. He clutched her and groaned.

"Oh, Susan," he muttered. "Much more of that and I won't be able to last very long."

Susan saw him draw in a ragged breath, and then she let herself do what she wanted to do. Though her body was crying for haste, she slowly and carefully began to unfasten his shirt buttons.

Kent watched her, loving her and feeling such tenderness for her. She was going about this task with such gravity; he was amused, but he was also sure that he might very well go crazy if she didn't hurry a little. He didn't want to rush either of them. But for once in his life, he was afraid his body was going to get the better of his brain.

Finally, he couldn't wait. He helped her. He got up and unclasped his belt buckle, and tugged off his slacks. Then he stood before her, the moonlight highlighting his naked body.

Susan watched him, and couldn't move.

He was magnificent.

He said huskily, "Your turn," and sat down on the bed beside her. He clasped an arm around her, drew her up so that he could tug her sweater over her head. And then he unfastened her bra.

For a moment, he was as riveted as she'd just been. Her breasts were touched by silver, her nipples taut, dark mounds.

Kent couldn't resist. He had to taste.

Susan, who'd always had her own kind of control, couldn't believe what was happening as Kent gently savored first one nipple, then the other. The desire-spiked pain and the pleasure were an almost unbearable combination.

He leaned over her, tugging off her slacks. He lifted her just enough to slide her satin and lace panties over her legs. Then he paused, transfixed by what he saw.

Susan's skin was pale, white gold in the moonlight, and so wonderfully smooth. Her breasts were proud, creamy mounds, centered by the taut, deep-rose nipples he had just explored. Her waist tapered, to merge with the soft swell of her hips. The very center of her was protected with a soft fuzz that looked pale gold in this light. Her legs were long, slim, with an enticing curve to her calves . . .

As he moved toward her, Kent did not once think of Elaine.

Susan felt as if Kent were the first man who had ever touched her.

She asked herself how a woman who'd been married and had had a couple of other relationships along the way could possibly feel so virginal?

But, heady though her thirst for Kent was, she suddenly felt a strange shyness as he again slid onto the bed next to her, then propped himself on an elbow and simply . . . looked at her.

The passion was still there. Her underlying need flowed strong as a tidal current. But just now there was a thin veil over her desire. Not reluctance, certainly, but rather a mix of wonder and fear.

Could she be everything to him she so desperately wanted to be?

She wanted to give him so much. All of her. All of her.

Kent's smile was gentle, as if he understood what was happening to her. And he probably did, she thought. She felt so completely in tune with him.

He reached out a long finger and gently touched first one of her eyebrows and then the other, tracing their curves as if he were drawing them.

With that same exquisite care, he gently outlined her nose, and then slowly, slowly, circled her lips.

Susan's lips began to tingle, and the fire inside her began to burn more and more and more. . . .

Now Kent's tongue traced her lips, as his fingers just had done, and then slithered on to the hollow of her throat. She felt his hands cup her breasts, massaging them with light, even strokes. Then his lips took over, teasing and sucking until Susan didn't think she could bear the ecstasy.

She clung to him, digging her fingers into his back. He held her just far enough away from him to start on a voyage of exploration that trailed lower and lower until he came to the mound that was the very core of her, and beyond to the most special place of all. And, as he touched her, Susan vibrated, writhed, then spun out of control.

Kent wanted this for her, God how he wanted this for her. But as her passion peaked, then as he felt her body go limp, he knew there was no way he could hold back much longer.

He muttered, "Sweetheart. Oh, Susan, oh, Susan." And Susan opened herself to him.

He entered her, and they rocked together. And Susan's hands were like magic butterflies, fluttering all over him, each gossamer touch leaving behind it another flame to fuel the fire of his desire. Then suddenly her hands stilled and her body took over, moving with Kent, matching his tempo, as they blended and blended and climbed and climbed until they shuddered convulsively, and shattered together.

In the aftermath, they clung to each other. It took time to come back down. They lay wrapped in each other's arms, each one still a part of the other. Then, after a while, it began again. The sweet yearning, the growing need, the hard response of Kent's arousal. And they set off on another journey that progressed more slowly, probed even more deeply, and took them into a stratosphere of exquisite culmination.

Susan, spent, fell asleep in Kent's arms. When, after a time, she awakened, she saw that his eyes were closed.

His long dark lashes fanned his cheeks. His breathing was deep and even. He looked so at peace. She felt so at peace. Fulfilled, complete, for the first time in her life.

She hadn't known it was possible to feel so much love.

Later, Susan and Kent lay side by side, hands clasped, not speaking for a long time because just then there was no need for words.

But finally Kent said, "There's something I have to get off my chest."

Susan wished she could hush him. They had been in their own wonderful world. Anything he might say about anything outside it would be an intrusion.

"There's something I should have explained to you sooner," he began, and she knew she'd been right. This was going to be an intrusion which, right now, she wished they could avoid.

But he continued. "When I realized you thought I might have something to do with those damned letters, it hurt so much...."

Susan pressed a finger against his lips. "Please," she implored him.

"No," Kent said. He propped himself up against the pillows, drew the bedclothes a shade higher as if to warn that there could be no more intimacy, for the time being. "It's not that I blame you," he insisted. "But I need to tell you this."

"Kent," she said. "I've already told you that I knew, in my heart, you had nothing to do with the letters."

"I know," he interrupted. "Thank God I *do* know, Susan. And I know you trust me. That's something for which I'll be eternally thankful."

"Please never doubt it."

"I don't. I won't." He smiled wryly. "It isn't that I have any doubts about *you*. I guess my problem is myself."

"I don't understand you."

The wryness lingered. "Maybe I don't understand myself. I seem to need reassurance."

"You, Kent? You're the most self-assured person I've ever known."

"Training, Susan," he said. "At the least, doctors have to appear to have a fair share of self-confidence, or they couldn't inspire much trust in their patients. But you're not a patient. And . . . oh God, Susan, I need you to believe in me."

"I do believe in you."

"Thank you," he said. "But try to understand that I have to let knowing that sink in. So damned much has happened . . ." Kent drew a deep breath, and continued, "There's still something I want to tell you, sweetheart. The difference is that now—well, I know that I no longer *need* to make this kind of an explanation."

Baffled, Susan asked, "Then why make it?"

"So you'll have my side of the story of what happened at Salzwald," Kent said.

Susan felt as if a chill had crept into the room, dispelling the glorious warmth that had been between them.

Salzwald. Elaine. Could she and Kent ever be entirely free of either?

"You may remember," Kent said slowly, "that last night I only danced with you a couple of times?"

"Yes."

"And I'm a lousy dancer."

She smiled. "Well, I wouldn't quite say that."

"You can say it. I know it. Also, last night I didn't dance with anyone else."

"I didn't really know that."

"You can believe it," Kent told her grimly. "I seldom attempt dancing. It's one of a number of things I don't do well, because I can't. Rock climbing, going up mountain trails, are two others."

"What are you saying?"

"I wasn't on the mountain when Elaine was killed, Susan, so I couldn't have had anything to do with her death."

"What are you telling me?"

"Just that. I couldn't have had anything to do with Elaine's death."

Susan sat up very straight. "Kent," she began, almost indignant about this now. "Aren't you convinced that I don't think you had anything to do with Elaine's death? Or, with the letters. So—" She broke off and stared at him, as what he'd just said really registered.

"You weren't on the mountain with the others?"

He nodded. "That's right. I stayed down at The Schloss, as I always have, and swam in the heated pool."

Susan said slowly, "Now I *don't* understand."

"When I was in college, I played football," Kent said. "Late in my last season, I was hurt. I was tackled hard, and twisted the wrong way as I fell. The result was a bad knee injury. A *very* bad knee injury.

"I had my share of surgery, therapy, rehabilitation. For a while, I thought I'd never get rid of the limp. But I do pretty well most of the time, unless I overexert myself.

"One thing the injury did was to kill my dream of becoming the world's greatest cardiac surgeon. There was no way I could stand up in an OR for hours on end, so I had to switch my choice of a medical discipline. Aside from that, the knee doesn't usually hamper me. But, as I've said, such things as rock climbing and mountain climbing and skiing, too, for that matter, are beyond me. Bicycle riding is out, as well, and I don't function too well if I dance much."

"I never realized . . ." Susan began.

Kent smiled. "Well, I'm glad you didn't. I guess that proves those grueling months of treatment worked pretty well."

He sobered. "But, as I say, those times when I went up to New Hampshire with the others I didn't attempt to keep up with them. Oh, I could have driven up to the picnic grove where they were all to meet, and sometimes I've done that. But on that particular Saturday, the idea didn't appeal."

His voice lowered, and he confessed, "I have to tell you that Elaine and I had a very bitter quarrel that morning. Not the first one...but one of the worst. I said things to her I've wished a thousand times I could take back. At the memorial service, when you came to Boston, my guilt was so damned heavy. Over the argument...but nothing more."

Kent went on, "As I said, at Salzwald, that Saturday, I stayed behind. I'm sure the other couples didn't think much of my doing that. They've always considered me somewhat antisocial, anyway. I suppose from their viewpoint I am. I don't have very much in common with them.

"They're basically good people, though. Their problem is that except for Clark—who has another problem, and that's the constant need to prove himself—they all have too much money, and it came too easily. I'd say they have very little real purpose or goal orientation in their lives, and that goes even for Harvey. He's damned good at what he does, but I wonder if he ever would have been a lawyer if his father hadn't been right at his shoulder, pushing him into the family firm. I can't say that Harvey's ever struck me as a person who's found fulfillment in his work."

Kent shifted position slightly, then continued, "Anyway, to go back to Salzwald three years ago. That Saturday morning I swam, had lunch, and then I stretched out in a lounge chair in the solarium at The Schloss and read a sci-fi novel and relaxed.

"Later in the afternoon, I got into a cribbage game with one of the other guests. An elderly man from Hartford, whom I'd met there before. I have to admit the time passed a hell of a lot more agreeably than I felt it would have if I'd gone up on the mountain with the others. But then, of course, they came back...."

Kent's face was grim and his eyes were bleak as he said, "It was so terrible, Susan. I will never, ever, forget standing by as they searched for Elaine. The darkness was coming down over the mountains and the weather getting colder, and a wind came out of somewhere that you could feel right through your bones.

"There was so damned little I could do. Normally I don't even think about my knee, I don't have to. But I felt like a helpless cripple as I trailed along after the others. One of the state troopers had driven me over to the lake. Then I lagged behind the search party, knowing there was no way I could be of any help if we had to start up one of the mountain trails.

"But then... they found her. And she was... so broken. There's a sheer drop from the edge of Castle Ledge. Nothing could have stopped her fall. She had gone straight down.

"I looked at her, and for an insane moment I thought I was looking down at you," Kent said. "Her face was unmarred, so she looked younger...and it was five years since I'd seen you. But, God help me, I nearly said, 'Susan.'

"That's when I thought my heart would break."

Chapter Thirteen

Joe didn't agree with Kent about Susan's going to Salzwald.

"I certainly don't *want* you to go," he told her Thursday morning. "But I don't see any other viable alternative."

He added gravely, "I think this is one of the few chances we may have to right a wrong by exposing the person who's been writing those letters. But there's another side to it, too.

"In my opinion, this is also a question of your futures—yours and Kent's. I'm afraid there may always be shadows between the two of you unless you find out who wrote those letters and why."

Susan had to admit that Joe was right. Much earlier that morning, she and Kent had gone a long way toward dispersing those shadows. But that didn't mean that they couldn't drift back again.

In the first daylight hours, Kent had gone up to her studio with her, but he hadn't lingered.

"I have to be at the hospital in a couple of hours," he'd said. "And you need to get some rest before you go to Joe's."

Looking back, it seemed to her that their hours together had been a separate part of life, a segment unto itself. Reality had come just before he kissed her goodbye.

His dark eyes had been intent as he'd said, "More than ever, Susan, I don't want you to go to Salzwald. I just can't let you take the risk. You have no part in this, there's no need for you to be there. I think you'll find that Joe feels the same way that I do."

But Joe hadn't felt that way.

Now Susan said, "Joe . . . Kent is *really* against my going, and I think he'll do anything he can to prevent it. I'm not suggesting that he's about to tie me up and lock me in a closet. But he'll be very angry with both of us unless we give in to him."

"Mmm . . . I admit that doesn't make it easy," Joe admitted. "My younger cousin has always had a stubborn streak a mile long. Though, like most things about him, he usually keeps it well under control." He thought a minute, then decided. "We'll just have to talk to Kent."

"I already went that route, Joe."

Joe grinned. "I'm sure you did, and I can imagine how Kent reacted. He can be hotheaded, as well as stubborn."

"Tell me more," Susan prodded.

"I learned a fair bit about Kent's nature while I was staying at the Davenport house on Louisburg Square when he was about five," Joe confessed. "I gave him a car for his birthday that he was crazy about. It was a remote control toy. I was afraid he might be too young for it, but he wasn't. He ran it all over the place.

"Then, one evening, he did something his father didn't like. Something trivial, I can't even recall what it was. Arthur took the toy car away from him, and Kent raised such hell he was sent to his room without any supper.''

"That was terrible," Susan protested.

"Arthur Davenport was a stern disciplinarian," Joe said. "I've always thought that had Kent's mother lived, Arthur might have been very different. The loss of someone you love can do strange things to a person."

Susan asked softly, "Was she beautiful, Joe?"

"Kent's mother?"

"No."

Joe nodded, knowing exactly who Susan meant.

"Yes," he said softly. "My Megan was lovely. She had coloring very much like yours, except that her eyes were brown. Like topaz."

His mouth twisted in a rueful smile. "I was such a fool," he said. "I let her go because of my stubborn, stupid pride. Then I waited to go after her until it was too late. She was from a strict Catholic family. She entered a cloistered convent. She died there."

Dismayed, Susan said quickly, "Joe, I'm so sorry. I shouldn't have..."

"Yes," Joe said. "You should have, and I'm glad you did. I still have so much about her bottled up inside me, despite all the years that have passed. Susan...nothing should be allowed to stand in the way of love. Going to Salzwald will not be easy for you. But stay with Kent, will you, and see this through? No matter how difficult it may be?"

"Are you saying that Kent has decided to go to Salzwald, Joe?"

"He didn't tell you that?"

Susan frowned. "No, dammit, he didn't tell me."

"When he brought those two letters out the other night, we talked for a long time, Susan," Joe confessed. "The idea of going back up there has always repulsed him, and I'm

sure it still does. It repulses me, too. But we both agreed that
he has to go.

"Don't hold it against him that he didn't tell you, Susan.
I can well understand why. He doesn't want you to go, because he doesn't want to risk having anything happen to
you, and I certainly can't blame him for that. I don't deny
that there's an element of danger involved. I can only say
that the situation could become even more dangerous if you
and Kent *don't* meet the challenge that's so implicit in those
letters.

"I think that would put our anonymous writer over the
edge. And there's no telling what might happen then. I very
much doubt that this person could take that kind of frustration without acting . . . violently."

Joe was determined to get Susan's mind off Salzwald, and
to keep her involved with his grandfather and Claude Monet for as long as possible.

Soon, at his instigation, Susan went up to the attic and
brought down the chest with the letters. And she quickly
became absorbed as Joe read her a letter written to Henry
shortly after Alice, Monet's second wife, died in 1911.

Then, only three years later, Monet lost his eldest son.
That same year—1914—he began a series of giant-sized
water lily paintings. His intention, he wrote Henry, was to
form a continuing frieze that could be observed from every
angle.

"He finished that project," Susan interrupted their
reading to tell Joe. "He specified exactly how the paintings
were to be hung in the Orangerie, in Paris, and they were."

In the early 1920s, Monet's eyesight was failing, and Susan found that so tragic that it was difficult for her to listen
to the letters he'd written Chase about his increasingly poor

vision—or to read aloud the comforting phrases Henry had penned back to him.

By then, Monet wrote Henry that he felt he was fortunate to have his daughter-in-law, Blanche, to care for him.

"Blanche was Alice's daughter," Susan explained to Joe, "so she had a dual relationship with Monet. He was her stepfather as well as her father-in-law. She'd lived in his household since she was a child, and she'd married the son who died."

The last letter of all, it turned out, was from Blanche to Henry. The year was 1926, and she wrote that the great artist had died peacefully, in his eighty-sixth year.

"It was Blanche," Joe reminded Susan, "who gave Henry the letters he'd written Monet when Henry made that final pilgrimage to Giverny as a kind of memorial tribute."

"You can be thankful to her," Susan said.

She stacked the letters back in the small wooden chest, then said sadly, "Joe, we've read all of them."

"So now our work really begins," Joe told her. "How are we going to handle this, Susan?"

"Well," Susan said, "I think that primarily the letters should speak for themselves. They're certainly fascinating enough to hold their own. All we really should do is provide a proper framework for them."

She closed the wooden chest, and set it aside. "I think that you should write a prologue about your grandfather and his amazing friendship with Monet," she said.

Joe's eyes twinkled. "You mean *you* should write it. I've no way with words."

"All right, we'll write it together."

"And I presume you want to use the sketches as illustrations."

Susan's face lit up. "That would be terrific! Imagine—sketches by Monet of some of his most famous works, brought to the public eye for the first time."

Joe found her excitement contagious, as she said, "This is going to be such a first in so many ways. Joe, they'll probably want you on all the talk shows, to say nothing of—"

"Hold it," Joe cautioned. "You're the one who's going public with this, not I. I'll work on the prologue with you, if you think that's the way to go. But the author is going to be Susan Evans. Let's get that straight from the start. This is your book."

Susan shook her head. "Share and share alike," she said sternly. "Or it's no deal."

"You drive a hard bargain, lady. But before you hammer in the last nail, pause a minute, will you, and think about how long I've had those letters up in my attic? Chances are I would never have done anything with them if Kent hadn't put the two of us in touch."

Kent.

Susan couldn't resist looking at her watch. It was late afternoon, and Kent hadn't called.

Joe said quietly, "You know, there's no law against your calling him, Susan."

"I always hate to call him at his office, or at the hospital," she admitted. "I feel like I'm taking him away from some life-death situation."

"If you were, Kent would tell you so. He'd never abandon a patient who needed him . . . much as I'm sure he loves to hear the sound of your voice. Why not put in a call to him, and ask him to come out for supper, as soon as he can break away?" Joe suggested. And added reluctantly, "The three of us need to talk."

* * *

Kent had been preoccupied most of the day by thoughts that had nothing to do with medicine.

Between patients, those thoughts took over—and, he mused wryly, they were a mix of gold and jet.

His love for Susan was like sunlight; but when he thought about Salzwald and the coming weekend he felt a black, starless night close in on him.

The intercom on his desk buzzed, and his secretary said, "Mrs. Evans is on the line, Doctor."

Time stood still as Kent picked up the receiver, and his voice was soft as he said, "Hi."

He was amused because Susan sounded so timid as she asked, "Am I interrupting something?"

"No," he said. "Your timing's perfect. This afternoon's schedule turned out to be relatively light. I may even be able to get out of here pretty soon."

"Joe has invited you to supper."

"And you'll be there?"

"Yes."

"Then how can I stay away? Have you and Joe had a good day?" *If only he could see to it that all her days were good days.*

"We finished reading the Monet letters," Susan told him. "Now Joe and I are arguing about the way we're going to deal with all this marvelous material."

"I refuse to bet on either of you," Kent said. Then added, "Susan?"

"Yes?"

"Did you tell Joe about Beth's invitation?"

"Yes."

"What did he say?"

Susan decided on evasive tactics.

"Let Joe tell you when you get here."

* * *

Joe said, "I know how you feel, Kent. I feel the same way. I want to protect Susan as much as you do. But if anything's to come out of this weekend, you both need to be there."

"The hell we do," Kent snapped.

"I wish that were so," Joe said mildly. He tapped the long white envelope that lay on his lap. "I might be more inclined to agree if it wasn't for this. I think you have to admit that this pretty much settles the matter."

Kent had stopped at his condo before driving out to Newton, and the envelope had been in his mailbox. He had taken it upstairs with him, intending to read it and then stash it away without saying anything about it. But it was so vindictive that he felt he had to let Joe see it.

Joe tapped the envelope again, and said, "This just underscores what I've been thinking. The person who wrote this is dangerously close to the edge. There's no telling at this point what he'll do—whether to himself, someone else, or both—unless he's stopped soon."

Kent asked dryly, "Are you foreseeing a murder-suicide at Salzwald, Joe?"

"That's not very funny, Kent," Joe reproved. "Maybe because it's possible."

Kent's mouth was tight. "And you're suggesting that we let Susan walk right into something like that?"

"Nothing in life is without risk, Kent," Joe said. "Sometimes the risk is worth it."

"Was it worth it for you?" Kent asked bluntly.

Joe winced ever so slightly, but he said, "Yes. Yes, it was. If I hadn't done what I did, a lot of innocent people would have been killed." Joe touched the arms of his wheelchair. "I'd rather be in this contraption than have deaths that shouldn't have happened on my conscience."

"Hell," Kent said contritely. "I'm sorry. You didn't deserve that."

"Be that as it may," Joe said, "perhaps I illustrate my own point. You do what you have to do, Kent, when it's important enough. If nothing comes off this weekend, neither Susan nor you will be safe anywhere. The anger this person feels has to be expiated somehow. Stop and think about that."

"I've already thought about it."

"Yes," Susan put in. "And that's why *you* decided to go to Salzwald yourself, isn't it? You might have told me, Kent. I really resent the fact that you didn't."

To her surprise, she heard Joe chuckle.

"Don't blame the man too much, Susan," Joe advised her. "I would say he's in love, and being in love can have a strange effect on a person's thinking." Joe was silent for a moment, and then he added, "I've always believed in that old saw about three being a crowd. But that's not going to stop me this time."

Kent frowned. "Exactly what are you talking about, Joe?"

"Why," Joe announced blandly, "I'm going to Salzwald with you."

They argued until midnight, and then finally Kent gave up.

"I know you too well," he told his cousin. "If I don't agree that we go as a trio, you and Susan will probably trek up there on your own."

"That's quite likely," Joe agreed. "It's been a while since I've tested my driving skills on a long trip."

Kent groaned. "And you're still capable of getting yourself in a hell of a lot of trouble," he warned. He turned to Susan and explained. "I found out *that* about him years ago, one time when he was visiting us. He snitched my father's Mercedes and drove all the way to Cape Cod in it, with another guy and a couple of girls."

Joe smiled reminiscently. "That was quite a weekend."

"My father really appreciated the ding you put in his fender."

"Your father tended to take a narrow view of a lot of things."

"Didn't he, though? I also remember that I wanted to go along, and you locked me in my room. I had to use considerable ingenuity to get out."

"Which was good for you," Joe approved. "Also, you were all of twelve years old, as I recall, and I was thirty-two. My friends and I would not have been suitable companions for you."

"Look at him," Kent complained to Susan. "He has an explanation for everything, and he usually gets his own way."

"That runs in the family," Joe said smugly. "Except that the older members do have an edge."

Kent laughed, and Susan laughed with him. And, looking at the two of them, Joe's heart ached a little. But his joy in having Kent respond as he was responding lately transcended the pain of an old and precious memory.

Kent was a combination son and brother to him. They were very much attuned, and so he'd recognized small changes that he'd been afraid would never come to pass. Kent was showing his feelings for Susan more and more, and Kent had never been one to reveal his emotions.

Also, tonight another milestone had been reached. Kent had spoken easily and naturally about his father. And since that terrible day when Kent had walked into the Louisburg Square house to find Arthur Davenport dead of a self-inflicted wound, the subject of his father, or anything connected with him, had been forbidden territory, even to Joe.

When the right moment came, Joe decided, he would tell Susan that. He wanted her to know the kind of miracle she'd already wrought in Kent's life. And the two of them had so much ahead of them . . . if they could just get through this weekend.

They were to leave from Joe's house on Friday afternoon, as soon as Kent could break away from his office.

Meantime, Susan packed a suitcase Friday morning, and drove to Newton with it. Then she tried to settle down with Joe on the sun porch and concentrate on their project. But today neither of their minds was on Monet.

They finally gave up by mutual consent. But as Susan was about to pick up the little wooden chest and take it back to the attic, Joe stopped her.

"I'm not suggesting we take any of the letters or sketches to Salzwald with us. It stands to reason that we shouldn't take anything irreplaceable," he said. "But I was thinking it might be a good idea if you run off a few duplicates on the copy machine. Put together a supply of notepads, pencils, and so on, too."

Susan sat down again and asked, "Why?"

"We need a decoy," Joe said. "If we have some working material on hand, it'll give more validity to my presence. Otherwise, why would you and Kent take a wheelchair-bound individual like me up to the mountains with you?"

"I wish you wouldn't talk about yourself that way, Joe. I very seldom think of you as being handicapped, and I mean that."

"Thanks, my dear," Joe said. "I think if I were twenty years younger—and didn't have Kent as competition—I'd court you myself, wheelchair or no wheelchair."

Joe grinned, and Susan had to smile. Joe's zest for life had triumphed over two personal tragedies, either of which could have been devastating, and she admired him tremendously.

Now she teased, "You're too sharp, Joe. But I already knew you'd figured out how I feel about Kent. I've seen you watching us."

Joe grumbled, "I must be getting obvious in my old age."

"Your old age isn't all that old. Think of all the famous men who are marrying much younger women these days. If it weren't for Kent, you might have *me* courting *you.*"

Joe laughed. "That's the best compliment I've had in many a day. If you ever fall out of love with Kent, let me know."

Suddenly he grew serious, his blue eyes steady on Susan's face as he asked, "You won't ever fall out of love with him, will you?"

"No."

"Good." Joe nodded, satisfied, and returned to more practical matters.

"Once you've copied some of the letters and whatever else you think might make a satisfactory bundle, come back down. I want to go over some things with you," he told Susan.

Susan went upstairs, and spent the next half hour copying some of both Monet's and Henry's letters, as well as a few other papers.

When she finally decided that she had enough material to put together a convincing bogus package, she carried the chest back to the attic.

She lingered in the attic for just a little while. This was such a special place, full of so many treasures. She loved it up here. And soon, maybe, she'd have the chance to explore more than she had. Joe had said that there were me-

mentos of Henry's friendship with Monet in some of the trunks, and they might want to include photographs of them in the book.

Once this weekend was over...

If only this weekend *were* over.

Susan locked the attic door, turned on the security system and went back downstairs.

Joe was on the telephone, and Susan heard him say, "Great. I'll be in touch."

He set the cordless phone back in its cradle, and turned to report, "That was a friend of mine who happens to be senior vice president of a major publishing firm."

"He called you?"

"No. I called him. I told him that I'm involved in a project with a very erudite young lady, and I think what we have in mind might interest him."

"And why did you do that?"

"I wanted him to give me a deadline for getting a proposal to him about a possible book."

Susan perched on the edge of a nearby chair, and complained, "I think you like to mystify me. Why do you want a deadline, Joe?"

"To lend credence to my going to Salzwald," Joe said. "I like to cover all bases when I'm on an assignment, Susan. And I feel this *is* an assignment. That's why I want to establish the fiction that you and I both need to spend most of our time working. That will be a lot more credible if we can honestly say that we have a deadline to meet. And," he added, "Howard Chisholm says that November 15 is fine with him."

"Wait a minute, Joe," Susan protested. "Is all of this with your friend Howard imaginary, too? Or...?"

There was a wicked spark in Joe's eyes. "Not at all," he assured Susan. "I didn't get into specifics about our book, but I did tell Howard enough to whet his appetite. He'd like to see a fairly detailed outline."

For a moment, Susan actually forgot about Salzwald.

"You agreed to a *November 15 deadline?* My God, Joe, that's not much more than a month from now," she moaned.

"I know," Joe said blithely, and let Susan mutter.

But he wasn't nearly as casual as he appeared to be. He hadn't slept well last night. And, he'd been on edge all day, though he was very good at camouflaging his feelings when he wanted to.

Actually, he was much more worried about this trek to the White Mountains than he wanted either Susan or Kent to know.

He hoped, he prayed, that he could be ready enough and act fast enough—if and when the time came—to prevent a tragedy.

It didn't help being chained to a wheelchair. Nevertheless, he still trusted his judgment and most of his reflexes better than he did those of a lot of other people.

Experience had its pluses. And, God knows, he had a hell of a lot of experience under his belt. Despite the terrible personal consequences of his last big case, he knew, without conceit, that he had a decided edge on nonprofessionals.

He would get Susan and Kent through the weekend at Salzwald . . . Joe tried to tell himself. Hell, they *had* to get through the weekend at Salzwald.

If Megan were around, Joe thought, he'd get on his knees and beg her to say a couple of prayers.

Was Megan around? Sometimes he had the strange feeling that now and then she watched over him.

Joe brushed by that, and concentrated on something else.

Whatever happened at Salzwald was bound to be traumatic, and that, too, worried him. With the circumstances of Elaine's death reenacted so devastatingly, Kent was certain to be put through a private hell.

Joe knew that for a long time before her death, Elaine and Kent had been married in name only. Nevertheless, she had been part of Kent's life for five years, and her death had been horrible.

And Susan—Elaine had been Susan's sister, after all. Though it was clear to him that they had not been close, they had been identical twins. This weekend, Joe suspected, Susan would go through private hell, as well.

There was no telling what might happen when two people in love were put under that kind of emotional stress. No telling what one or both might do.

Thinking about that, Joe had called his editor friend and snagged a deadline date with one definite purpose in mind.

He wanted to make sure that, after Salzwald, Susan didn't run away.

He wanted to guarantee that she would come back to Boston, both to him and to Kent.

Chapter Fourteen

Salzwald—5 Miles.

Susan saw the road sign at the edge of the highway and tensed.

The northern New Hampshire countryside was spectacular. The huge harvest moon brightened the sky so that the mountains were like black surrealistic silhouettes cut against a dark cobalt background.

One of those peaks she was seeing was Mount Schloss. And high on the side of Mount Schloss was Castle Ledge....

Susan shuddered.

Kent, who was driving Joe's van, saw her involuntary movement, sensed exactly what was causing it, and swore silently.

Even now, when they were almost there, his temptation to turn back was strong.

He didn't want Susan to be any part of this, no matter what Joe said. Joe's arguments were very convincing, but if

Kent thought he could take Susan back to Boston and somehow convince her to stay there, he knew he'd reverse directions, regardless. He and Joe could drive back up here in the early morning hours tomorrow, and be on the scene in plenty of time . . . for whatever was going to happen.

Kent also knew he didn't have a prayer of doing that. Susan had committed herself, and she had a strong will. He admired that. And in this case, he also deplored it.

They'd had a later start out of Boston than they'd planned. He'd had to stop by the hospital to go over some details about the patients he was leaving with the colleague who was going to fill in for him this weekend.

Even Joe had been on edge by the time he got to Newton, and Susan—though she'd put up a brave front—had been a bundle of nerves.

Joe had elected to stay in his wheelchair during the trip, saying, "It'll make logistics easier when we get there."

Kent had been relieved when Joe didn't insist on taking the wheel. He'd preferred to drive, not because he worried about Joe's driving but because he needed action of almost any kind right then. So Susan was in the front seat next to him, and Joe and his wheelchair were locked into place behind them.

They'd barely gone beyond the outskirts of the city when he and Susan had come close to an argument, and Joe had immediately been called upon to play peacemaker.

It had been his fault, Kent admitted. His fuse was short right now.

They'd agreed, yesterday, that he should be the one to call Beth and tell her that Joe, as well as he and Susan, would be coming to Salzwald. But he hadn't done it.

So, when Susan had said, "I take it Beth was able to make arrangements for us," he'd automatically gone on the defensive.

"I didn't call her," he said.

"But you promised you'd take care of that," Susan remonstrated. "Kent, without any reservations we may not be able to find a place where we can stay. Beth warned me that this is one of the most popular weekends of the year."

"We have reservations, Susan," Kent informed her. "For better or worse, I'm pretty well-known at The Schloss. The manager will see to it that Joe has a ground-floor room in the lodge, and you and I will have separate rooms on the second floor."

"Far apart, I take it?"

It wasn't like Susan to be snide, but that's the way she sounded, and Kent slanted a curious glance at her.

"Why the sarcasm?" he demanded. "I was thinking of you."

"Of me? Oh, you're telling me you were thinking of my reputation, is that it?"

It wasn't like Susan to be cynical, either, and he didn't need this from her right now. Irritated, Kent retorted, "Is there anything so wrong about my considering your reputation?"

"I'd say it's late in the day."

"Exactly what do you mean by that?"

"I think we can both take it for granted that your friends have already connected us, Kent, and there's not much we can do now to negate that."

"Kids," Joe urged, "we need to keep peace in this inner circle."

Kent smiled slightly. "So we'll stop bickering, cousin, okay?"

After that, Kent decided that in the interest of the peace Joe was talking about, he'd better shut up. He'd spoken only when Joe made an occasional comment. And now, when he observed Susan's shudder, he decided he'd still better keep quiet.

Susan had been monosyllabic throughout much of the trip, too. Now she had to admit that Joe was the only one of the three of them who seemed to be taking this safari in stride.

Maybe Joe's easy confidence was a front. If so, she had to hand it to him. No one would have suspected that he was doing any more than going to the mountains with the thought of enjoying some autumn foliage, and doing some work with her at the same time.

Kent turned off the highway, and Susan's pulse thudded.

He turned again, onto a road that seemed to be heading straight into the mountains. Then he said, "Up there, ahead," and Susan saw the black bulk of a mountain, and the brightly lighted resort complex that nestled at the foot of it.

As they neared the complex, she felt as if she'd suddenly been transported to Switzerland. Alpine chalets dotted the grounds around The Schloss, and the long, two-story lodge that centered it was a larger variation on the same theme. Carefully positioned lights illuminated the whitewashed exterior, the stained crossboards and roof overhang, and the window boxes were filled with red geraniums that still bloomed in profusion.

Susan asked Kent, "When is someone going to start yodeling?" and she was rewarded by his chuckle.

"Don't be too surprised," he told her. "The help does wear either lederhosen or dirndls. Depending, of course..."

The attendants who came to assist with their baggage wore lederhosen and rimmed hats with feathers in the bands, and Susan nearly giggled.

Kent came around to help her out of the van, and he held her hand as he said, "Before we go in, sniff."

"What?"

"Just sniff."

Susan drew in a deep breath, and felt as if she'd become part of a fragrant pine forest. She closed her eyes for a minute, savoring the scent. "Wonderful," she said.

"And so are you." Kent's voice was soft, his words meant for her alone. "Sweetheart, I'm sorry I was so edgy earlier."

Susan smiled up at him. "That makes two of us."

"Susan, don't look at me like that. There's a limit. I won't be responsible—"

Joe cut in. "Ready, children?"

"As ready as we'll ever be," Kent said soberly, his mood of the moment before broken.

He and Susan followed Joe up the ramp that accommodated Joe's wheelchair. Inside the lodge, giant logs blazed in a huge stone fireplace. Evidently someone had alerted the manager about Kent's arrival, because he immediately appeared from an inner office, and practically ran to greet Kent.

The manager was a big, ruddy-faced man, who spoke heavily accented English. His welcome to Kent was hearty and effusive. But when Kent turned to include her in the greeting, Susan saw that familiar flash of recognition on the man's face, and knew she'd jolted him.

The lodge manager, of course, had known Elaine. And there was no doubt that she reminded him of Elaine. But he was very smooth. He covered his shock quickly, and he was smiling again when Kent introduced them.

Kent said, "Klaus, this is my sister-in-law, Mrs. Evans. Susan, Klaus Bergstrom, who keeps this place functioning."

Bergstrom bent over her hand, touched it to his lips in a gesture that was charming and very European, and said, "I am delighted to see you here, *madame.*"

Susan mumbled that she was very happy to be there. But she was afraid that her attempt at a smile was pretty sorry.

She felt so strange.

My sister-in-law.

She *was* Kent's sister-in-law, Susan reminded herself. But she'd never wanted to be, and that held true now more than ever.

Suddenly Susan felt as if Elaine were standing in the shadows watching, her lips curved in a mocking smile.

She'd never believed in ghosts. She still didn't, she insisted to herself. Nevertheless, just then she felt as if she were being haunted.

Joe, helped by a lederhosen-clad attendant, disappeared in one direction.

Susan and Kent were ushered to their second-floor rooms, which, while not at opposite ends of the building, were well separated.

Susan unpacked, showered and slipped on comfortable slacks and a sweater. The dress code at The Schloss was casual, Kent had told her, except for Sunday nights when the women, anyway, tended to get a little fancier.

She had just put on her shoes when someone knocked on the door.

She froze, and her pulse began to thump faster. Annoyed at herself—she'd be in big trouble if she panicked as easily as this—she was frowning as she flung the door open. In the brief interim, she drew herself up defiantly, as if determined to be in readiness for whatever might confront her.

Kent, standing on the threshold, gauged her expression, gauged her position, and wished more than ever that he'd followed his instinct and driven Susan back to Boston.

"Well," he asked gently, "are you going to let me in?"

"Of course," she said stiffly, making way for Kent, then closing the door behind him.

She had a corner room, with windows on two sides. Kent looked around, and commented, "Nice. When you wake up tomorrow morning, you'll find that you have a spectacular view."

He reached in his pocket, brought out a tiny package and handed it to her.

"A small reminder of a wonderful time," he said.

Susan glanced up at him first, and melted when she saw the tenderness with which he was looking at her. Then she unwrapped the little package, and her eyes misted. The silver filigreed earrings she'd admired so much last Sunday, when she and Kent were strolling through Boston's North End, nestled on a soft cotton bed.

"You went back and got them!" she exclaimed.

"Yes."

"When did you ever find the time?"

"I snatched the time."

"Oh, Kent, they're so pretty. I want to put them on right away."

"All right. But there's something else, first..."

Kent drew Susan into his arms, and teased, "Don't you know that there's a special way to say thank you, when you get a gift?"

"Teach me," she urged.

"Like this." He brushed her lips with his.

She asked, "That's all you have to do?"

"Well," Kent said, "it depends how thankful you are."

"Then..."

Susan drew his head toward her, and kissed him. Then she nuzzled her lips against his and kissed him again, and again. She could feel her pulse thudding, but this time it wasn't from fear. A wave of sweet heat began to chase away everything else, and she moved closer to Kent, her body seeking and finding the core of his desire.

Kent, breathing hard, grasped her and moved her away a little. "God, sweetheart," he moaned between breaths, "I didn't know you could be such a witch. Have pity, will you? I told Joe we'd be down in just a few minutes. . . ."

Susan stood back, slowly, slowly, simmering down herself.

As she fastened the earrings Kent had given her, she marveled at what this man did to her. She couldn't believe the kind of initiative she'd just taken.

Kent watched her secure the second earring, and said, "They're very becoming. Susan . . ."

His tone alerted her, and she swung around.

He admitted, "I saw the expression on your face when I introduced you to Klaus Bergstrom as my sister-in-law. I . . ."

"Hush," Susan said. "You don't have to explain."

"Perhaps not. But I want to explain. I introduced you that way because I thought it would be best for *you*. Just as I thought that booking separate rooms was the right way to go. I felt I should be discreet, for your sake."

Kent smiled, an endearingly lopsided smile. "Blame it on my stilted upbringing," he said. "But not on much else. I love you, Susan. I love *you*. Do you know what I'm saying?"

She nodded.

"I want you to fix that in your mind, no matter what," Kent told her. "Sweetheart, never have any doubts about my love for you. No matter what anyone tries to throw up to you this weekend, please don't let them get under your skin. Believe in me, will you?"

"I do believe in you."

"Oh, God, I wish we could shut out the world and go to bed with each other right now," Kent groaned. "I think then I could make you a believer, even if you aren't already."

"But I am," Susan protested.

"I know, I know. But I want you so damned much." There was a ragged edge to Kent's laugh. "I'd call Joe and tell him we'd meet him for a late dinner a couple of hours from now, but unfortunately it isn't that simple. Before I came to your room, I went back downstairs to check on Joe, and I ran into Harvey Farragut in the lobby."

Some of the lightness went out of Susan's heart.

"Harvey said the Benedicts haven't arrived yet, but they're due any time. He told me everyone is meeting in the lounge for drinks, and he hoped we'd join them. They've scheduled a late dinner, and he asked us to team up with them, too. I felt I had to accept for you and Joe, as well as myself."

Kent added, "Incidentally, the Farraguts and the Benedicts are in one of the chalets. The Donavans and the Whitfields are sharing quarters in another. Harvey seemed a bit aggrieved because I'd made arrangements on my own. He said Beth had planned for both of us to stay in their chalet, which is one of the larger ones, and there'd be room for Joe, too. I explained to him that I'd had to wait till the last minute to make a decision, because I wasn't sure I could get anyone to cover for me at the hospital."

He finished reluctantly, "I suppose we'd better go along, get Joe and catch up with the others."

Kent and Susan discovered that Joe had gone ahead on his own, and left a note on his door telling them to join him in the lounge.

He, the Farraguts, the Donavans, and the Whitfields, had commandeered a corner of the lounge, and evidently Joe had been regaling the others with a story.

As Kent and Susan approached, Lilian Whitfield said, "Joe, you're outrageous. But that was very funny."

Beth made room for Susan next to her, and when a chance presented itself, she murmured, "Why didn't you tell me you were coming, after all? When I didn't hear from you, I assumed you'd decided not to."

Susan copied what Kent had told Harvey. "It had to be a last-minute decision, Beth."

"Well, I think it's a shame that you and Joe intend to work while you're here."

"Only part of the time," Susan assured Beth, and hoped that was the right thing to say. She ventured, "I suppose Joe told you about our deadline."

"Yes," Beth said. "And I think it's absolutely fantastic that the two of you have a nibble for your book before you've even written it. That was really quick work."

"Joe's doing," Susan said. "He's the one with the connections."

"Well, don't let him also become a slave driver," Beth cautioned. "See to it that you save some time this weekend for fun."

How could Beth imagine that anyone in their group could possibly have any fun this weekend? Susan wondered.

The Benedicts arrived, and when they put in their drink orders, most of the others opted for seconds. Susan was surprised when Harvey Farragut didn't. Was Harvey actually trying to stay sober this evening?

Finally, the headwaiter—who also wore lederhosen—came to tell them that their table was ready.

The dining room was beautiful, a semicircle framed by windows. There were snowy-white tablecloths, flickering candles, and a nosegay corsage at each woman's place.

Before any seating arrangements could be decided upon, Mandy Benedict said, "Let's not sit next to our spouses. Either two men or two women are going to have to sit next to each other as it is."

"Quick on the logistics, isn't she?" Kent whispered in Susan's ears.

Mandy was directing things. "Let's put you at the head of the table, Joe," she decided.

"Does that mean I'm a fatherly figure?" Joe quipped.

"No," Mandy said. "It means I want to be sure to sit next to you."

Mandy promptly chose the place to Joe's right, and Beth preempted the chair to his left.

Susan wished she could sit next to Kent who, after all, wasn't a spouse. But she found herself wedged between Phil Donavan and Bert Whitfield, and she saw that Kent was between Beth and Lilian.

Phil, she discovered, was on his best behavior tonight. He was polite, quiet, made no passes, either verbal or physical.

Bert, too, was quiet. In fact, as the excellent dinner progressed, it began to seem as if a pall had been thrown over the group. There was none of the boisterous camaraderie they'd shared in the lounge a little earlier.

The mood change was disturbing. Susan felt as if all of these people had suddenly become immersed in their own deep, dark thoughts.

They were almost finished with the meal before anyone said anything specific. Then Heddy Donavan suddenly blurted out, "This is the same table we sat at last time."

Phil Donavan reacted quickly, and savagely. He turned on Heddy and snarled, "What the hell prompted you to bring that up?"

"I remembered, that's all," Heddy retorted defensively. "*She* was sitting where Susan is sitting, and you were next to her."

"Christ," Phil grated. "You've just never learned to shut up, have you?"

Bert Whitfield said sedately, "That kind of talk isn't necessary, Phil."

Before Phil could retort, Mandy Benedict said, "You're absolutely right, Bert. Phil, just because you can't bear to talk about Elaine doesn't mean the rest of us can't. That's why we're here, after all. To remember her."

"Mandy's right," Clark Benedict said, and no one looked more surprised than his wife. "We came here to honor Elaine."

Harvey Farragut got to his feet. He kept his voice low so that other late diners wouldn't hear, as he said, "This is disgusting. I, for one, can't stomach any more of it. Couldn't the whole bunch of you at least have waited until tomorrow?"

Kent stood, too. He said, "If you'll excuse us, I think Susan and I will call it quits. We've both had a long day."

There was a sudden hush, broken by Lilian Whitfield.

Lilian said softly, "Susan, please excuse *us*. I think we all became a little bit unnerved when we realized this *is* the same table we sat at the last time we were here. I guess that brings back more memories than some of us seem to be able to handle. But we all owe you an apology."

Heddy, on the verge of tears, said, "I'm sorry, Susan. It just hit me all of a sudden."

"All right," Mandy conceded. "I was out of line, too, and I apologize, Susan."

"Please," Susan said, feeling as if she were about to suffocate from all of this. "I can understand how you all must feel. There's no need for apologies."

Joe put in mildly, "Susan's right. What we need to do is to go forward instead of backward at this point in time, people, and I have a suggestion. Why don't we finish up here, then move back to the lounge? Klaus Bergstrom told me earlier that they'd scheduled some great late entertainment. Why not ask him to serve our desserts in there, and take advantage of it?"

As they left the dining room, Susan managed to slip behind Joe's chair, and under the pretense of pushing it murmured, "You missed your calling. You should have been in the diplomatic corps."

"In a way," Joe murmured back, "I *was* in the diplomatic corps. Susan, thank you for not taking off as soon as Kent suggested it."

Susan admitted, "I wish we were back on your sun porch, making plans for the book."

"We will be, my dear."

Kent came up alongside them. "Susan," he said, "there's no need for you to sit in on this entertainment."

Joe muttered in a low voice that didn't carry, "I'd like her to be there, Kent."

"Damn it, Joe." Kent, too, kept his voice low. "I think she's had enough."

"What happens tonight will be of great help to me tomorrow," Joe said. "I need to listen to people. I need to watch them."

"Are you saying you need to watch them watch Susan?"

"In part, yes," Joe admitted.

Kent snapped, "I didn't bargain for this."

Kent saw Mandy Benedict approaching them, and he muttered one short expletive that startled Susan.

What had happened to Kent's former cool reserve?

As soon as Mandy was within earshot, Joe said to Susan, "So, it seems to me that we might enjoy this weekend more if we work tomorrow, and then take Sunday off. What do you say? We don't have to leave for Boston till after lunch on Monday."

Susan decided she was becoming better at game playing. "Fine with me," she told Joe.

Mandy Benedict hurried up to them. "Did I hear you just say that you and Susan plan to work *tomorrow?*" she asked Joe.

Joe nodded. "As I pointed out to Susan, if we spend tomorrow doing what we need to do, we may have some playtime the rest of the weekend."

"But you can't do that," Mandy protested. "The picnic is tomorrow."

"The lunch you take up on Mount Schloss?"

"Yes."

Joe touched the sides of his wheelchair, and said, "I doubt that would be an excursion for me, Mandy."

"But it would be, Joe," Mandy insisted. "You can drive right to the grove.

"We always meet there on the Saturday after we get here," Mandy added, eyeing Joe anxiously as if she was afraid he might be the instrument of destroying everyone's plans. "We elect someone in the group to drive up with a lunch prepared by the staff here. It . . . it's a ritual."

"A very important one, evidently."

"Yes, but not just to me," Mandy said quickly. "It's important to all of us. Especially this time. That's why we came. . . ."

"I wondered about that," Joe admitted. "Mandy, just why did all of you come up here this year?"

"To remember Elaine," Mandy said. "But, believe me, it wasn't my idea."

"Whose idea was it?"

"You might ask Heddy Donavan."

With that, Mandy flounced off.

Joe said softly, "Spot Heddy, Susan, then push my chair as close as possible to where she's sitting. I think I'm about to make a nuisance of myself."

Heddy Donavan was glad to make room for Joe. But she didn't seem very happy about including Susan.

The message was clear to Susan: *I am not her favorite person. If I hadn't already gotten a clue to that at the Whitfields' the other day, I surely would now.*

She decided to let Joe deal with Heddy by himself, and moved toward the back of the lounge.

A platform had been set up near the bar, and a comedian was regaling his audience with jokes that must be funny, Susan thought, because most of the audience seemed to be in stitches.

Kent loomed up at Susan's side, and said, "Let's cut out for a few minutes."

"Suppose someone notices?"

"Right now, I couldn't care less."

"Well," Susan suggested, "suppose you let me go first, and you follow in a few minutes. We can meet in that corridor that leads to the rest rooms."

Kent chuckled. "I think Joe has been giving you lessons."

"I could use a few more," Susan told him. Which was only too true.

She paid a visit to the rest room, and by the time she went back into the corridor, Kent was sauntering toward her. They went out a side door, then Kent led Susan to the far end of the wide porch that bordered three sides of The Schloss.

He guided her down a short flight of steps and along a path that led toward the woods. And, once they were in the shadow of the pines, Kent drew Susan toward him and his kiss was slow and deep, both giving and demanding. Then he nuzzled her hair and admitted, "I don't think I could have made it through the night without that. I may not be able to make it through this damned night without coming to you."

Susan let her heart speak. "I hope not," she told him. Then she smiled faintly and said, "If you're still so worried about my reputation, why would anyone have to know? If you wait for a while, the others will all be in their chalets, except Joe."

"I'm not worried about Joe, sweetheart. He's on our side."

"Then just be sure the others really have left . . ."

Kent drew Susan toward him. "Joe really *has* been giving you lessons, hasn't he?" he quipped. But his voice was husky, and held such a promise of passion that Susan's sensual response was sharp and swift.

She whispered, "Regardless of the others, don't wait too long. All right?"

Kent's laugh was low, and very, very seductive. "Have no fear," he promised.

Susan went back to the lounge first. She tried to do a head count, tried to see if all the members of the group were present. But now there was a blues singer on the platform, and the lights had been turned so low she couldn't be sure.

She wanted to be near Joe, and as she approached his wheelchair, she saw that Heddy Donavan was no longer sitting next to him, but Lilian Whitfield was.

Lilian made room, and Joe looked up with a welcoming smile.

The blues singer had a terrific voice. Susan let herself flow with the music, and then wanted Kent so much, she was astonished at herself. It took all her willpower not to turn around and search through the dimness to try to see if he'd come back.

A magician followed the blues singer, and then a guitarist. It got later and later, but no one seemed inclined to leave. Then finally the house lights came up, and Susan looked around.

People were drifting back into the lobby, and she was sure Kent wasn't in the room.

She said good-night to the Farraguts and the Whitfields, and watched them head out the front door toward their respective chalets. Joe came along, and as she was about to say good-night to him, he told her quietly that he'd persuaded Kent to share a nightcap in his room, and wished she'd join them.

Susan had been getting wearier and wearier, and now she was so tired she didn't see how she could possibly hold her head up long enough to assimilate anything Joe might say.

Joe, she saw, was taking a long, hard look at her, and evidently he made a decision. He said, "I'll see you in the morning, Susan. Get some rest."

Susan was confused. Was Joe excusing her from the session with Kent and himself, or was his saying that merely a ploy in case some of the others were within earshot?

He repeated, again keeping his voice low, "Definitely the morning. You're done in. Get some sleep."

He meant it, Susan decided, and she bent and kissed him on the cheek before she said good-night.

As she went up the stairs to her room, she wondered where the Benedicts and the Donavans were. She was sure they hadn't left, so probably they were having a last drink at the bar, which must be staying open a while longer.

Susan undressed, put on a robe and tried to fight an overwhelming drowsiness as she waited for Kent.

While the others were listening to the blues singer, Kent had managed to procure a key to Susan's room simply by going up to the desk and asking for it.

The night clerk couldn't have been much out of his teens, Kent thought, and he spoke very little English. Kent summoned up some of his scanty German, and told him the number of Susan's room. The clerk responded by giving him a key, and a deep bow along with it.

That didn't say too much for the security at The Schloss, in Kent's opinion, and that worried him.

Now, as he turned the key in the lock, he wondered if Susan had put on the door chain for safety, but she hadn't. That worried him, too.

It was very late. He and Joe had talked for quite a while as they sipped some excellent Irish whiskey Joe had brought along. They'd still not been in complete agreement about the scenario for tomorrow when they finally decided to call it a night.

Kent had hoped that he'd find Susan in bed, and his heart turned over when he saw her sitting up in the armchair, fast asleep.

He didn't want to frighten her. He made as little noise as possible as he went over to her bed and turned back the covers. Then he lifted her tenderly, carried her to the bed and gently laid her on the smooth, crisp sheets.

He carefully pulled the covers up around Susan, his heart overflowing with love for her. Then he switched off the bedside lamp, kicked off his shoes and stretched out alongside her.

She turned toward him as his arm encircled her, and pillowed her head against his shoulder. He smelled so wonderful, she thought drowsily. He felt so wonderful. He was warm and strong and everything a woman could ever want in a man.

More than everything.

Susan thought she must be dreaming, yet she knew that Kent was with her, and she wanted to make love to him. But she couldn't separate herself from sleep.

They'd make love in her dreams, she decided. She and Kent would make love forever and ever and ever.

She loved him so much.

So much. So much . . .

Chapter Fifteen

The sunlight that splashed into the room seemed to be mixed with gorgeous tones of red and orange. Susan got out of bed and padded to the window. A giant maple stood in a clearing between her side of the lodge and the pine forest that swept up Mount Schloss. Its leaves were a blend of the most glorious autumn colors she had ever seen.

She went back to the bed, and gazed down at the pillow next to the one she'd been using. Yes, she could still see the impression made by Kent's head.

She hadn't been dreaming. He'd really been here.

She had awakened early. He'd already been gone.

Saving her reputation again, she thought with a wry smile.

The room phone jangled, and it was Joe.

"I didn't wake you, did I?" he asked.

"No."

"Susan, have you had breakfast?"

"No." She admitted, "I haven't been up *that* long."

"How about having breakfast with me? I'll order from room service for both of us."

"That sounds great." Susan hesitated, then said, "Joe, about last night. I feel I should have gone back with you and Kent...."

"Quite all right," Joe said, and to Susan he sounded cautious.

Was it possible that even the in-house phone system in The Schloss could be made to sprout ears...?

God, how she hated this.

She couldn't resist asking, "Have you talked to Kent this morning?"

"He stopped by a while ago. They have a heated pool here, and he was going for a swim. He'll join us a little later. Meantime...shall I go ahead and order breakfast? They're so busy here it may take some time to get it."

"That would be fine," Susan said, and didn't have the heart to tell Joe that never in her life had she felt less like eating.

As she crossed the lobby a little while later on her way to the wing where Joe had been given a small suite, Susan saw Clark Benedict turning away from the newsstand, a copy of the *Boston Globe* tucked under his arm.

"Well, hi there," Clark greeted her. "Up early, aren't you?"

"Not as early as I should have been. This is a working day for me," Susan told him.

Clark grimaced. "Are you saying that Joe Chase is really going to make you work today?"

"This morning, anyway. But it's a mutual decision, Clark."

"You must be dedicated. Could I tempt you to join me for breakfast first, Susan?"

"Thanks," Susan said, "but Joe's expecting me." Then she looked around, and asked, "Where are the others?"

"When I left our chalet a little while ago, Mandy and Beth were just waking up," Clark said. "Harvey was watching the news on TV.

"I haven't seen either the Whitfields or the Donavans, but Phil is probably already running up and down the mountain. He seems to have a perpetual need to work off some of his surplus energy. I've told him he should bottle it, and peddle it to the rest of us."

"I didn't realize he was such an athletic type," Susan said.

"I wouldn't call him athletic. He's just possessed of a hell of a lot more drive then most people have, and his problem is that he doesn't know what to do with it," Clark diagnosed. "Sure I can't interest you in even a cup of coffee?"

Susan was tempted to accept his invitation. Maybe, over coffee, she could draw out further information about some of the others. Clark wasn't exactly garrulous, but neither was he closemouthed.

But Joe was waiting for her, so she went along to his suite.

Breakfast arrived a few minutes after she did. Under Joe's watchful eye, Susan munched a croissant, nibbled at scrambled eggs and bacon, and drank a glassful of orange juice.

Kent arrived just in time to finish off the remaining croissant, and the rest of the coffee. His hair was still damp from the swim he'd taken, and there was an enticing wave to it that he subdued when it was dry. Susan yearned to twist the moist tendrils around her fingers.

"I just ran into Phil Donavan," Kent reported. "He's already been out jogging. He said he and the Whitfields plan to climb to the top of Mount Schloss the hard way—that's via a steep trail on the far side of the mountain. They'll be starting out shortly.

"Clark and Mandy and Harvey are going to take off later this morning, and follow some of the easier trails," Kent continued. "Beth and Heddy will be driving the food and drink up to the grove in one of The Schloss's vans. Everyone's to meet at the grove as close to one o'clock as possible."

Kent scowled. "Joe, I like this less and less. Ever since I got here, I've been waiting for someone to make a move, or at least some kind of slip. But no one has."

Joe nodded. "I know. Frankly, I'm as frustrated as you are. Last night, I managed to get most of these people alone at one time or another, long enough to try to find out who originated the idea of their coming up here this weekend.

"I know where the plan was hatched. At the party the Farraguts gave for you, Susan. But I think by the time it was brought up, most of the people must have had enough to drink so that their recollection is very fuzzy.

"Almost every one of them identifies a different person as the originator. The same name comes up only twice. It would seem that for once, the Donavans are in accord about something. They both think that it was Bert Whitfield who came up with the idea."

"I can't see this coming from Bert," Kent said.

"No? He had a hard time realizing that Susan wasn't Elaine the other day, didn't he?" Joe pointed out. "And he said some rather odd things about Elaine to Susan later."

"Even so," Kent said, "regardless of whatever Elaine may have meant to Bert—or he to Elaine—I can't think he'd go for something as bizarre as drinking champagne toasts and throwing bottles off Castle Ledge."

"They still plan to do that?" Susan asked.

"According to Phil, yes. And I have to say that *he* didn't seem at all keen about the idea," Kent replied, as he tried to coax a little bit more coffee out of the pot, and failed.

Joe said, "There's one of those do-it-yourself coffee machines in the bathroom, if you're interested. Or I can phone room service."

"Later, maybe," Kent said. "First . . . well, I think you know there's something we have to settle, Joe."

"Yes," Joe said with a weariness that was unlike him. "I know."

Susan looked from one to the other of them—and was sure something had brewed between the two of them during their talk last night.

She didn't mince words. "You're holding out," she accused. "Give."

Joe sighed, and said, "Kent isn't content to sit back and wait."

"And what is that supposed to mean, Joe?"

"We have two different theories, Susan. In a situation like this, my contention follows the old saw that if you give someone enough rope they'll hang themselves."

Kent said dryly, "Joe expects a full confession when everyone's assembled up on Mount Schloss."

"I never said that," Joe protested. "What I did say is that I expect there will be a revelation. Enough so that we'll know who's been writing the letters, and we can take it from there."

"Take it where?" Kent demanded. "Suppose we all go and picnic—if you can possibly imagine such a thing—and nothing happens? What do we do then?"

"We go back to square one and start again," Joe said.

"I don't see that. You've said yourself that the rendezvous today is the one real opportunity we'll have of getting this person to come out in the open."

"I still say that. I've already told you I think the pressure's been escalating for a long time now, getting stronger and stronger and consequently harder to take. I think when everyone's together at the actual scene, the boiler will blow.''

"And I,'' Kent stated, "think that's wishful thinking.''

Susan, dismayed at this first sign of real disagreement between the two cousins, protested, "Kent, you've said all along that Joe is the one with experience about things like this.''

"Joe *is* the one with experience, I know that. And if Joe were in my shoes, I think he'd do exactly what I propose to do.''

"What do you propose to do?''

"I'm going to stand up in front of the whole crowd of them, and I'm going to start reading the damned letters, Susan,'' Kent said. "I'm not going to wait for this person to worm out of the woodwork. I'm going to smoke him out.

"Joe can watch as I read, and I think he'll get all the re-action he wants. I think he'll soon separate the wheat from the chaff, for want of a better expression. I think he'll elim-inate until we're down to one individual. And I think the pressure, by then, *will* make the individual blow. I'm not going to sit back and *wait* for that to happen. I'm going to *make* it happen.''

Kent went on, "Joe's problem is that he's trying to pro-tect me. Just as he's trying to protect you. But—'' he turned to his cousin "—if you were in my shoes, that's what you'd do, isn't it, Joe?''

"Yes,'' Joe admitted reluctantly.

Joe was walking. Susan tried not to stare openly as he awkwardly propelled himself toward the van, using two aluminum crutches.

Strange, she was so seldom conscious of his handicap when he was in the wheelchair. But she couldn't avoid be-ing aware of it when he was on his own two feet.

Susan remembered Kent saying that Joe could manage to get along on crutches, but it was painful for him. As he sank down onto the front seat of the van and gave her a wry grin, she could believe that.

He said, "Whew!" as he stashed the crutches at his side. Then he went on frankly, "I guess maybe you can see why I don't do this too often. I once thought it might get easier with time, but it doesn't."

"Why today?" Susan asked him.

"I thought it might work better," he said, and didn't elaborate.

The early-morning sunlight had given way to clouds. Joe, as they set out, said, "Looks like we may run into rain before the day's over. At least it's not cold enough to snow."

"Don't bet on it," Kent advised. "The temperature around here can drop faster than you can count. But I hope we don't even have rain. That road can be a mess when it gets wet."

"Does the road go straight up the mountain?" Susan asked.

Kent smiled. "Not quite. It spirals around. But the last part's pretty steep."

"Does this picnic grove belong to The Schloss?"

"No, it's state-owned. But I think you could say The Schloss has a kind of proprietary right to it. Most of the people who use it are guests at the resort."

"How is that?" Susan asked. "With all the people who come this way at foliage time, I'd think it would be crowded everywhere."

"Almost every place is," said Kent. "But though Mount Schloss is technically within the White Mountain National Forest area, it isn't especially famous as mountains go. There are any number of much more famous mountains around here to attract tourists.

"The Presidential Range has eight peaks over a mile high, with Mount Washington the giant of them all. And there's an assortment of other mountains with a lot more to interest visitors, like Cannon with its tramway, and Cranmore with the skimobile that takes people up to the top off-season. The list goes on. Mount Schloss is pretty inconspicuous in comparison, and the road up to the grove is not exactly publicized, as you'll see."

They had been traveling along a fairly narrow state road, and, as Kent made the turn onto the narrower road that led up the mountain, Susan wondered how he had ever spotted it. It looked to her like a narrow break between the pines.

Soon, the road grew narrower still, so that there was room for only one car. Every now and then there was a turnoff to allow passing, and Kent said, "I've always been just as glad I've never met anyone coming in the opposite direction when I've been driving along this road."

The pines grew thicker as they climbed, and the underbrush on both sides of them was so dense it looked impenetrable.

Joe said, "Klaus Bergstrom was telling me that the bear population's increasing. Sometimes in the winter the bears get hungry enough to go down around The Schloss to forage for food."

Kent nodded. "You'll also find deer roaming around, as well as moose. And there are bobcats. This is wild country, easy to get lost in. If a person goes very far into those woods they can lose all sense of direction." He warned lightly, "I'm not about to let you out of my sight, Susan."

"Don't worry," she assured him. "You won't get the chance."

Kent didn't answer, and Susan saw that he suddenly looked grim.

"Almost there," he announced.

Kent swung the van around a final curve, and Susan saw a dirt parking lot ahead. Beyond the parking lot, a large area had been cleared, and there were picnic tables, grills and trash cans.

Susan scanned the scene. Near them, a couple with three small children was having a picnic. Then she spotted a group of people at the far end of the grove, and though she couldn't identify them from this distance, she had little doubt of who they were.

Kent frowned, and said to Joe, "You're going to have a hell of a time covering that distance on crutches. I brought the wheelchair along. Why don't I get it out?"

Joe shook his head. "I'll manage. I'll take it slow."

"I'll stick with Joe," Kent told Susan. "You go on ahead and catch up with the others."

Susan would have much preferred to stay with Joe herself, even if it took him forever to cross the grove. But she moved on, as Kent had asked her to. This wasn't the time to raise a needless fuss.

Clark Benedict met her halfway.

"We thought you were the girls with the vittles," he said, nodding toward Joe's van. "The Schloss van is pretty much the same color. Welcome aboard, Susan."

"Thank you."

"Did you come straight from the lodge?" Clark asked.

"Why, yes, we did."

"Any sign of Heddy and Beth?"

"No."

Susan glanced at her watch. She, Joe and Kent deliberately had elected to arrive on the late side, and it was almost one-thirty. "I imagined they'd be here by now," she admitted.

"So did we all," Clark said. "Well, they shouldn't be much longer."

As Susan walked along with Clark, he said, "Mandy and Harvey and I were the first on the scene here. For a while, we thought it might start to snow, it got so cold. But it doesn't seem quite so bad now.

"Lilian came down the trail from the top a while ago. She cut around to this side of the mountain, and took an easier route. Phil and Bert are still up there somewhere."

Clark lowered his voice, though there was no one near enough who was apt to be able to hear him. "I thought Chase was paralyzed," he said.

"No. He prefers to use a wheelchair because it's more comfortable for him."

Since Susan wasn't sure of Joe's rationale for using crutches today, she invented a reason for him. "I gather he thought it might be difficult to maneuver the wheelchair over this kind of terrain."

They were nearing the cluster of picnic tables that the members of the group had appropriated, and Mandy came toward them rubbing her arms.

"I'm freezing," she complained. "I hope Beth and Heddy will remember to bring some blankets along with the sleeping bags. Are they far behind you, Susan? I'm not only half-frozen, I'm also starving."

"Susan didn't see them," Clark told his wife.

Harvey Farragut had been sitting on a picnic bench. He got up and greeted Susan, and she thought he looked strained and was acting wary.

But then, she conceded, her imagination could be playing tricks on her.

Clark said, "Next time I do anything like this, I'll stuff my pockets with nips. A shot of bourbon right now would be therapeutic."

Susan tried not to center all of her attention on Kent and Joe, who were nearing the picnic tables. Joe's halting progress was hard for her to watch. As Kent pulled out a picnic bench, Joe propelled himself forward and sat down on it, making no secret of his relief.

Then, finally, the van from The Schloss arrived, and Clark, Harvey and Mandy headed toward it to start ferrying the food across the grove.

"I suppose we should help," Susan murmured to Kent.

"We'll ask when they get back with the first load. Where are Phil and Bert?"

"Clark says they're still climbing around the mountain."

Heddy and Beth had brought an astonishing number of hampers filled with food, thermos jugs, charcoal and utensils.

As she started putting some of the things out on one of the picnic tables, Beth giggled and said, "There's enough for an army. Sorry we took so long. The kitchen help at The Schloss weren't exactly swift today."

Heddy was watching the couple with children. They were putting away their things, and going toward their station wagon.

"Thank God they're leaving," Heddy said. She looked uptight and sounded disagreeable.

"They weren't bothering anyone," Clark commented.

Heddy scowled. "Well, I'd just as soon be alone right now."

"I doubt we'll have any more company, the way the weather's turning out. Not like last time," Clark said. "There were other people around until pretty late in the day, remember?"

"Yes, I remember. Though maybe I don't have as much cause to remember as you do," Heddy told him.

Clark's customary smile faded. "What's that supposed to mean, Heddy?"

Beth interrupted. "Will you men get a couple of the grills going, Clark? Klaus included some small filets mignons and some special sausages he has flown in from Vienna."

Beth and Heddy had brought a huge jug of what they called Klaus's special toddy, a hot beverage that Beth promised would warm up anyone. And they were all sipping it when Mandy looked around and asked, "Where did Lilian go?"

"Maybe to look for Bert," Harvey said.

Clark laughed. "That would be the day."

Susan remembered that Clark had said Lilian had come down from the mountaintop a while back. But Lilian hadn't been in evidence since she, Kent and Joe had arrived on the scene.

Now, as if she'd heard her name being called, Lilian emerged from a woodland path past the end of the grove, and sauntered toward them.

When she was close enough, she announced, "I went up to Castle Ledge."

There was a stunned silence, and then Clark Benedict asked, "What the hell made you do that?"

Lilian accepted a mug of toddy from him, and shrugged. "That's why we're here, isn't it?" she said. "To pay tribute to Elaine? Let's say I went up to the ledge to communicate."

Mandy Benedict said slowly, "You have such damned poor taste, Lilian. Even Bert's money didn't do much to help there, did it?"

"Enough, Mandy," Mandy's husband commanded.

Mandy turned away, but there was a strange mix of anger and triumph on her face.

Finally, Bert Whitfield appeared. And it was at least another five minutes before Phil Donavan came across the grove to join the group.

With Phil's arrival, Susan automatically did a head count. Everyone was here.

Time passed, and they ate and drank, but it certainly couldn't be said that they made merry. Susan tried and failed to analyze this strange mood that seemed to hover over the mountain grove like an added cloud.

She knew that darkness would come early, especially on a gray and cloudy afternoon like this one. And she remembered Harvey Farragut telling her about that other afternoon, three years ago.

Harvey had said that it had been a beautiful day. After they'd eaten, some of the group had stretched out in sleeping bags to take naps. Others had wandered around. As he recalled, the last he'd seen of Elaine she was heading toward Castle Ledge, and she was by herself.

They'd been ready to go back to The Schloss when they missed her. Then they'd begun to call her name, but she hadn't answered. . . .

Now, Harvey stood up with a suddenness that startled Susan, walked over to two large plastic pails that had been placed a few feet away from the picnic tables and took the lid off the first pail.

Harvey withdrew two bottles and held them up.

"I think it's time we get this damned charade over with," he announced. "You're all stalling. I say let's get the show on the road and get out of here. Beth, I think you brought along some of those plastic champagne glasses?"

Beth nodded, "Yes."

"So we'll do our toast," Harvey decided. "Then anyone who wants to can go up to the ledge and toss bottles over the side."

Kent stood up.

Susan looked at him and thought her heart would stop beating. His face could have been carved from stone, except for his eyes, which were like glowing coals.

He was wearing a heavy red wool jacket. She watched him take a packet of long white envelopes fastened with a rubber band out of an inner pocket, and she felt a sudden, terrible premonition.

It was all she could do not to shriek at him and beg him to stop.

He said, "Before anyone drinks any toasts, I think there's something you need to know."

Heads turned toward him.

"Ever since Elaine's death, I've been receiving anonymous letters," Kent told them. "At first, they weren't so terrible. But then they got worse and worse. And, I discovered the writer had another victim. Susan. The seed was planted in Susan's mind that I was somehow responsible for Elaine's death—even though all of you who were here that day know I wasn't even on the mountain.

"These letters," Kent went on, "are the product of a distorted mind, the work of a psychopath. The person who wrote them is sick, very sick . . . and very dangerous. None of you is safe from this coward who hides behind filthy phrases and horrible accusations in order to try to work out some kind of a vendetta so that he can live with his own guilt."

Kent went on steadily, "You see, it's this person, this coward, this paranoiac, who is responsible for Elaine's death. Let me read these letters to you, and I think you'll see that for yourself. . . ."

Bert Whitfield sprang to his feet, his face white. "For God's sake," he accused Kent. "Have you no respect? Oh, I know what she was, but she was also *Elaine*. And she's here with us, can't you feel her? She wants to lead us up to

Castle Ledge. Then we can each drink our own kind of toast to her, to love or to hate. And we can each throw a bottle over the ledge, so there'll be champagne splashing all the way down to where she died.

"The bottles will crash down to the shore of the lake, right where we found her body. Maybe some of the glass will stab her soul."

Harvey Farragut faced Bert, his fists clenched. "Have you lost your mind?" he demanded.

"No more than any of us," Bert said. "She had each of us in turn, didn't she? I don't know who came first, but you were the last, weren't you, Harvey? So you should have the honor of opening the first bottle of champagne. Elaine told me the last time we were together that she was going to ditch Kent and you were going to ditch Beth and the two of you—"

"No!"

Beth Farragut's scream was bloodcurdling. And suddenly Beth darted to the plastic pail that held the champagne bottles, and grabbed a bottle.

"Damn you, Harvey," Beth said, her voice low and deadly. "And damn you, Bert. And all the rest of you. She just took you and tossed you away when she'd had enough of you. But you were all too stupid to see that, weren't you?

"But—" Beth's voice rose "—she also took *you*, Kent, and I couldn't forgive her for that. Bad enough that she stole my husband...but she already had you."

Beth smashed the champagne bottle against the edge of the nearest grill, and Susan flinched from the poisonous hatred that transformed Beth's pretty face into a malevolent mask.

Holding the shattered bottle with its jagged edges thrust in front of her, Beth faced Kent. Her eyes flashed as she said, "Do you really think Elaine wanted you? Oh, you knew she didn't. But I wanted you. God, how I wanted you. And if she hadn't come back, I would have had you.''

Beth swerved with incredible speed and came toward Susan, her hand clenched around the broken bottle.

''You,'' she screeched. ''*Why did you come back?*''

Susan was hemmed in by the table at which she was sitting. Before she could move, Kent hurled himself at Beth, and Susan saw him wince, and go off balance. Before he could steady himself and grab Beth, she swung the broken champagne bottle toward him and slashed his arm...again, and again, and again.

Then she turned back to Susan.

Joe's voice rang out. ''Beth, stop!''

Beth halted, and stared at Joe. And Susan, momentarily oblivious to Beth, slipped out from behind the table intent only on reaching Kent. He was clutching his arm, and his red sleeve was turning darker and redder.

Joe commanded again, ''Stop!'' And Susan turned.

Joe was standing, and there was a gun in his hand.

Beth let out a long, anguished cry that no one who heard it would ever forget. Then she turned and ran.

''Good god,'' Clark Benedict shouted. ''She's making for Castle Ledge. Head her off!''

Susan was aware that Clark and the other men were running toward the trail to Castle Ledge. But she ran in the opposite direction. Toward Kent.

Epilogue

They were in Joe's suite in the lodge. Joe was in his wheel-chair. Kent, his left arm heavily bandaged and in a sling, sat in an armchair, his long legs thrust toward the fire that blazed on the hearth. Susan sat on the floor next to the chair, partially propped against Kent's thigh.

"She looked so terrible," Susan said. She stared at the flames and hoped she wouldn't see Beth's tortured face in her dreams.

"They'll keep her in the hospital here tonight," Joe said. "And take her to Boston tomorrow." Joe's eyes rested on Kent. "You let her off light, cousin."

"Because I didn't tell the state cops that she assaulted me?"

"Yes."

"What good would it have done?" Kent asked. "Any psychiatrist's evaluation would be enough to keep her from being convicted of anything she might be charged with. She'd be sent to a state hospital, and I'd rather see her receive private treatment. There may still be hope for her. Anyway," he added ruefully, "if my trick knee hadn't let me down, she couldn't have done much."

"She is so... twisted," Susan said. "She thought at that last moment that I was Elaine. Do you think from the beginning she thought I was Elaine?"

"No. Only at times, I'd say."

"It was *Beth* Harvey wanted to talk to me about. I wish I'd let him."

"I doubt if it would have altered events," Joe said. "It's true that Harvey has been increasingly concerned about Beth, but even he didn't know how paranoid she is."

"And Elaine, and the affairs..." Susan didn't dare look up at Kent.

But he touched her cheek with his fingers and said without bitterness, "Let it go, Susan. Elaine paid a very heavy price."

"Do you think Beth had anything to do with Elaine's death?" Susan had to ask that.

"She thinks she did," Joe said. "I talked to the emergency room doctor at the hospital. Beth had been unloading a lot, and most of the time she was pretty lucid. Evidently there was a confrontation between Beth and Elaine at Castle Ledge. It's likely that Beth went into a rage similar to the one she went into today. Probably she advanced on Elaine, and Elaine stepped backward, and fell. That would be enough for an intolerable guilt burden to build up in someone like Beth.

"Also, I have to say that she was—is—in love with you, Kent. My guess is that she sensed that special something between you and Susan at Elaine's memorial service. So you became a rival to her, Susan. That's why she wanted to lure you to Boston. She wanted to keep an eye on you. Enough, kids. This old man needs to get to bed. It's been quite a day."

Susan bent and kissed him good-night, and said, "I love you, Joe Chase."

Tired and hurting though he was, Kent protested, "Hey, wait a minute."

It was Saturday night. There was dancing in the lounge. As Kent and Susan crossed the lobby, they could hear music and laughter. And they were glad that none of the other guests at The Schloss had any idea of the danger and drama that had taken place up on the mountain back of the lodge, just a few hours earlier.

On the second floor, Kent asked, "Your room or mine?"

"Mine... if you'll stay in it."

"If you're asking me if I intend to creep out in the small hours of the morning so that I won't be seen, the answer is no. Your reputation will have to take its chances."

As they entered Susan's room, she was very aware of the ordeal Kent had gone through today. He'd had quite a number of stitches taken in his arm in the emergency room at the small hospital in town. He was pale, weary, and Susan knew that he must be in considerable pain. Still he gave her a smile that threatened to melt her bones.

Then he said, "If the breath of scandal gets to be too much for you to take, I suppose I could make an honest woman of you." The smile faded, and an anxious look crept into Kent's dark eyes. "Susan," he began, "do you suppose you could ever..."

Susan. Yes, she was Susan. And the strange thing was she knew, now, that she'd always been Susan to Kent.

They'd been so different, she and Elaine. And Kent had realized that, right from the beginning.

Susan thought of her twin sister, and wondered if things might have turned out differently if the two of them had been closer. Maybe, if Elaine had been able to confide in her twin, she wouldn't have felt so impelled to upset whatever small world she moved into.

She'd been such a restless spirit. To her surprise, for she wasn't much for that sort of thing, Susan found herself forming the silent hope and prayer that after today Elaine would find peace.

And as for herself?

She looked at Kent, and knew she didn't have to go very far to find everything her heart desired.

He said unsteadily, "You're making me wait an awfully long time for an answer."

Susan said, "I think I'd love to have you make an honest woman of me."

She was surprised to see the look of deep relief that crossed Kent's face.

"Did you have any doubt?" she asked him, wondering how that possibly could be.

"No longer," Kent said. And added, "Never again."

Susan went to him, and grasped his good arm. She led him toward her bed. She urged him to lie down, then she pulled off his shoes.

Amusement mixed with fatigue in his dark eyes as she tugged the covers up over him. And love. Lots of love. He had never known it could be possible to love anyone so much, Kent thought drowsily.

Susan switched off the bedside lamp, then nestled next to him. "Now go to sleep," she instructed.

"Susan . . ."

"I fell asleep on you last night," Susan said. "Now it's your turn."

There was all the promise in the world in her voice as she added, "But tomorrow..."

* * * * *

For all those readers who've been looking for something a little bit different, a little bit spooky, let Silhouette Books take you on a journey to the dark side of love with

SILHOUETTE *Shadows* ™

If you like your romance mixed with a hint of danger, a taste of something eerie and wild, you'll love Shadows. This new line will send a shiver down your spine and make your heart beat faster. It's full of romance and more—and some of your favorite authors will be featured right from the start. Look for our four launch titles wherever books are sold, because you won't want to miss a single one.

THE LAST CAVALIER—Heather Graham Pozzessere
WHO IS DEBORAH?—Elise Title
STRANGER IN THE MIST—Lee Karr
SWAMP SECRETS—Carla Cassidy

After that, look for two books every month, and prepare to tremble with fear—and passion.

SILHOUETTE SHADOWS, coming your way in March.

 *Silhouette®*

SHAD1

Take 4 bestselling love stories FREE

Plus get a FREE surprise gift!

Special Limited-time Offer

Mail to Silhouette Reader Service™

3010 Walden Avenue
P.O. Box 1867
Buffalo, N.Y. 14269-1867

YES! Please send me 4 free Silhouette Special Edition® novels and my free surprise gift. Then send me 6 brand-new novels every month, which I will receive months before they appear in bookstores. Bill me at the low price of $2.71* each plus 25¢ delivery and applicable sales tax, if any.* I understand that accepting the books and gift places me under no obligation ever to buy any books. I can always return a shipment and cancel at any time. Even if I never buy another book from Silhouette, the 4 free books and the surprise gift are mine to keep forever.

235 BPA AJCH

Name	(PLEASE PRINT)	

Address	Apt No.	

City	State	Zip

This offer is limited to one order per household and not valid to present Silhouette Special Edition® subscribers. *Terms and prices are subject to change without notice. Sales tax applicable in N.Y.

USPED-93   ©1990 Harlequin Enterprises Limited

It takes a very special man to win

She's friend, wife, mother—she's you! And beside each Special Woman stands a wonderfully *special* man. It's a celebration of our heroines—and the men who become part of their lives.

Look for these exciting titles from Silhouette Special Edition:

January **BUILDING DREAMS** by Ginna Gray

February **HASTY WEDDING** by Debbie Macomber

March **THE AWAKENING** by Patricia Coughlin

April **FALLING FOR RACHEL** by Nora Roberts

Dont miss THAT SPECIAL WOMAN! each month—from your special authors.

AND

For the most special woman of all—you, our loyal reader—we have a wonderful gift: a beautiful journal to record all of your special moments. See this month's THAT SPECIAL WOMAN! title for details.